O, LUCIFER,
FALLEN, FALLEN, FALLEN.

DELPHINE M. SHANNON

Oh, Lucifer, Fallen, Fallen, Fallen.
Copyright © 2019 by Delphine M. Shannon

All rights reserved. No part of this publication may be reproduced, distributed, or transmitted in any form or by any means, including photocopying, recording, or other electronic or mechanical methods, without the prior written permission of the author, except in the case of brief quotations embodied in critical reviews and certain other non-commercial uses permitted by copyright law.

Tellwell Talent
www.tellwell.ca

ISBN
978-0-2288-0613-4 (Hardcover)
978-0-2288-0612-7 (Paperback)
978-0-2288-0614-1 (eBook)

TABLE OF CONTENTS

Dedication..iv

Acknowledgement...v

References..vi

Forward: Attestation of Enki by Scribe, Endubsar...................vii

Introduction: About This Book...........................ix

Chapter 1: Creation and the Fall of Lucifer.............................1
Chapter 2: The Rogue Planet Nibiru....................................11
Chapter 3: The History of Nibiru......................................17
Chapter 4: Earth's Beginning..31
Chapter 5: Toil and Frustration Continue..............................41
Chapter 6: Establishment of Five Cities...............................53
Chapter 7: A Grave Decision...67
Chapter 8: The Igigi Saw that the Daughters of Men Were Fair..........87
Chapter 9: The Great Deluge/Tsunami...................................95
Chapter 10: Gone are the Olden Times.................................101
Chapter 11: King Anu's Last Visit to Earth...........................119
Chapter 12: The Bombing of Mount Sinai/Sodom and Gomorrah............135
Chapter 13: All Roads Lead to Rome...................................153
Chapter 14: The Life of Christ.......................................165
Chapter 15: The Book of Revelation...................................195
Chapter 16: The Curtain was Rent.....................................215

Appendices..225

DEDICATION

This book is dedicated
to our Lord and Savior Jesus Christ.

ACKNOWLEDGEMENT

I wish to thank Zecharia Sitchin for without his brilliance in translating ancient Sumerian texts, manuscripts, ancient artifacts, scrolls, clay tablets, cuneiforms, temple carvings, and writings, this book would have been incomplete.

Without Zecharia we would not know who the Elohim (Anunnaki gods of the Old Testament and the Nefilim) are. These brave astronauts, our ancestors, landed on Earth off the coast of the Indian Ocean many of thousands of years ago.

With much respect for the determination and hard work of Mr. Sitchin, I am grateful.

REFERENCES

Nine books of Zecharia Sitchin translated by him.

King James Bible, the creation of the Universe, creation and fall of Lucifer and the life of Jesus Christ.

MY own book, Dominus Vobiscum; published in 2011 from which chapters 2 through 10 were used as reference.

NASA scientific reports using Cosmic Microwave Background Radiation (CMBR). This determined when the Universe originated which helped determine, along with the Bible, when Lucifer was created and his fall.

Cosmic Mysteries of the universe by space scientist and bible scholar, Adrian V. Clark.

The teachings of the Catholic Church before 1960.

WWIII and the Destiny of America by Dr. Charles Taylor.

My own serious studies of fifty years, learning from brilliant minds, and hope to give logical explanations for some mistranslations.

The Lost autobiography book of Enki as told to his scribe, Endubsar, in 2024 B.C. and translated by Mr. Sitchin. Enki related all he experienced from his birth on Nibiru and his 450,000 years of experience on Earth. His people are many thousands of years ahead of earthlings. Mankind has forty years to make a name for himself (ages 25 to 65). Enki has thousands of years, about 700,000 years to make a name for himself; he lived all that he wrote, so his words are indisputable.

FORWARD

ATTESTATION OF ENKI BY SCRIBE, ENDUBSAR

About 2024 B.C. The following is written from the words, in part, of Enki, Lord of the Old Testament as told to his scribe, Endubsar. In the seventh year after the Great Calamity, (bombing of Mount Sinai and the total of five cities including Sodom and Gomorrah) in the second month on the seventeenth day, Lord Enki Summoned Endubsar. He wrote that he was among the remnants of Eridu who had escaped the Evil Wind from the nuclear bombing. He wandered off to find twigs for firewood when a whirlwind came out of the south. It had a reddish brilliance and made no sound. He said that as it reached the ground, four straight feet spread out from its belly.

Endubsar lifted his eyes and saw two men, their garments sparkled like burning brass. They called him by name and spoke to him and said they would take him to Enki's domain in Africa on an island amid the River of Megan where the sluices are. When they arrived, he collapsed and fell to the ground, overcome by brilliance. He was taken to an enclosure and heard someone call him by name.

"Endubsar, offspring of Adapa (Adam), I have chosen you to be my scribe, that you write down my words on the tablets." He looked to see a tablet and a glistening stylus. The voice said, "Endubsar, son of Eridu City, my faithful servant. I am your Lord Enki. I want you to write down my words. I am much distraught over what has befallen mankind by the great calamity. It is my wish to record the truth to let gods and men know that my hands are clean."

He continued, "Not since the Great Deluge which was destined to happen by natural events, not so with the bombing of seven years ago. It could have been prevented, and I, Enki did all I could to prevent it. I failed. In the future shall it be judged, for the end of days, a Day of Judgment there shall be."

Continuing, Enki said, "On that day, the Earth shall quake and the rivers shall change courses and there shall be darkness at noon and fire in the heavens and in the night, the day of returning celestial God it will be. And who shall survive, who shall perish, who shall be rewarded and who will be punished gods and men alike, on that day shall be discovered for what shall come to pass and by what had passed shall be determined; by the will of your heart for good or evil will judgment come. I will tell you of the Beginning, of Prior Times and of the Olden Times, for the past and the future are hidden Olden Times. I will be with you for forty days to relate to you."

INTRODUCTION

ABOUT THIS BOOK

This is the story of creation, the fall of Lucifer, the history of Nibiru, Earth's history, Christ's mission on Earth and the Vatican's control of the Earth until the present.

4.5 billion years ago, Lucifer was cast out of heaven via Planet Nibiru. He created its heavens and the planet to be livable. He created the Nibiruans.

Psalms 82; v. 6. God's admonition to the Nibiruans: "I have said, "Ye are the Elohim/Anunnaki, and all of you are the children of the Most-High. But ye shall die like men and fall like one of the princes."

Psalms 99. 3: "Before the Elohim/Anunnaki upon Olam/Nibiru, he Yahweh/Lucifer sat."

The Anunnaki are Nibiruans who came to Earth to live.

Psalm 6:18. Explained "Just as the Anunnaki had been on Earth before Adam, so was Yahweh/Lucifer on Nibiru/Olam before the Nibiruans."

445,000 years ago, Planet Nibiru was becoming a dying planet due to a hole in its atmosphere which was causing droughts, lack of food, water, illness, and children not being born.

Enki with fifty astronauts came to Earth to mine gold to make gold dust to fill the breach.

The Nibiruans/Anunnaki landed on the Indian Ocean, the Persian Gulf (Kuwait) which would become Eden. When they landed on the ocean, they donned their fish suits (similar to our Navy Seals fish suits) to swim to shore. Enki became known as the fish god and the Pope, Cardinals and Bishops to this day wear his fish miter to honor god Enki.

They immediately started their quest for gold and built the first city, Eridu. German; erde/Earth.

Gold couldn't be mined fast enough; the toiling was severe, so 600 Nibiruans came to labor on Earth and Mars (a way-station). Still, it was not enough. Enki decided to create workers to hasten the gold on its way. Because of his creation, medical practices, and his emblem, a serpent coiling around the staff, representing DNA double helix, he became known as the serpent.

Enki, after many years of toiling and suffering and doing the best anyone could do under the circumstances, was devastated when he learned that his rival brother, Enlil, decided to come to Earth to be commander. Their rivalry continued on Earth.

This is an exciting story of their toiling, suffering, building cities, rearing their children, wars and brother rivalries. Also, the creation of man, the natural calamity of the flood and the bombing of Sodom and Gomorrah.

Come with me on this exciting journey of your ancestors as they walked the Earth and prepared the way for YOU.

CHAPTER 1

CREATION AND THE FALL OF LUCIFER

In the beginning was the WORD and the WORD was with God, and the Word was God. He/Jesus was in the beginning with God. All things were made through Him and without Him was made nothing that has been made. In Him was the Light, and the Light shinith in the darkness.

All things that are made have an established principle of logic/science/reality. That is the principle of causality, something that has a beginning has a sufficient cause. The principle is, "Everything that has a beginning has an efficient cause. The cause must be sufficient or adequate." The cause of the Universe must be nonmaterial (supernatural) because it is not subject to decay. All material things decay in time, the Universe does not.

God said, "Let there be light." Light is the first physical thing that can be detected by our senses. This was the beginning of selective creation, the Universe. In the beginning, God, this Master Builder, prepared a plan, a blueprint before the construction began. This is in full agreement of the religious teaching that the Master Builder existed before the Universe was created (John1: 1-1. KJV) "In the beginning was the WORD and the Word was with God,"

The Universe was filled with light before the Big Bang. Light is a form of energy called electromagnetic radiation. In the Universe every star emits light in every direction. The light begins its journey for billions of years until it reaches another object. This is a continuous ray of light from every point of the Universe.

The supernatural God by WORD, commanded the Big Bang to happen about 123.8 billion years ago, thus creating the Universe and about 200 billion galaxies. The Universe began to cool sufficiently about 380,000 years after the Big Bang to create solar systems and planets. This was determined by NASA using Cosmic Microwave Backward Radiation.

The Universe consists of light, normal matter, dark matter and dark energy. It is the habitation of billions of galaxies, planets, stars, dust clouds, atoms and more. There are an estimated 100 billion habitable earth-like planets in the Milky Way and an estimated sextillion planets in the Universe. Within this Universe, God created planets, stars, time, space, atoms and light. God placed His Headquarters in the upper, northern, central part of the Universe: Mission Control Center. This all-knowing spiritual computer whose webs, grids reach out to the farthest ends of the Universe and with a tracking device, receiving and recording all happenings: thoughts, words, deeds of all living beings into its core to be recorded eternally. (Luke. 12: 7.). "indeed, every hair on your head is numbered."

(Matt. 12: 29.). "not one sparrow will fall to the ground without Your father knowing."

For any human to comprehend and explain the Universe is impossible. The vastness, magnificence and bewildering awesomeness is indescribable.

As the Universe grew in age, God needed spiritual beings to aid in the inhabitation and to rule and care for billions of planets. In this magnificent, beautiful Universe, God created spiritual beings out of light and a love that is all-encompassing. Among them was the most beautiful Lucifer.

The Creation and Fall of Lucifer

Lieutenant Lucifer was one of God's most treasured cherubs, the most beautiful anointed one in the heavens. He was brilliant, efficient and self-assured. He had been in the Universe for billions of years before Earth was fashioned. He was not an ascendant. He was a created son of the Local Universe and was perfection from the day he was created. (This compiled information is from several different accounts that I have read throughout fifty years of serious study).

Lucifer resided in Eilat in the mid-way part of the Universe. He grew to become the high counselor of his group, distinguished for sagacity, wisdom and efficiency. He was very high on the list of credentials when commissioned by the Melchizedeks, and was designated as one of the 100 most able personalities in more than 700,000 of his kind. He oversaw over 600 habitable planets, so perfectly capable of making the right decisions. He would have attended many meetings on the Mount of Assembly with those of high stations' masking important decisions.

He had a magnetic, brilliant personality and stood next to the Moat High of the Fathers of the Constellations in the direct line of the Universe authority.

Lieutenant Lucifer, in his realm, was responsible for making the planets habitable. In order to do so, he must first create an atmosphere to protect the earth from the Sun's rays. He would need to extract ash from volcanoes and gasses from the earth. For water, he would need to extract hydrogen and oxygen from the stratosphere, more so from the troposphere which is the layer closest to the planet which contains 99% of the water vapor of the atmosphere.

He would have been a teacher on many planets. Lucifer would have used the Universal cloud seeding method to seed the earth with life. Within this method, the clouds carry seeds, insects, small creatures such as toad's frogs, etc., and when these take hold, the Lord saw that it was good. (Gen.1:12). "And the earth brought forth grass, seeds…and God saw that it was good. In our time, clouds have been seen passing in front of the moon.

Lieutenant Lucifer would have traveled from galaxy to galaxy teaching many planets how to make planets habitable. He no doubt traveled through the Universe in a living molecular cloud that Jesus traveled while on Earth. (Acts. 1: 11), "Ye men of Galilee, why do you stand ye gazing up into the heavens? This same Jesus which is taken from you into heaven, so shall he come in like manner in a cloud as ye have seen Him go into heaven."

Just as we living beings mount a living horse and guide it with our minds to our hands, so the angels enter a living molecular cloud and guide it with their minds.

In the meantime, about 4.6 billion years ago, our solar system was a cloud of dust and gas Solar nebula. Gravity collapsed the material on itself as it began to spin in the center of the nebula. With the rise of the Sun, our galaxy was formed. Then Tiamat/Earth formed and while forming, she twirled, twisted, danced and swayed in front of the Sun gathering and holding the golden rays deep into her core to become the only planet to contain the precious gold.

Tiamat became totally covered with water and became known as the Blue-Water Planet; very beautiful to behold. Then Mercury was formed. His and Tiamat's waters mingled to help form Mars and Venus. Before they grew in size and stature, Saturn and Jupiter formed and surpassed their brothers in size. Uranus was formed in the distant heavens and lastly Neptune.

Lucifer was with Jesus when the Earth was created. (Job. 38: 4.). "Where was thou when I laid the foundations of the Earth? Declare for the angels sang and all of you shouted."

Lucifer was sent to Ashdod. It was during his time there that the idea of self-assertion took place, then resentment slowly crept in. He became critical of the entire plan of the Universe administration. He became critical that he could not be sovereign over his system and although he and the angels had free will they were not permitted to be self-assertive and he was angry of the right that

Jesus had to assume sovereignty over his domain. All the while, he kept a cordial relationship with Jesus.

Year after year, little by little, over and over he talked to Abaddon, chief of the staff of Tiberias of his resentments, hoping to sway him to his way of thinking which he eventually did. Lucifer then went to Beelzebub, the leader of the disloyal and mid-way creatures who allied themselves with the forces of the rebellion of the traitorous Tiberias. He also convinced Beelzebub to join him in the future rebellion. Lucifer then went to his second in charge, recruited him and then to his third and fourth and so on until he had a large following.

In the meantime, Lucifer stood next to the Most High on the Mount of Assembly, many times in counsel with them. They did not know that he was harboring feelings of resentment, rebellion and criticism of the administration. In their presence, he controlled his thoughts and always professed whole hearted loyalty to the supreme rulers. There was no condition which suggested rebellion.

However, as time went on, word got to Jesus. Jesus was merciful and willing to forgive, knowing all angels are given free will, and that Lucifer may see the wrong in what he was doing and stop. But he became more insincere and evil evolved into deliberate sin.

Lucifer was now causing such an uproar in the Universe peace and harmony. The Fathers set up a meeting and decided to have a hearing on Mount of Assembly in a few days to hear Lucifer's claims. They sent Gabriel to give him the opportunity to repent and call off the meeting. Lucifer declined and in anger stated that he has a manifesto written and wants to present his grievances. He had gone too far and his mischief-making pride would not let him stop.

The meeting was to be and Gabriel was certain that there would be a riot there. He and the Fathers determined what measures would be taken to prevent it from happening.

Lucifer was notified to appear at the Mount of Assembly to explain himself. The moment came and the Most High and officials were present. The entire cabinet of Lucifer's rebellion were allowed to enter and sign in. The meeting was called to order and Lieutenant Lucifer was called forth to present his case. Tension filled the room.

He walked self-assuredly to center stage. His manifesto was on the wall and one was given to each one present. He stood powerfully tall and handsome, but a certain beauty was gone from his face. His anger could be seen and felt by all.

"I have here in hand my Manifesto, the 'Declaration of Liberty' and as you can see I had one just now placed on the wall. One has been given to all present. For years, I have been unheard, and all the while tormented by feelings of low self-worth from the Most High. You ask me what are my grievances? Let me tell you what they are:

"#1. He, the Most High, is my first grievance. The reality of a Universal God is ignorance. I accept the fact that He and Jesus are my creators, but they are not my God.," There was a shocked gasp from those present and a stirring. He continued, "I know everything that they know, there is nothing more they can teach me. I now have the wisdom and knowledge to be on my own. I should have my own realm under my own authority."

"#2. My second grievance is that of the Universal government of the Creator, Jesus. He should not control everything. He should not sovereign over my systems. Local systems should be autonomous. Who should know better than the one who made them habitable, cared for them and governed over them. I know what is best for their present and their future. We have been given free will but can't be self-assertive."

He raised his voice, "I know better than Jesus what is the right thing to do for my systems!" His followers were applauding and getting loud. On and on, Lucifer ranted.

"#3. My third grievance is that there is too much time training the mortals on some planets. There should be a new system for teaching and training that would save us time to do more important things."

His followers shouted and swayed back and forth. The leaders were shocked with Lucifer's reasoning, his demands and disrespect for the Universal laws. Lucifer continued on and on passionately speaking in detail, inciting anger in his followers. They rose up and the tensions grew. Those of the Most High tried to reason with him, but his years of pent up emotions of anger, jealously and pride increased. Back and forth went the arguments. The stand-by army of the Most High showed themselves and seen by Lucifer which enraged him further. He began to exit, and his men enraged and shouting followed him.

Lucifer reaching his height of anger, realized that he must leave. As he was exiting, raising his fists, he screamed out, "I will ascend into the heavens. I will exalt my throne above the stars of God. I will sit on the Mount of Assembly. On the farthest sides of the North!" (Isaiah. 14: 12-15.).

He left with those heated words. Nothing was solved only now deepened hatred. He was allowed to leave and return to Eilat, and fully permitted to establish and organize his rebellion government. The Constellation Fathers did confine the rebels to their system of Caligastia. Jesus allowed Lucifer to run free for 200,000 years and Jesus still remained aloof.

Lucifer never succeeded in gaining a thing he asked for at the meeting on the Mount. He became more vengeful that he never received the admiration and respect that his pride demanded, that he was above God. He continued to rebel and recruit followers.

From a magnificent beginning, through evil and error, he embraced sin, and now is numbered as one of the three systems sovereign who have succumbed to the urge of self. He surrendered to the sophistry of spurious liberty-rejection of Universal allegiance and disregard to fraternal obligations and blindness to cosmic relationships. Lucifer is now the fallen and deposed sovereign of Satania, the exalted personalities of the celestial world of Lucifer.

By deliberately sinning against God, the angels and all living beings, he was deliberately going against peace, harmony, order and UNIVERSAL LOVE. Lucifer lost his true beauty and his emotion of love, dealing with logic without love. He has now become a sociopath, filled with hatred and jealously. He will eventually develop into a psychopath to become the most dangerous entity that could ever happen to the Universe.

Jesus, realizing that the situation was worsening and that Lucifer would never repent, could take no more. He summoned Michael and told him to notify Lucifer by messenger to prepare for war and of the time and place. "Gather your army, Michael, wear my banner of war to contest and counter work Lucifer."

At the amphitheater, Michael with his large army of angels entered, boldly displaying the Banner of Jesus. He stood fearless and blew the trumpet of war. Lucifer appeared at the amphitheater with his large army, displaying his banner as a call to battle. He, in turn, blew his trumpet in such a way that its sounds were rocketing between his gasping in anger. He was about to fight a war with all the rage that had built up for thousands of years.

The battle began with a furious lunge from Lucifer. Michael struck back. Back and forth they went. Striking, falling, rising, falling. One and then the other, over and over, fighting while going backward at times, then violently lunging forth with flashes of lightening bolting heavenward.

They fought on and on, using violent forces of pressure; Michael with the cosmic forces of Love and Lucifer with forces of hatred; the forces of good and evil. Also using electromagnetic mind control, laser beams; all this producing lightning flashes bolting heavenward. The war waged on continuously in heaven.

We cannot understand a spiritual battle, but this one was horrific. The war was terrible, although not like Earth's savage wars, this was far deadlier as it was fought in terms of life eternal.

For a long time, backward and forward they fought furiously, now inching Lucifer backward, unbeknown to him to the point of exile. Michael was winning as they forced Lucifer and his army backward toward a cliff. Below was the waiting space ship Nibiru. Michael and his army, in this final battle, pushed violently with Lucifer falling, falling down backward.

This last thrust was extremely humiliating to the falling Lucifer as he and his angels were violently pushed backward and down onto the waiting planet of exile. As they were falling, still in the motion of battling, Lucifer's fists raised in anger. He screamed curses at the victors as the planet was given its final thrust as the WORD rocketed it out into space and out of the sight of God.

(Isaiah. 14: 12). "How have you fallen from the heavens. O, day star. son of the Morning. How have you been cut down to the ground?"

O, LUCIFER, YOU HAVE FALLEN, FALLEN.

CHAPTER 2

THE ROGUE PLANET NIBIRU

About 4.5 billion years ago, an awesome event occurred. Rocketing through space, a rogue planet, seeded with primitive life from the cosmos, came in from the east, soared in from the deep. Nibiru, 40,000 miles in circumference, reddish in radiance, truly beautiful to behold, rocketed toward our solar system. It was traveling in a clockwise motion in its own path when suddenly, it was pulled in by the gravitational pull of Neptune.

As he passed Neptune, his side began to bulge from Neptune's pull. The bulge of Nibiru was torn away and became Neptune's moon, Triton. Nibiru entered the solar system, counter to that of the other planets which rotate counter clockwise. That is why Triton has a retrograde motion and the cause of highly elliptical orbits of the other satellites and comets.

Sparks and flashes bolted from Nibiru to Neptune, and from Neptune, Nibiru carried four satellites: North Wind, South Wind, East Wind and West Wind. Then Nibiru bolted sparks and flashes at Uranus and more satellites were created as Nibiru passed by. Uranus picked up four moons and Nibiru gained three more satellites.

Nibiru went from Neptune to Uranus and then to Saturn. He then passed Neptune and Uranus and would no doubt have continued away from our area, but he was drawn to the planetary system as he reached Saturn and Jupiter; the destiny of Nibiru was changed forever.

It was also then that the chief satellite of Saturn, Pluto was pulled away in the direction of Venus and Mars. This was a dire direction made possible only by the retrograde force of Nibiru making a vast elliptical orbit. Pluto eventually returned to the outermost solar system. This upset gave Pluto an inclined and peculiar orbit that sometimes takes it between Neptune and Uranus.

The new destiny of Nibiru was irrevocably set toward the olden planet, Tiamat/Earth. The path of Nibiru was on a collision course with Tiamat/Earth which would not take place for five hindered years after he entered the pull of Neptune.

In the meantime, the planets were still wobbly in their orbits. Tiamat was unstable and she was being pulled in many directions by the two large planets, Jupiter and Saturn which were behind her and Mars and Venus between her and the Sun. This resulted in her gathering a host of satellites swirling furiously. The moon was the most dangerous to the stability and safety of the other planets. Its name was Kingu; it was of planetary size and about to break away from Tiamat to have its own orbit around the Sun. (Binary planetary hypothesis: the size of the moon in comparison to the size of its planet).

Nibiru with its seven satellites continued on its collision course with Tiamat and her eleven satellites. It was Nibiru's seven satellites that smashed into Tiamat. The North Wind satellite hit hard; cracking her.

Nibiru was close enough to Tiamat so that they affected each other, Nibiru's magnetic field enfolded her and he shot immense bolts of electricity/lightening at the old, blue water planet, Tiamat. She was filled with brilliance, slowing down, heating up and distended. Wide gaps opened on her crust, emitting steam and volcanic matter. Nibiru's main satellite, North Wind, cracked Tiamat.

Except for the planet-like Kingu/Moon, all the moonlets orbiting Tiamat were caught in the magnetic pull of Nibiru. They were shattered, broken up and thrown off their precious course and forced into new orbital paths, but still rotating counter clockwise. Thus comets were created.

Kingu/Moon was deprived of his almost independent orbit and became a lifeless mass of clay. He has now devoid of atmosphere and radioactive matter and forever to face in one direction. Nibiru then crossed the heavens and circled the Sun. It was forever caught in its new orbit, making it the 12th planet in our system.

One Nibiruan year later, 3,600 years, Nibiru passed Neptune, Uranus, Saturn and Jupiter without mishap, but the new orbital path took him straight toward Tiamat again. And again, Nibiru did not strike the cracked Tiamat. It was again his North Wind satellite that struck her so hard, breaking off 8,000 miles of her lower half, hurling it out into space to become the Asteroid Belt traveling counter clockwise.

This force carried off Tiamat's upper half, 28,000-mile circumference and the Moon from fourth position between Mars and Jupiter to the third position between Venus and Mars. She was forever caught in this new third position from the Sun.

Tiamat now had a large hole in her western half toward the Sun. This hole became full of most of the planet's surface water and exposed the soil, mostly on the eastern side. She was no longer the Blue Water planet but became firm ground planet. Because of the magnetic pull of Tiamat, she had pulled primitive live from Nibiru and life was seeded on Tiamat/Earth. Tiamat once 36,000 miles in circumference had become about 28,000 miles in circumference.

Nibiru went on its own circuit, returning 3,600 years later. This time Neptune and Uranus were again given their final make-up. Each had its own satellites. Pluto had been a moon of Saturn, but he was torn away during Nibiru's first intrusion. Now Pluto had its own moon, Charon, which was torn from Neptune, and Pluto was sent to his final destiny…'The Hidden Place in the Deep' with an inclined and peculiar orbit. Pluto became second to the last planet from the Sun.

Nibiru became the last planet from the Sun. His orbit from the Apogee, in the 'Distant Abode' back to the Apogee is 15 billion miles. This takes 3,600 years and is One Nibiruan year.

Lucifer readies his new abode.

Lucifer took his rage with him to his new prison planet. The hatred he bore would continue to grow. Since he had sinned against the Most High and turned his back away from the Light, he lost the Love of the Universe. He had no love in his being for anyone but himself and the power he longed for. Without the Universal love, he became ugly.

He was no longer permitted beyond this Solar System. Thus, he became known as the 'Prince of the Airways'. His craft were no longer the beautiful white Celestial Universal Clouds, but plain silver saucers. For a long time, Nibiru soared through space until it was caught in the Solar System. About 7,000 years for it to settle in its orbit. Shortly after settling, Lucifer called a group of his angels to reconnoiter the land with him. Then he called all to attend a council meeting to determine what must be done and the steps to be taken to make the planet habitable. He wanted it pleasant for his men and livable for future intended mortals that he intended to create to begin his own planetary system.

During council meeting, it was determined the following must be done:

1. Temperatures must be kept at 15 degrees to 115 degrees F.
2. An atmosphere must be made. There were volcanoes there from which the ash could be used and rocks that could be pulverized into ash. The atmosphere would have to be 100 miles thick to protect the earth from the Sun's rays, to keep the surface warm, to protect it from radiation and to keep out the small and medium sized asteroids.
3. Suitable abodes must be built.

4. Water must be regularly assessible: oxygen and hydrogen from the stratosphere, but also by digging wells from the water tables. mostly from the troposphere as it contains 99% of the waters from the atmosphere.
5. Energy; a steady input of light or chemical energy cells to run the chemical reactions necessary for life.
6. Nutrients. All solid planets and moons have the same genetic make-up, so nutrients are present. Nibiru has a water cycle and volcanic activity and they can transplant or replenish the chemicals are the chemicals required by living organisms. (Quora, "How to make a planet habitable?" A question and answer site answered by its community of uses.) Lucifer would have had over 5 billion years of experience in all these matters.
7. Lucifer would also capture the Universal clouds that seeds the planets throughout the Universe and use them to seed his planet.

He and some of his angels visited near-by planets and found one of them, Uranus, habitable and also several moons. So, millions of years of tasks to be performed had begun, including creating his own mortals. He had every intention of having his own planetary system, free to create, free to rule, and have his own mortals to adore him.

He and some of the angels visited near-by planets.

Psalms 99: 3,

Before the Elohim (Nibiruans/ANUNNAKI Upon Olam/Nibiru, he (Yahweh/Lucifer) sat.

CHAPTER 3

THE HISTORY OF NIBIRU

A thick 100-mile atmosphere is constantly fed by volcanic eruptions, that enveloped Nibiru. This atmosphere sustains all life and without it, all living things would perish. It is like a constantly renewed warm coat which keeps the planet warm while in the deep Apogee and cool in the Perigee near the Sun's scorching rays.

The atmosphere holds and releases rain to lakes and streams, feeding and protecting lush vegetation and causes all manner of life in the water and on the land to sprout. It was seeded by Universal cloud seeding. From the beginning, Nibiru was comprised of hill and dale.

It took millions of years for Nibiru to evolve to the point where mortals could live on it. When the Lord/Lucifer saw that it was good and ready to receive mortals, he created them, male and female he created. The mortals evolved over millions of years. It was as if he created them and then flew away.

The Nibiruans grow to be tall, the men about 6', 8" tall and the women about 6' 5" tall. They are very beautiful, pleasant to look at with blond hair and blue eyes. They are easy going and calm. They live to be about 600,000 years old. In their gardens is the Tree of Life and also Water of Life. There is no illness, they just simply die of old age. (The further away from the Sun is a planet, the longer the people live).

Advanced man turned hill and dale into agricultural farms and dairy lands, ewes, cattle, turkeys and chickens. There are fruit and nut trees and all sorts of vegetables and plants. These were planted and used as food millions of years ago. Dogs, cats and small animals were pets. They went from primitive life to hunters and gatherers to settlers who grew a variety of plants, fruit and nuts and killed wild life for food.

They progressed slowly until a certain point and then everything happened rapidly; from hunters and gatherers and roaming to settlers, they decided it was safer and better to settle in one place to grow food and have animals.

Time passed and the number of people grew and spread throughout Nibiru, some lived in the hills, some in dales, some tilled the soil while others shepherded the animals. Some made their homes in the mountains, some in villages and some in the cities. Some of the cities were beautiful.

Rivalries, encroachments and clashes occurred, sticks became weapons. After many shars, clans gathered into tribes, these separated into two great nations; The North sand the South.

More shars passed and the hand-held weapons turned into thrusting missiles. Terror increased and a long and fierce battle engulfed the planet, it was brother against brother.

For many years, death and destruction nearly diminished life. Then a great war ensued, a nuclear bomb devastated the land terribly: beautiful cities, homes, universities were destroyed and many people and animals died.

This shocked them into doing something about the violence. A truce was declared, "Peace and union. Let there be one throne either from the north or the south. Whoever is selected as king, let him choose a wife from the opposing factor, thus uniting the globe."

A northern king was chosen and a southern woman chosen as his bride. A royal title, An, to be given to the king. This means 'a celestial one'. An.tu was the name given to his wife. A splendid city, Agade, was built for rulership, and it was now the capital of Nibiru.

The new king made many wise decisions and changes such as: governors to restore and reclaim one's rightful land, restore peace and unity, build new cities, canals, provide food for all and to restore record keeping.

All kings were descendants of An. The following are the records of all the kings since the nuclear bomb:

1. An married An.tu. They had sons, An.ki, An.ib and Enuru.
2. An.ki married, had no sons.
3. An.ib married his niece, Nin.Ib. She bore An.shar.Gal.
4. An.Shar.Gal. married An.Shar.Ga, his half-sister. He loved knowledge and understanding; studied the heavens and Nibiru's circuit around the Sun. He called one circuit a shar and pronounced two festivals one

   Females outnumbered males. So he decreed that a male could have more than one woman for copulation and one 'official wife' whose son should rule. But if a son was born of a concubine half-sister, the son is a double seed of the king and his son should rule. Hence, "The Law of the Seed", he is to rule. An.Shar.Ga bore a son, An.Shar

5. An.Shar married his half-sister, Kishar. He was the first : "Law of the seed."

   It was during the reign of this king, An. Shar that the breach /hole in the atmosphere occurred. Little by little, the heat entering the earth began to diminish their yields, fruits and grains lost abundance. Nearing the Sun, the heat grew stronger and in the Apogee, coolness was more biting.

   To understand what was happening, counsels were held, savants were called to examine the soils, lakes and streams. Then they examined the air and found the breach in the atmosphere. The volcanoes were not emitting enough ash to supply the atmosphere.

The breach became wider: lakes and land began to dry up and pestilences of the field made an appearance. He was the fifth king to reign since the nuclear war took place.

6. En.Shar married his half-sister, Nin.Shar who bore him no sons. A concubine bore him the next king. Du.Uru.

    En.Shar studied the five planets outside the Asteroid Belt. He named the planets; he called Pluto/ Gaga, Neptune/An, Uranus/Antu, Saturn/Anshar, and named Jupiter/Kishar. He sent space craft to these planets to carefully study their atmosphere, but to no avail. It was known that gold was needed to fill the gap, but the only planet that has gold is Tiamat/Earth.

    Suffering increased; dried soil, little water, little food, women were not bearing children. For many more shars it continued. The leaders tried everything they could think of to help solve the problem: bombing the volcanoes to produce ash, grinding stone for ash, several times lifting up domes only to have them fall to the ground. Wells were dug to supply water, but it was never enough.

7. Du.Uru married Daura. She bore him no children. One day she found an abandoned male child at the palace gate and took him as her own. Her husband adopted him and named him Lahma, meaning dryness. The suffering continued.

8. Lahma married Lahama. He was not of An's seed. Things remained the same for the four shars he reigned (14,000 years) nothing was accomplished. Unity was gone, accusations were rampant, savants came and went with advice. Yet, great calamities came.

    The next in succession was Anu a seed of An. But a rogue prince, Alalu usurped the old king Lahma and sat on the throne. This was unforgiveable to Anu.

9. Alalu had a daughter, Damkina, who married Ea, son of Anu. He reigned for nine shars. He made all kinds of promises

to the people that he would fix the breach but failed as did the others.
10. Anu battled Alalu and took the throne. He married his half-sister An.tu. She bore him a son, Enlil. He would one day become commander of Earth. Previously, Anu had two other children by two concubines; a son, Ea who would become Enki, Lord of Earth and a daughter, Ninmah who would become Mother of Earth and a medical doctor. Anu had just battled Alalu for the throne and won.

When the 9th King, Alalu took over the throne from Lahama by lying that he was a descendant of An., he deprived Anu from his rightful kingship. Anu never forgave him, and being made Alalu's cup-bearer added insult to injury causing further humiliation. Anu knew he would fight Alalu to win kingship that was rightfully his.

Anu's first son, Ea, would have followed his father in line to be king, but when Alalu stole the throne that wouldn't happen. When Anu married his own half-sister and bore Enlil, Ea's hopes were shattered. His kingship and hopes were dashed. Enlil would surely inherit the throne by the 'Law of the Seed'. To make matters worse Ea had fallen in love with his beautiful, brilliant half-sister Ninmah, and she had fallen in love with Enlil. This resentment between the brothers would last for thousands of years.

Time passed and Ea married Damkina, Alalu's daughter. She bore him a son, Marduk. All the while, the droughts and suffering continued. They continued irrigation in some areas, wells in others. This enabled them to produce plants, berries, etc. to eat and to make powdered vitamins. Always just enough to get by, but never enough. They knew that their only salvation was gold from planet Earth/Tiamat. Throughout the years, astronauts were sent to travel through the Asteroid Belt in hopes of reaching Tiamat, but they and their craft would be crushed soon after entering the Belt.

After Alalu had reigned for nine shars, Anu finally saw the opportunity to battle Anu. It was in the public square when he was unguarded. Anu could no longer bear to serve one who is lesser than he, one who lied about his lineage to acquire the throne. He, whom he had to serve as his cup-bearer.

"Alalu," he screamed as he grabbed his arm and threw him to the ground. "Take off your clothes and weapons (as was the custom) I challenge you to the throne you stole from me. You have not fulfilled any of your promises to save our planet you made in the beginning of your reign."

Startled shoppers watched in shock as a horrific battle ensued; falling, rising, thrusting. Hand to hand combat in naked bodies they went. Door posts trembled, walls shook, on and on they went, rolling, jumping up and screaming curses. Alalu was becoming weaker. Anu, still strong as he kept in shape awaiting this day.

Anu jerked him from behind and Alalu, exhausted, fell to the ground on his chest. Immediately, Anu forced his foot on the fallen man's back and declared, "I am the winner, I have taken the throne from one who stole it from me."

The crowd cheered, shouting praises to Anu. They put him on their shoulders to carry him to the palace.

Alalu seized this moment to escape and he ran to the space ship hangers for he too, had a secret plan feeling this day would come. He knew his fate was either death or exile. He hurried to the large space craft, Triton, that he prepared for this very day. He sat in the commander's seat. And quickly turned on the dashboard/panel which contained a cosmic map and the Tablets of Destinies. He fired up the engines, set the destination course; Tiamat/Earth. Up, up, up he soared.

He looked back at his beloved planet. It was hanging like a ball in void, belching fire blazed forth. He saw it as a sustaining envelope, reddish in color and moving like a churning sea. Alalu could see the breach that gaped at him like a darkened wound. Then Nibiru looked like a small tub. He cried aloud, "Gone…gone."

He raced past by Pluto knowing then that he was on the right course. He raced past Neptune, Uranus, Saturn and Jupiter. Fear gripped him as he saw the Asteroid Belt come upon him so swiftly. He was frightened, but now he knew that he must put his plan into operation. He had loaded 10 nuclear missiles into the Triton with the hope that he could blast his way through the Belt. Just as he was about to enter the dreaded death trap, he blasted forth the first nuclear missile and it made a path for him, forcing the deadly boulders out of the way, following close behind.

Beads of sweat streamed down his face, fear gripping him. Then another and then the third missile continuing through the opened path followed closely behind it. The door was opened before him. He shrieked when he saw the Sun, then he saw the sixth planet and said aloud, "There is Mars. White at both ends, reddish in the center and there are lakes."

His craft was following its predetermined course from Nibiru to Tiamat/Earth. He looked upon the Earth with fascination. He found it to be smaller with a gravitational pull weaker than Nibiru. The tops and bottoms were white with blue and brown between. Alalu spread his craft's wings to slow down and circle the ball, coming in closer. Fearful to land on the water, not knowing if he would live or die, not knowing if he would ever see his family again, he left his life to fate.

Fully caught in the Earth's gravitational pull, his craft was moving faster. It crashed and the craft shook, emitting a thunder… **Alalu did not move.**

Back on Nibiru, it had been seven days since the coup and Alalu was nowhere to be found. It was thought that he had escaped to the mountains. Ea was called from his classroom to go to the palace conference room immediately. Upon entering, he was surprised to see the sages, savants and Enlil seated with King Anu. They all had a puzzled look on their faces. Ea sat down not knowing what to expect.

King Anu said, "Gentlemen, I am about to tell you some shocking news. I received a radio beam from Alalu. He is on planet Tiamat/

Earth. I told him I would assemble you to hear him directly. He is waiting to speak to you."

Totally agog, disbelieving what they had just heard, couldn't' speak. Their mouths were agape. Anu turned on the radio and told Alalu to speak, "Men of Nibiru, I am here on Tiamat. I have planned this trip for a long time. I stored 10 nuclear missiles on the Triton to blast my way through The Hammered Bracelet to reach the planet of gold. I have found GOLD…Did you hear, I have found gold. If you don't believe me, check from where the radio beam is coming."

Thus, they did, still in shock, they listened as he continued, "I had a frightening trip through the system, almost being pulled into planets by their pull. I got through the dreaded Belt in much fear. After I crash landed, I slept for three days. When I awoke, I checked the air and found it habitable, then I found the water drinkable.

Then, I donned my fish suit and followed the water flow to come upon a pool of silent water…static…testing it, found it drinkable. While testing, I heard a hissing sound and saw a slithering body moving. It frightened me so I used my laser to kill it. It is a sight never before seen on Nibiru. It's body is like a long rope without hands and feet and its small head had piercing eyes. Out of its mouth a long tongue was sticking."

"I then put my gold tester into the water and it registered gold…gold. Do you hear me? I will send you proof, a sample of gold in the beam. You owe me, Anu I am your savior. We will keep in touch. For now, I will say good-bye."

Totally dumbfounded, filled with disbelief, they discussed what they had just heard and decided what was to be done; who would travel to Tiamat and what plans to be made. All savants were called to decide what to do.

Council was held, Ea and Enki were present. Ea decided he should be the one to go since he is Master of Waters and knows how to extract gold from the waters and he is Alalu's son-in-law. He had no reason to stay on Nibiru as mating with Ninmah to have a son was impossible, this would have guaranteed him kingship as she was also a child of Anu. He would never inherit kingship.

All agreed and plans began immediately: how many astronauts to take, which equipment for gold extracting, food for the journey, medicines, etc. Alalu would send a map as to where to enter the path in the Asteroid Belt he made with missiles. Ea decided to use water to blast through the Belt. He decided on 49 astronauts, each one with his own particular ability and contribution to the mission. The commanders had a shar/3,600 years to prepare for the journey.

The astronomers selected the proper time for lift off. When the time for the departure arrived, a multitude gathered at Cape Gaga/Pluto to bid farewell to the astronauts and Ea, their leader. The largest space craft, Kishar, ever made took the awe of the populace.

When the time for departure arrived, a multitude gathered at the Cape to bid farewell to the astronauts and Ea. The Nibiruan Anthem was proudly played with many tears falling as they stood at attention.

The men entered the craft one by one each bearing an eagles helmet and carrying a fish suit, a wet suit with fins. Ea's mother, Nimul held him to her heart. He kissed his wife, Damkina tenderly. He locked arms with his son, Marduk. Next with Enlil, he locked arms. "Be blessed Ea, be successful."

The band played softly as Ea knelt before his father to receive his blessing. "My son, fIrst- born, a far journey you have undertaken to be endangered for us. Let your success banish calamity from Nibiru. Go in safety and come back."

Ea rose to his feet, father and son locked arms. With a heavy heart, he entered the craft, turned to wave good-bye as his eyes scanned for Ninmah. He spotted her a short distance away, smiled and nodded a good-bye. She wiped away tears as she waved good-bye. The engines started with such a force that it shook the land. The people wondered how any craft so large could lift off.

Here then is the account of the journey to the seventh planet and how the Legend of the Olden Times/ the Legend of the fish that originated. (fish miter worn by those of the Vatican today).

Ea sat next to Anzu who sat in the commander's seat because he knew the heavens so well. He powerfully soared toward the Sun. Ten leagues, a hundred leagues, a thousand leagues toward Pluto who came out to greet them, it showed the way to the beautiful enchantress, Neptune.

"Let's examine her waters" said Anzu.

"No, no," shouted Ea. "You must continue on for it is the planet of no return!"

Anzu said excitedly, "There is Uranus. He is on his side (from the collision of Nibiru 4.5 billion years ago) with his moons swirling about him.!"

The tester's beam indicated there was water if needed. Anzu continued on to Saturn with its colored rings, the astronauts admired and feared him. They could feel the gravitational pull. Anzu deftly guided and cleverly avoiding the crushing danger.

"Look there is Jupiter. For certain, he is of firm ground as the tester beam indicates. Great Cosmic God, he is pulling us in. The net force is overpowering us!" Shouted the pilot. With fury, Jupiter was thrusting lightnings at the craft. The host of satellites seemed directed to the uninvited astronauts. Anzu with great skill diverted the craft making their way to encounter the next last enemy, the Asteroid Belt.

Ea said, "Anzu, there is the Hammered Bracelet and it is coming upon us quickly. It's time to test and pray my invention works… Engur, prepare the water blaster, make haste as our craft is rushing toward the host of turning boulders."

Ea's heart was pounding, he could feel it in his throat. In the cool cock-pit, he could feel beads of sweat on his forehead and his hands felt damp. He was frightened and hopeful that his water force would work. If not, they would all die. The turning boulders looked like a sling-shot furiously aimed at the craft.

"Ready, aim, fire. Go for it!" Shouted Ea. With the force of a thousand astronauts, the stream of water was thrust and one by one, the boulders turned face, making a space for the craft. As one boulder fled another was attacking in its stead. Their number was beyond account. It was as if old Tiamat was seeking revenge for Nibiru's satellites, North Wind splitting her in half. Again, and again Ea gave command to Engur to keep whirling the water thruster again and again. The water was directed at the host again and again. The boulders turned their faces, making a path for the Kishar.

Then at last the path was clear, the craft unharmed came out of the Hammered Bracelet. The Sun shone so bright, bright beyond what they had ever seen on Nibiru and it blinded their eyes. "We made it!" They acted like little children, jumping, laughing and filled with disbelief.

All at once, an alarm signaled danger, they were running low on fuel (water); excessive waters had been consumed to power the water thruster. Water to fuel the space craft's rockets for the remaining of the journey was insufficient. Ea's heart pounded in fear, "We will crash!" he shouted.

There in the dark deepness was Mars, the sixth planet. They could see it as it was reflecting the Sun's rays. The water tester indicated that there was water on Mars. "Anzu can you bring the craft down?"

"I'll give it a good try," he said as he headed for Mars and made a circle around it. "The planet's gravitational pull is not too strong, it is easy to handle."

Mars was a sight to behold with its many hues, snow white at both ends, reddish hued in the middle with lakes and rivers aglitter. Anzu made the huge craft go slower and carefully landed it by a lakeside. They could not believe what they were seeing; they had actually landed on another planet. Ea told his men to stay put as it wasn't known if Mars was compatible.

Anzu and Ea donned their helmets, stepped down to the firm ground. They smiled at each other with disbelief. "Engur, have the men lower the siphoning line into this lakeside. Fill the tank," hollered Ea through his microphone. They walked around and examined the area. They stretched out the air tester and water sampler and these indicated that the water was good, but the air was insufficient; they could not stay too long. All of this Ea recorded in the craft's annals from the time they left Nibiru.

They looked ahead to see the seventh planet, Tiamat (Earth) and its companion, the Moon and found them thrillingly inviting. They looked upon the planet of their destination. The planet that was Nibiru's salvation or doom. The craft circled the Moon to make slowing circles. They noticed it was lying prostrate and scarred from the North Wind satellite striking it 4.5 billion years earlier. Anzu lowered the craft and it was noticed that that two thirds of the planet are snow, and dark-hued was its middle where they could see firm land. They searched for the signal beacon from Alalu.

"Look yonder, I can see the beacon," said Anzu excitedly. "It's coming from the ocean near dry land. There are four rivers swallowed by marshes. The craft is too large and heavy to land on the marshes. Where Alalu landed, the earth's gravitational pull is too powerful for us to land on dry land. We are in a dilemma!" He said with trepidation.

Ea screamed, "Splash down, splash down in the ocean's waters" Anzu obeyed and he made one more circle around the planet, and with great care, he lowered the craft toward the ocean's edge. He filled the unoccupied chambers with air and splashed down in the water's depth in the Persian Gulf, an inlet of the Arabian Sea (Indian Ocean) and it did not sink. Far away they heard "To Tiamat (Earth/Ki) be welcomed," coming from Alalu's loud speaker.

What welcomed words they were. They determined his whereabouts by the direction of his beamed words. Anzu directed the floating craft toward Alalu. Soon the ocean narrowed and there was dry land on both sides. On the left there were brown-hued hills and on the right, there were mountains. Ahead there was some flooding of the dry land and marshes.

They put on their fish suits and with a strong rope they attached to the craft, and pulled it to shore. While swimming toward Alalu, his words became more powerful. "Hurry, hurry, this way." There, at the edge of the marshes, low and behold, they could see Alalu's space craft from Nibiru glowing in the sunlight. The men quickened their swimming, thus quickening their pull.

Ea, impatient his heart beating like a drum within his chest, put on his fish suit and jumped into the marsh. With hurried steps, he went toward the marsh. The marshes deeper than expected, he changed his gait to swimming and then he advanced forward toward with bold strokes, He could see green meadows ahead of him as his feet touched firm ground. He stood up and walked on dark-hued earth. He stood, filled with disbelief and said, "How can this be?" He wondered, still shocked of his daring trek.

"Here I am," called Alalu. He waved his hands vigorously and ran toward Ea. He powerfully embraced him. "My son, my son by marriage. Welcome to a different planet. One shar since I've seen you and since I talked to another person."

Ea embraced his father in-law, Alalu in silence, tears of joy filled his eyes, and he bowed his head in respect for this daring pioneer, his father-in-law. The 49 astronauts were advancing, some still donning their wet suits and more were rushing to dry land. "Keep the craft aloft, anchor it in the waters and avoid the mud ahead." Commanded Alalu.

Once ashore, the men bowed before Alalu. Anzu was the last to leave the craft and then, he too, bowed before Alalu. When he rose, Alalu welcomed him with locked arms. To all who arrived, Alalu spoke words of welcome.

When all were assembled, Ea stood up and spoke words of command, "Here on Earth, I am commander. We are here on a life or death mission. It's up to us whether or not our wives, children, parents and friends live or die. In our hands, is the fate of our beloved Nibiru."

THUS, THE LEGEND OF THE FISH GOD WHO CAME OUT OF THE WATER WAS BEGUN.

CHAPTER 4

EARTH'S BEGINNING

It was during the Philistine Ice Age, 445,000 years ago that the space craft with fifty astronauts splashed down in the Arabian Sea. They met their ex-King Alalu who had been residing on earth alone for 3,600 years.

Ea did not let them bask in their success too long. "There's a lot of work to be done and the sooner we dig in to do it, the better."

He looked for a place of encampment and spotted the reed hut that was erected by Alalu. "Heap up the soil and fashion mounds there where Alalu built on firm ground. It is close enough to our treasured gold in the water. We must get our shelter built. Alalu deliver my words to Nibiru to my father. Announce our successful arrival."

The men began to level the ground and dig with equipment they brought from Nibiru . . . they worked for hours stopping only to eat. Soon the hue of the sky was changing a brightness to a reddish color, a sight they had never seen before. The Sun as a red ball was disappearing on the horizon. Fear seized the men as they were already afraid that a great calamity was about to occur. "What is happening to Apsu (Sun)?" Screamed one of the men.

"What is going on?" Screamed a horrified Engur.

"Watching in the background, quite amused, stood Alalu, until he saw the seriousness of the situation. "It is the setting of the Sun," he said laughing. "I suggest that you lie down for a quick rest as a night on Tiamat (Ki) is unbelievably short. Before you know it, the Sun will be up and it will be morning."

Darkness came quickly and brought storm clouds, and lightening pierced the darkness and thundering rains followed. The strong winds blew water from the gulf, making the men chilled. They huddled in the craft. The men did not rest because they were upset, so agitated they were from excitement, and apprehensiveness as Kishar was being tossed to and fro from the strong winds. The first day ended on Earth.

The Sun returned and when its rays appeared, there was rejoicing and did much back slapping. After breakfast, Ea issued orders, "Engur, because of your knowledge of waters, you will be master of sweet waters. You will provide drinking water."

Alalu went with Engur to the snake pond to test it, but the evil serpents were swarming in the pond. So, in awe was Engur of these ugly, squiggly things that he took his wand and poked at them, laughing. He turned round and round and extended his foot into the water.

"Stop," cried Alalu. "Their bite will kill you! I've seen them strike large animals and kill them." They left for the water of the marshes and considered the abundance of rain water. Engur made a hole to gather the rainwater to separate the sweet waters from above and the marsh water below.

Ea ordered Enbililu in charge of the marshlands; telling him to mark out the thicket of reeds. He told Enkimdu that he was in charge of ditch and dike. "Make a boundary for the marshes." He ordered the others to continue on as yesterday.

The next day, they assumed their assigned tasks. The men announced that they were sick of eating manna and were running out of the ingredients to make it. So Ea with his vizier, Isimud, a horticulturist, went to the orchard to see and distinguished the herbs from the fruits. Isimud named them and took some to cook for the men. He was placed in charge of food. Now, food and water they had.

On the fourth day, the men were told to bring tools from the Kishar and start building abodes. "Mashdammu, you and half the men lay the foundations. Kulla, you and the other half of the men make bricks."

All day, the Sun shone, invigorating the men and they worked until night time. And it brought a beautiful sight never seen on Nibiru. A marvelous sight to behold they saw in the heavens… the Moon. It was a full moon and it cast a pale light on the earth.

"A lesser light to rule the night." said Ea. "It is the ending of our fourth day on earth." He marveled at all the earth had to offer them.

On the fifth day, they resumed their tasks. Ea told Nihgirsig to make a boat of reeds to measure the marshes and swamp land. He commanded Ulmash to distinguish between, and separate the good fish from the bad as he had great understanding of fish and fowl. Here, there were many he had never seen before. He was bewildered by their vast number and astonished that the good carp were swimming with the bad fish.

"Enbilulu and Enkimdu, in the marsh lands, make a barrier with cane breaks and green reeds to separate the good carp from the bad fish. Also make a snare to capture good fowl."

On the sixth day, Ea assigned Enursag the task of distinguishing all that creeps and all that walks. Enursag was astonished of their ferocity and wildness. "Kulla and Mashdammu, I want the abodes to be completed and surrounded by a fence."

The men laid the bricks on the foundation quickly and with reeds, they made the roofs. With cut down trees, they made the fencing. Anzu brought a laser gun for killing from the space-craft, and set up a speaker at Ea's abode. By evening, the encampment completed, the men could rest within. Ea, Alalu, and Anzu saw all was good. Thus, ended their sixth day.

On the seventh day, after breakfast, Ea assembled the men. "Heroes, a hazardous journey we have undertaken from Nibiru to the seventh planet, Earth/Ki. We arrived safely and in six days with much hard labor, we have established an encampment. Let our encampment be called Eridu which means, 'Home in the Faraway'. From the word Eridu we get the name Earth. (German; erde/erda).

Every time we say Earth, we are honoring the first settlement on Earth, Eridu, of 445,000 years ago. Every time the Pope, Cardinals, and Bishops don their fish hat (Miter) they are honoring the fish god Ea/Enki, our god of Nibiru, who came from the water and created man.

Thus, the seventh day of rest was originated at this time and held true until this day. EA continued, "Those on our home planet will be proud of us. Let Alulu be declared Commander of Eridu." All agreed.

Alalu spoke up, "Let Ea be called Nudimmud, the 'artful fashioner'. Now let us feast and rest on this seventh day."

It was morning on the eighth day on planet Earth. Ea started the task of obtaining gold from the marsh waters. He started Kishar's engines and extended its siphoning tube into the water. For six days, all the metals within the area was extracted from the marshes floor. They were sucked up and filtered through the crystal sieve vessel and the water ran from the sieve into the marsh water. All the metal remaining in the vessel for future examination. The men toiled for six days.

The metals were emptied into a separating vessel, separated and taken ashore by the heroes. So disappointed they were when they looked over the smallest accumulated pile which was the gold. Six more days of hard labor and the same result, little gold. This continued for weeks and during this time.

Ea was fascinated with and studied the Moon, waxing and waning. He named the Moon's circuits a 'month'. He noticed luminous horns which signified the month's start. The Moon's half-crown announced the seventh day. Fullness of the Moon indicated the half way of the circuit. Eventually, it lost its brightness. Then with the Sun's course, the Moon's circuit was appearing.

As Ea studied the Moon, feelings of sex, longing, romance and nostalgia stirred within his being. He was feeling the effects of the

Moon, unknown in Nibiru. He called for Ningirsig and instructed him to make harps, flutes, banjoes and any other musical instrument he could think of. "Make them out of wood, strong reeds and gourds. We must have music and song." So affected by the Moon was Ea. He noticed that every six months, Earth got a new season. Enki named them winter and summer. He called these two seasons one year.

The heroes toiled on and on, day after day, month after month, they labored for Nibiru. The craft siphoned out the metals. By the end of the year, the accumulated gold was counted. There was not enough to send to Nibiru. King Anu was notified by radio waves of the bad news.

"We must move out into the deeper ocean to find more gold. Men move the Kishar out further into the ocean and lower the siphoning tube to the ocean floor." This was done and metals and sparkling gold were found, great joy filled Ea's heart. He beamed the good news to his father. Ea did keep in touch with him often. On and on they worked, year after year. The men missed their families very deeply and knew the must carry on for the sake of saving Nibiru and their lives.

Ea again radioed his father and was surprised to hear the voice of Kumarbi, Alalu's grandson. He hastened the king to the speaker. He told his father that gold is sparkling out in the ocean, yet not enough gold is being produced.

Anu said, "It is nearly one shar since you left. Nibiru is nearing the Sun. This will bring us close to Mars and Earth on our solar circuit. Is there enough gold to send us as we near Earth?"

He replied, "No, father, we have not collected enough. You must let another shar pass, then, hopefully there will be enough."

Saddened, Anu said, "We must continue on in doing what we can do to survive. We are keeping alive, but not really living." He related that Marduk and Damkina, Ea's son and wife are well. He related that Marduk is showing signs of aggression. "He is resenting Enlil for trying to command you on earth on your quest for gold."

"We will work hard to save our planet. I will pray to our Creator of all that we succeed in finding enough gold. I miss you and all my loved ones. I will watch for beautiful Nibiru and wave to you as you pass. Good-bye, father." Ea choked up and wiped away tears as they fell.

Ea did resent Enlil bossing and telling him what to do, but he could not really control him. He thanked god that Enlil was on Nibiru. He cried for his loved ones and wondered if he would ever see them or his beloved Nibiru again. It was so boring on earth as compared to Nibiru. The only entertainment the men had was sitting by the fire at night. They played and sang songs of Nibiru, talked and reminisced.

One night, Isimud called from the small observatory atop a high, flat rock. "Look," he screamed in excitement, "There is Nibiru nearing Mars."

The men took turns looking through the scope and marveling as each man got to see the craft and converse with his loved ones. They could watch their home planet until it could no longer be seen. Many tears were shed, but life must go on and the toil for their loved ones. Each man hoped that one day, he would be able to return to Nibiru.

Time and toil continued on and once again it was determined that there was not enough gold to be shipped to their home planet when it neared. The time passed so quickly for the men on earth in comparison to Nibiru, that a year went quickly. Time had a different meaning on the slow- motion existence on Nibiru. On Earth the 12-hour day sent them into a dizzying spin of life, work during the day, only a short sleep and it was time to get up and start all over again.

Ea's heart was filled with sadness over the lack of gold. "There is something wrong. Gathering gold is a much slower process than we anticipated. We can never give up, we must continue siphoning the gold. We have been her 5,400 years, one and a half shars on Nibiru."

Months, years passed. "Anzu, something is not right. There is so much gold in the Asteroid Belt. The part of the Earth's from which the belt was torn must also contain much gold. We must take some of the parts we brought from Nibiru and make a sky chamber (helicopter). We need to survey the planet, this has been let go for too long."

From the storage room in the Kishar, they took the needed parts to assemble a sky chamber. Ea put Abgal in charge of the assembly. He was not only an excellent pilot, he knew the mechanics of flight. Ea ordered the men to build a hanger for the craft near Alalu's craft, the Triton.

Daily, Ea had Abgal fly him all over the earth. "We must find the cut-off part of the earth from where the belt was torn. This is where the large quantity of gold must be, I must learn the secret. In fact, I must learn all the earth's secrets."

Daily, he studied the viewing crystals (visual tapes in Alalu's craft to understand what their beams discovered and registered) He wanted to know where on Earth is earth's gold.

Ea and Abgal soared over the earth to learn its secrets, covering thousands of miles. They roamed over the mountains, valleys, rivers and forests, recording their findings. The beam from the helicopter scanned and penetrated the soils. One day, after they landed, Ea was called to the radio. "Ea, this is your father," said Anu.

"Hello, father. Abgal and I just returned from reconnoitering the lands in search of gold. How are you?"

"Not good, my son. Our patience is expended. We are growing desperate. Our efforts here are waning. My people are crying out for gold protection. Listen, my son and listen hard. Nibiru's completed shar near earth is close at hand. Assemble the gold and on our nearing, you must deliver the gold that you have. Do you understand? No more playing around and promising. We are desperate."

"But how can we deliver the gold? In what?" Asked Ea.

He answered, "Repair Alalu's craft, the Triton for bringing the gold to Nibiru when we near Earth. We will make use of any and all the gold you have. Do you understand?"

"Yes, father, it will be done." Answered Ea.

The next evening, after their reconnaissance mission, Ea and Abgal landed their copter near the Triton and entered it. They were agog when they spotted the seven nuclear missiles that Alalu had stored for his flight many, many years ago. Ea recognized the possibility of danger while working around them. He thought that there could be a serious accident while working around them. He and 'Abgal loaded them, took them to another land (Africa) and hid them inside a cave. Ea made certain that the encasements were sealed, locked and secured. He knew that they would be safe there.

Then, they soared back to Eridu where he told Anzu to repair the Triton. "Have it ready to travel to Nibiru when its circuit brings it near us."

Anzu and a few men worked hard and long on the craft. They repaired the engines, carefully tuned up the gears maps and panel. Not too long after he started,

Anzu discovered that the seven missiles were gone. In a fury, he headed for Ea. Irate with fists in the air, Anzu screamed out in anger. "Where in --- are the nuclear weapons? Without them or the water thruster, no one can pass through the Hammered Bracelet. The danger surpasses the endurance. What have you done?"

"Now, wait a minute, Anzu," fumed Ea. "Foreworn is the use of nuclear weapons; neither in the heavens nor on firm ground shall they never be harnessed!"

Alalu, commander of Eridu, heard the arguments and understood the dangers of working around missiles and the need to deliver gold to the coming Nibiru, and agreed.

Abgal, hearing the arguments and dangers of delivering the gold, volunteered to pilot the gold for the sake of Nibiru. "Let the stargazers of Nibiru select an opportune day to deliver the baskets of gold to our beloved Nibiru," said he.

On the appropriate day, Abgal entered the Triton and sat in the commander's seat. Ea took the Tablets of Destiny (maps) from his Kishar and gave them to Abgal. "May these tablets show you the way. God speed you to safety," said Ea as he shook hands with and hugged him.

The Triton was closed, the engines fired up and the rockets were enlivened, casting a red brilliance as the multitude of men bade them farewell. The chariot, Triton, soared heavenward.

On Nibiru, words of the ascent were radioed and there was much expectation from the inhabitants.

GOLD WAS ON ITS WAY!

CHAPTER 5

TOIL AND FRUSTRATION CONTINUE

On Nibiru, 434,200 years ago, excitement ran high, gold, thus their salvation was coming. "I will stay by our radio to receive and report to you the arrival of Abgal to Nibiru," said Anu.

Abgal reported with confidence, "I am now heading for the Moon. It has been three shars since I have traveled this way. I will circuit it twice to gain speed from its powers."

"Abgal, how do you feel about coming through the Hammered Bracelet?"

He replied, "I'm scared. Please pray that Ea's crystals will locate the open path he made three shars ago. I will have to enter it at a slant, and keep it slanted as I fly through the moving hole."

Time passed while the anxious Nibiruans awaited. Kumarbi stood close to the radio anxious to hear any news of his grandfather, Alalu. He never forgave King Anu for taking the throne from his grandfather.

Abgal saw the opening of the Bracelet and headed directly toward it. Slanting the Triton to glide into it, the craft was handling beautifully. Getting at the opening, he entered into it safely and glided through safely. "I am homeward bound. Ahh, the eye of fate has looked upon me with favor and has brought me through safely," he said softy to himself. Then, he screamed aloud, "I'm receiving signals from Nibiru. I'm homeward bound!"

Those on Nibiru were thrilled to see the large, beautiful craft coming through the thickness of the atmosphere which is hundreds of times thicker than Earth's. The crowd joyfully greeted him as he exited the craft. "Abgal," they shouted. "You have brought us salvation, Our hero!"

He was taken to his quarters to freshen up before they dined. There, at the long table, were the royalty; King Anu, Ninmah, Enlil, sages and others. All were delighted to hear about Earth. He told them of the dizzying earth, the Sun, Moon and their circuits, seasons and the hours in a day. He told them of the constant toil for gold.

Enlil asked in length about Ea. Abgal answered with uneasiness as all knew of the feud between the brothers. "Ea is working very hard, he is loyal and dedicated to the salvation of Nibiru. He gets homesick for Nibiru and each of you. He misses his family very much and hopes to visit here one day."

"I must tell you about the serpents. They are unseen on Nibiru and very frightening to behold. They are like a rope, they are without hands and feet and slither on the ground to get from one place to another. They have a small face, with small beady eyes and a tongue that strikes fast to kill. One bite can kill you." He shivered as he spoke of them.

On and on went the questions and answers. He told them of all the fruits, berries, herbs, and how Isimud, skilled as a horticulturist named all the plants, fruits and berries. He mentioned the ferocious beasts.

But very important was the subject of the dizzying planet and its effect on them; speeding up the time. He told them of the beautiful Moon and its strange effect on the men; romance, longing, nostalgia and longing for their home, Nibiru. After a lengthy conversation, they retired to their quarters.

The gold brought by Abgal had been taken immediately to be pulverized and shot into the breach. It would be determined that the gold was sufficient for another shar. The shar passed and when they neared the earth, gold was delivered to the craft; there would be enough gold for another shar. At that time, Abgal decided to stay on Nibiru for another shar to return 3,600 years later.

When they returned the same scenario took place with Abgal saying he wished to return to Nibiru. He would do this for a total of 4 shars. Each time, there was always just enough gold for the following shar.

The Nibiruans on Earth were happy to keep their home planet alive, but it was never enough to make them feel secure. It had been a long time since Ea had traveled over the earth, looking for gold. He knew there was gold; a lot of it…somewhere…but where? Again, he and Abgal began traveling the earth every day searching. Then, one day, traveling lower Africa (Absu), Ea saw something glistening. He let out a scream, "Universal God, GOLD…GOLD…GOLD. Look Abgal, GOLD!"

It was the end of the Pilestine Ice Age 416,200 years ago the snow and ice were melting and gold was showing itself everywhere. "We must radio father and tell him the good news, "Gold is found, much gold, father!"

Enlil immediately suggested that he go to Earth to be in command. The savants agreed and plans began immediately. King Anu radioed Ea to tell him that Enlil was coming to Earth to be in command. Ea's heart sank. He thought about Enlil taking away his kingship on Nibiru, taking away his beloved Ninmah, who bore Enlil's son, Ninurta.

Now his thoughts were that "He will come to Earth to bask in my hardships that I've gone through for 28,800 years." When Kumarbi heard of Enlil's new position of commander of Earth, he was furious as his thoughts were; "Now, Enlil will take away my grandfather's rulership on Earth." His resentment would continue to grow. And then, there was Marduk, Ea's son, who was furious for a long time over Enlil being made king of Nibiru one day, and now to rule over planet Earth.

While he, Marduk, has had no recognition or position at all as grandson to King Anu. He too would grow more resentful. Enlil and his crew immediately headed for Earth. When he arrived, he immediately took over. The brother's rivalry immediately returned. Ea tried to conceal his anger as Enlil started to boss everyone. Alalu was angry also as Enlil was taking over his rulership of Eridu. King Anu decided to come to Earth to settle who would control what. The salvation of Nibiru was at stake.

King Anu also arrived 416, 200 years ago. He was welcomed, fed and shown to his quarters. The next day, he held counsel and as he issued orders, Alalu went to get a plate of food and as he returned, he saw Anu in the reeds, gathering three reeds. He witnessed Anu cut them to different sizes and hold them a certain way in his hand in order to control the choices.

Anu said, "Let us three choose lots to see who will become King of Nibiru and who will rule which areas on Earth. The one who chooses the longest reed will become King of Nibiru, the second longest chosen, will remain in Eridu and the third will take over Africa."

Anu continued, "I will draw first. When you draw a reed, hold it in your hand until I tell you to open it."

Anu drew first and kept the reed clenched in his fist. He told Enlil to draw the second and as he held the closest one to him, he nodded to Enlil that one was the one to take. Then to Ea to take the last one. All three held his firmly in his hand and when Anu gave the orders to open the hand at the count of three, they did so. They opened their fists and a shocked Ea, after glancing over the three reeds, gasped in emotion. "Oh, my god," he whispered, "My beloved Eridu!"

Anu said, "By fate, have we chosen. I will return to Nibiru. Enlil, you are allotted Eden; over it, you will be Lord of Command. You must establish more settlements. You will take charge of the sky ships. Then the men from all the lands from the Eden to the sea, you will be the leader."

Enlil's smile was more of a smirk. Ea, unable to speak, let out a silent scream, his heart was broken. Anu raised his voice in a manner of importance to have Ea feel as if he had done him a favor, "Ea, the land beyond the water you will govern. You will be Master of the Abzu (Africa) where you will procure the gold with your ingenuity."

Enlil pleased, bowed to King Anu. Ea, still shocked unable to speak. He choked up, his eyes filled with tears as he did not wish to be parted from his Eden and his Eridu.

To comfort him, Anu said, "Let Ea retain his home in Eridu, being the first to splash down, he must be remembered. Let Ea be known as Master of the Earth. From here on, he will be known as Enki. Lord of the Earth (lord of Earth/Ki)."

The men were called to assembly, where Anu spoke to all his decisions. Alalu, angry since the arrival of Enlil, was now filled with extreme anger, and remembering him catching him off guard to steal the throne of Nibiru from him, and seeing what he had just done to Ea, Alalu was foaming.

Alalu stepped forward to Anu, his fist in the air, he shouted, "A grave matter happened eight shars ago. That was the promise when I announced I discovered gold on Earth. Nor have I forgotten the claim to Nibiru's throne."

With eyes popping, neck veins bulging and a reddened face, Alalu went on, "You took the throne from me, you then promised I would be master of Earth. You said Ea was the first to splash down." He screamed, "Liar, now you take it all from me. You took the throne from me and that is unforgiveable. And now, you share all of this with your sons, a grave abomination. I challenge these decisions!"

Then, he neared Anu in a daring manner and in a lower tone, through clenched teeth, he screamed, "Liar, thief, I challenge these decisions."

In the beginning, Anu was startled, without words. Then, he swelled and spoke in anger, "By a second wrestling our dispute will be decided. Let us wrestle here. Let us do it now!" he screamed. Anu was well prepared to fight as he kept in shape knowing one day, he would be confronted by Alalu.

With a look of distain, Alalu removed his clothing; Anu did likewise. The two royals grappled and a mighty struggle ensued on the counsel room floor. Round and around they went, back and forth, over and over. The men shocked with disbelief as they watched the royals battle. Hatred could be seen on their faces, spit and sweat was flying.

All the while Alalu was weakening more. Anu saw this and knew his time had come, he lunged at Alalu, bent him backward bending his knee, causing him to fall backward onto the floor. Anu swiftly placed his foot on Alalu's chest, thereby declaring victory.

Anu said loudly, "By wrestling, the decision is made. I am King and you, Alalu will never be permitted to return to Nibiru." He removed his foot from the fallen man.

Then, totally shocking the onlookers, Alalu as quick as lightening, sat upright and in a fit of anger grabbed the unsuspecting Anu's legs and pulled them down. In a heated frenzy, with his mouth wide open and screaming from the bowels pulled himself upward and bit off Anu's testicles. Not meaning to, he took a deep angry breath and swallowed the testicles.

In pained agony, Anu screamed a cry to heaven, wounded he fell to the floor. The onlookers dazed with disbelief as Enki ran to his fallen father. Men carried Anu to his hut as he screamed curses, "Alalu, you are a doomed man."

Enlil rushed to grab the enraged Alalu and held him captive. He then was shocked when he saw Alalu laugh hysterically. Enlil shouted above the commotion to his lieutenant, "Let justice be done. Kill Alulu with your laser!"

"No, no," Enki fiercely shouted. "Justice be within Alalu. His innards are poisoned by Anu's semen. Bind his hands and feet and take him to his hut."

Enki returned to his father who was in much pain. Enki, deep in the knowledge of medicines applied a healing to his father's wound.

In his reed hut, Alalu was sitting and began to vomit spittle. In his innards, the male hood of Anu was becoming a burden as the semen was impregnating his innards and like a pregnant woman, his belly grew swollen. He was poisoned. Anu's pain subsided on the third day, but his pride still greatly wounded. "To Nibiru I wish to return. But first, there must be a judgment on Alalu, a sentence befitting the crime must be imposed."

In the square of Eridu, the men assembled to observe the trial of Alalu. By the law of Nibiru, seven judges must be present and seven seats provided. He was brought before the seven judges with hands and feet tied.

Enlil spoke, "In fairness, a wrestling match was held and kingship was forfeited to Anu. Having been vanquished, Alalu performed an abominable crime. He bit off the testicles of King Anu. Death is the punishment. What say you, Alalu?"

Alalu, pale and sickly, spoke slowly, "On Nibiru, I was king, reigning by right of succession. Anu was my cup-bearer. For nine shars, I was king of Nibiru. Anu challenged me and took the throne of my sons. To escape death, I made a dangerous journey to this distant planet. I discovered salvation for Nibiru."

Then Anu came here and by lots tricked Ea. I saw what he did in the drawing of the reeds. Then to appease Ea, he named him Enki, Lord of Earth. For eight shars, I have been commander over Eridu and now this was taken from me." He was weakening but got no sympathy from the men.

Anu spoke up. "By royal seed, by law and by fair wrestling did I gain kingship of Nibiru. You bit off my manhood, swallowed it and now my offspring line is discontinued."

Enlil spoke up, "For the crime thus accused let the judgment come. Let death be the punishment." All agreed except Enki, "No, death to Alalu will come by itself. What he has swallowed in his innards will bring death."

Others spoke up, "Anu, in anger and pity said, "To die in exile be his punishment. Neither on Earth nor Nibiru shall he be exiled. On planet Mars it shall be. We made a stop there for water. I have been thinking of making it a way station. It is endowed with water, air and atmosphere. Although not the best air, it's livable."

They sailed by boat to reach the space craft for departure. Anu told Enlil to prepare a landing place on firm ground in the Eden for the space ships to land. He said since the gold is coming faster, a flight plan must be made to transport gold from Abzu/Africa to Eridu/Kuwait and also begin to utilize Mars as a way station.

Anu limped to the craft. Alalu was taken, hands tied as he entered with Anzu, his kin. There were farewells, both of sorrow and joy. Nungal circuited the Moon and headed for Mars.

There, Nungal circuited the planet twice and came into the strange planet. They noticed that it had tears on its surface and they marveled at its high mountains. They observed the lakeside where Enki's chariot landed eight shars ago to water up.

They readied the sky chamber/helicopter for Alalu's descent. He was untied, escorted to and strapped in the seat. Anzu was expected to land the craft and let Alalu off with supplies, but he made an unexpected statement, "I will land Alalu on firm ground. I do not wish to return in the sky chamber to the mother ship. I will stay with him on this strange planet until he dies. I will protect him and when he dies of the poison. I will give him a burial befitting a king."

There were tears in Alalu's eyes and amazement in Anu's heart as he said, "Your wish shall be granted. Here by I make a promise to you, by my raised hand to you I swear that on the next chariot to Earth, the pilot will circle Mars, land and pick you up. If you are found alive, you will be proclaimed Master of Mars. When the way station is established on Mars, you will be the commander."

Nungal had loaded into the craft two eagle helmets, two fish suits, food and supplies. Anzu as the pilot, entered the sky chamber and departed from the mother ship. Anu and Nungal watched the descent until it disappeared. They continued on their way to Nibiru.

King Anu received a joyful welcoming. The next day, he summoned the savants and told them all that occurred on Earth during their stay. "I have plans for gold extraction and devise methods of delivering it here. We must manufacture machines here that will extract the gold. Enki will figure a way to extract it and he will radio us on what equipment to make. There must be way stations established on Mars. All the planets will be one family."

He continued, "I am also considering a way station on the Moon. On the other planets, or their circling satellites, way stations will be set up. There will be a constant chain of caravans of space ships to supply and safe guard the gold without interrupted."

The savants saw promise of salvation. Chariots and sky ships were made and a new kind of rocket ship was added. Men were placed in tasks for which they had talents and were given extended learning. These plans were radioed to Enki and Enlil and were told that they must speed up their preparations.

Enki replied that he told Alagar, overseer of Eridu and mapped out a route from Africa to Eridu which will hasten the golds transport. The gold will be from the bowels of the earth, "I need more men to excavate and tools for extracting; an earth-splitter to reach the innards, the motherlode by way of tunnels. Also need is an earth crusher to be able to extract."

Father, we also need medications. One in particular for Enlil's dizziness caused by the spinning Earth. He also suffers from the Sun's heat. He longs for coolness and shade.

Anu responded that he would send herbs and medicines. And he would begin manufacturing the equipment needed. Enlil, in his flying disc, surveys the extent of his Eden. He spotted where to establish a place for the landing of the craft. He saw a place that quickened his heart to build his home on the snow-covered mountains on the north side of Eden amid the tallest trees, in the Cedar Forest.

He had his men begin construction on the landing place and his home. They flattened the surface with power/laser beams. They quarried and cut great stones from the hill side and carried them by sky ships using anti-gravitation and placed them as a great foundation for the landing place. He said, "This landing place will be for future generations to marvel."

The men made from the cedar trees a strong foundation for his home so beautiful to behold; secluded by many shade trees. He called it, 'The Abode of the North Crest'.

On Nibiru, Ninmah was summoned by her father, King Anu. Beautiful to behold she was with her long blond hair and blue eyes and very kind. He told her shocking news, "Prepare during the next shar to gather all that would be needed to go to Earth and set up a medical center."

She sat there, her mouth agape, she could not speak, just stare.

He continued, "You will need medicines, medical supplies, herbs, growing seeds, plants. I will give you a list. You will choose seven of your best and brightest nurses. You must train them in all medicines and administering treatments to our men on Earth and for future men who will arrive. You are an exalted woman, greatly learned in succor and healing treatments of all ailments."

She just stared in amazement, shocked and her head was spinning, "Oh, yes, I will do all you say…Oh, father, what of Enki? Do you think he can forgive me for having a son by Enlil?"

He replied, "So concerned he is over getting gold for our salvation, I'm certain he has forgotten it. I'm sure both brothers will be happy to see you. I am sending fifty astronauts with you also."

"Thank you so much for sending me." Ninmah departed and jumped for joy.

Time passed and when Nibiru neared Earth, the ship was readied for take-off, King Anu said, "Nungal, do not forget to stop on Mars to see if Anzu is alive. If he is, he may need care. Use your detection beam to follow the signal that is coming from his helmet. If he is alive, tell him my promise to him that he will be commander of Mars still holds."

Tears flowed and good-byes were said as 58 Nibiruans entered their huge craft. Ningal smiled and gave a salute as he boarded. Into the heavens they soared, they landed on Mars and a small group of men and Ninmah exited the craft to locate Anzu. A faint beam was picked up from Anzu's helmet and they followed it, they found him beside a lake shore. He was prostrate and motionless, he lay dead.

Ninmah listened to his heart and declared he was dead, she asked for the pulsar from her pouch. She placed the pulsar on his heart. She then took the emitter from her pouch and placed it directly to his body. On the sixth time, Anzu opened his eyes and motioned words from his lips. She poured water of life on his face and slowly poured some in his mouth. Gently, she gave small bits of food; so gentle was Ninmah.

Anzu awakened and smiled as he looked into her beautiful face. "I thought you were an angel."

When he improved, they questioned him about Alalu. He told them to follow him. Barely able to walk, he led them to a rock. It protruded upward from the planet.

He related, "Soon after we landed. Alalu began to scream in pain. From his mouth, he was spitting up his innards in agony, he peered over the wall (died). In a great rock, I found a cave and therein I hid his corpse. I covered the entrance with stones."

They found a pile of bones lying in the cave. Ninmah said, "For the first time in our annals, a king of Nibiru has died outside our planet and buried there. Let him rest for eternity rest."

They covered the cave entrance with stones and held a burial service. With a laser beam, they carved the image of Alalu upon the top of the great rock mountain. They depicted him wearing his eagles helmet and left his face uncovered.

Ninmah declared. "Let this image of Alalu forever gaze toward his beloved Nibiru that he once ruled as king for nine shars." She choked back tears saying, "Let his image also gaze upon Earth whose gold he discovered and from where he commanded for eight shars."

*#1 THUS, THE FACE ON MARS FOREVER GAZING AT TWO PLANETS.

A short pause, "And to you, Anzu, Anu's promise that you will be commander of Mars will be. Twenty men will remain on Mars with you to begin building a way station. Ships from Earth will deliver gold ores to Mars. Celestial ships shall then transport the gold to Nibiru. Hundreds of men will make their home on Mars."

Supplies and equipment were unloaded from the craft. The twenty-one who remained bid a sad farewell to those departing. From the planet Mars, the chariot departed toward Earth carrying precious cargo….women.

Toward Earth did Ninmah journey to fulfill her destiny.

Mother of Mankind

Ninmah

Mamah

Mamma

CHAPTER 6

ESTABLISHMENT OF FIVE CITIES

The crew of fifty men and eight women arrived on Earth 412,600 years ago. So happy were Ea and Enlil to see their sister. Over supper they discussed many things that happened on each planet. The brothers were pleased with the equipment, especially Ea and the medicines from home.

"You will be able to see Alalu's face on Mars through the telescope," said Ninmah. "And oh, Kumarbi took the exile and death of his grandfather very hard. He retreats to his quarters every time he can since he heard of it."

That night the sleep was welcomed. The following morning Enlil took his sister to show her his home and the landing place for the sky ships. When they exited the craft, he picked his sister up in his arms and quickly took her to his abode. Rushing her to his bedroom he said, "Oh, my sister. my sister," while tearing off her clothes, "It has been so long." He passionately made love and then they nestled and talked in each other's arms. He asked her about his son, Ninurta.

"He is a handsome man, like his father. He wishes to come to Earth to be with you. He cries out for this adventure."

At this time, Enki flew over Enlil's abode and knew they were making love. Knowing that his beloved Ninmah was in his brother's arms broke his heart. He was still in love with her and still hoped for a son by her. He started speeding in his craft, raising his voice, he said, "Enlil, you took my throne on Nibiru, thus taking the throne from my son, Marduk. You took my parents from me, you sired a son by my love and you have taken Eden from me."

"Now your son, Ninurta, will be coming here and taking away from my sons. You will use here the 'Law of the Seed' of Nibiru of Nibiru to take everything from me."

He soared, screaming out in emotional pain as he flew to the Abzu, soaring over and over. He then spiraled downward to speed land with his ship spinning round and round. He stopped, shouted out and then sobbed. His siblings were unaware of his of his pain.

In the meantime, Enlil took Ninmah to look over his Eden and to see the wonderful plans for the great landing platform he planned. "It will forever be." #2 Baalbek. He then took her to the place to plant her grape seeds. A place that would produce juicy fruit to make elixir for the men.

"Come, I will show you the place where I will build your Medical Center, Shurubak will be its name." So delighted was Ninmah. "My own Medical Center, how very wonderful," she said as they flew over the area. Enlil said,

"There will be five cities in my Eden; Sippar (Bird City), the landing place, Nibiru-Ki (Mission Control Center, Shurubak, Lagar and Lagash (Beacon City/Lebanon." The five cities that were first built.

In the Abzu, Enki began to make plans for the building of his abode in the South East. It was a land bursting of riches and perfect fullness. A mighty river rushes across the region with great waters flowing in the wind (Victoria Falls in the west of Zimbabwe in South East Africa.

Then Enki decided where the place of deepness was and men began to use the earth splitter to descend into the bowels of the earth. A gash was made and the men began to work, gold was brought up. Near by the earth crusher was placed and work began to crush the earth to remove the gold ore and placed on sky ships to carry to the landing place near the Cedar mountains.

Night and day, the men toiled working in shifts. In the evenings by the moon light the men would sing, drink Ninmah's wine, play and listen to music. The women would come from Shurubak to be with the men. Not so for the men on Mars; they could enjoy music, drink wine, but no women. They became resentful.

Time passed, cities on Earth were continuing to be built. Some tired Anunnaki were returning to Nibiru to rest. More Nibiruans were arriving, some to Eden, to Mars and some to the Abzu. The men on Mars were establishing way stations with Anzu as a tough task master.

409,000 years ago, the two hundred fifty men in Eden, the three hundred in the Abzu and the and the three hundred men on Mars were radioed to assemble near their radios to hear and watch the first lift off of gold being transported from Sippar to Mars.

King Anu announced, "Men of Earth, Nibiruans those on Mars, you are saviors. The fate of Nibiru is in your hands. From this time on, those who reside on Earth will be called the Anunnaki (those who from heaven to Earth came). You on Mars and the way-stations, Phobos and Deimos will be called the Igigi, (those who observe, the Watchers)." These men were peons from Nibiru).

Anu shouted, "May the God of the Universe watch over us. Blast the first rocket. Let the gold come! . . . **Count down. 10, 9, 8, 7, 6, 5, 4, 3, 2, 1…LIFT OFF!**" With a mighty roar, up it soared. Shouts of joy pierced the day. GOLD was on its way directly from Earth to Mars.

Sometime later, shock ran out through the Earth when Enlil was arrested for date rape by a young nurse, Sud. He had an eye for her and seduced her to his abode. He gave her wine, but she resisted his advances telling him she was a virgin, but he heeded not. Later, Ninmah saw her weeping and when she was told what Enlil did, she was furious. Enki was called in on the matter. It was taken to the Seven Judges who pronounced that he must into exile forever.

He was taken there by Abgal who showed him the seven nuclear missiles in the cave if he wished to use them as a bargaining tool to return home. Some time passed, Sud went to Ninmah to tell her she was pregnant. Before the judges, Sud said she forgave him. They decided he was forgiven, but he must marry her.

Abgal was sent to return him to his abode in the Eden. Sud was given the title Ninlil. At the allotted birth time, Ninmah assisted her in child birth, a son, Nannar, was born.

With the pleading of Enki, Ninmah went to live with him in the Abzu. She bore him two daughters. Both times, he was furious that she did not give him sons and would have nothing to do with his daughters.

So disappointed was he that after the first daughter was born, to appease himself, he would go to the jungles to escape. One day, he spotted a creature that shocked him. "What is it? It walks upright." It's body was covered with hair and had head hair like that of a lion, and it used its two front legs as hands. He watched them climb trees, eat bananas, frolic, mate and was totally filled with disbelief as to what he was seeing.

For the third time, he went after Ninmah violently, sexually, tearing at her clothes, and through clenched teeth screamed, "Give me a son!!"

"Enough," screamed Ninmah. "Enough, I'm leaving." And so she did. Enki continued to go to the jungle to study the creatures.

Enki summoned his wife, Damkina and his son, Marduk to come to Earth the next time Nibiru neared. At that time, Kumarbi asked permission to be left off at Mars. He said that he wished to be near the body of his beloved grandfather, Alalu, but he had a secret plan, a plan of revenge...rebellion to take over Earth.

When Damkina and Marduk arrived, they went to Enki's home in Eridu. She was given the title Ninki (Lady of Earth).

When the three cities in the Eden were completed: Larsa, Lagash and Shurubak, Enlil notified Enki that he needed his talents and his earth-splitter in the Eden to build the city, Nibiru-Ki (bond between heaven and earth). For six shars (36,000 years), Enlil lived in Larsa while his city was being erected. Back and forth went Enki, from the Abzu, to Eridu to govern his city where his wife and son lived. He was needed in both lands. When over worked or disappointed with his life, Enki would go to the jungles to watch and study the strange creatures. They were getting used to his presence and accepting him.

Kumarbi on Mars, for a long time had been stirring up rebellion; telling the three hundred Igigi that they have no say in anything, they have no pleasure, they should have rest areas on Earth when loading the gold before returning back and they should have women.

Often, the Igigi would go to their supervisor, Shamgaz. "Tell Anzu to speak up for us. Let him go to Enki to plead with him that we need rest when we come to Earth. We unload gold on Mars, return to Earth to load, and return to Mars to unload. Those on Earth have rest and entertainment."

"We have little sleep, no green grass and no freedom to walk the soil without apparatus. We watch the Nibiruan children grow on Earth. We want our own wives, children and abodes. Our lives grow tiring and boring."

Anzu took these grievances to Enki and he promised they would get some of their wishes.

In the Abzu, there was much toil, the miners worked in three shifts. They did have pleasure; in the evenings there was wine, music and sometimes women. They enjoyed watching the children grow, playing with them, teaching them, but discontent over the hard labor prevailed.

Gold was shipped from Africa to the landing place in Sippar and from there to Phobos, Deimos, Mars and then to Nibiru. This time when Nibiru neared the Earth, Anu called a meeting to assemble.

The Anunnaki praised Enki with this poem:

Great gods who had hither come, Anunnaki gods who to court assemble come!. My son had for himself

> a house built: The Lord Enki, Eridu like the mountain on Earth he raised His house, in a beautiful place Eridu, no one uninvited can enter. In its sanctuary, from the Abzu the divine formula Enki deposited.

A hymn to Eridu edited and translated by A. Falkenstein, Sumer Vol, VII.

In Nipper, the beautiful Nibiru-Ki was completed. Placed on a stone mountain, it had a beautiful domed observatory, and a tall pillar/radio tower to speak directly to Nibiru. There was Mission Control Center and a dark chamber which held the secret formulas/discs.

These contain all information, creation, evolution, history of the Solar System, all information of astronomy, astrology, medicines. Herbs, laws, cosmology, science, genetics, food, beer, life, death, illness of Earth and cures, everything and all things. There were cameras that Enlil could see all his cities and even behind their walls.

On Earth, the Anunnaki, tired and worn out were sent back to Nibiru. Fresh, young men arrived and were gung-ho. But the Igigi complaining loudly, they demanded rest. Enlil said angrily, "You are selfish. Think of the salvation of Nibiru. You will have a rest area here one day."

The First War on Earth; The War of the Titans. 355,000 years ago.

On Mars, Kumarbi was furious at what Enlil said. He told his men to prepare for battle and leave for Deimos. Shamgaz seeing the danger, radioed Anzu, told him of Kumarbi's rebellion and to prepare twenty chariots. "Leave for Deimos immediately as I want Kumarbi to see your show of power, he wants to battle Enlil and Enki for control of Earth."

Anzu radioed Enlil to tell him of the impending battle. He said he would try to delay the battle by threatening him with a show of the twenty chariots. "Something must be done immediately."

Enlil radioed Enki and Anu. The king suggested that Anzu come to Earth to discuss any possibility to calm Kumarbi. Shamgaz, with his twenty chariots was told to go close to him, show his strength, threaten him that Anzu was on Earth discussing the grievances. Kumarbi saw the dangers of Shamgaz and heeded.

On Earth, Enlil decided to show Anzu all that he accomplished; his five cities, the observatory, his beautiful abode. He showed him the cameras in the five cities where he could see and hear all and everyone, even within the walls. He took him to the dark chamber where the wealth of the world's information was kept, the Mes and the Tablets of Destinies with power to light all things.

Anzu welled up in jealously. He, who descended from the heavens to resolve the Igigi's problems was about to do the unthinkable. He knew he was of royal blood, a kin of Alalu. Anger, jealously and hatred welled up inside of him. He had a plan.

Anzu told Enlil that he would go to Deimos to console the men; tell them that Enlil will start immediately to give them their wishes. He soared into the heavens with jealously in his heart. There, he told them of his evil plan; to steal the power of the Tablets. They were delighted.

"I plan to take away the Tablets of Destiny, take control of the decrees of heaven and Earth and his instrument of power." He departed for Eden. "I will remove Enlil from his lofty position. I will rule the Igigi."

> Etched in stone about 355,000 years ago. "I will take the celestial tablets of Destinies; The decrees of the gods I will govern, I will establish a throne, be master of the heavenly decrees; The Igigi in their place I will command."

Anzu arrived back at Nibiru-Ki and headed for the dark chamber. Enlil greeted him and they further discussed the resting place for the Igigi. Unsuspecting Enlil left the sanctuary and went for a cooling swim. With evil purpose, Anzu seized the Tablets. In his chariot, he flew away to the mountains of the sky chambers to the landing place and there, the Igigi were awaiting him. They were preparing to make Anzu king of Mars and Earth. By that time, the brilliance in the sanctuary of Nibiru-Ki petered out. The humming had quieted down, silence had prevailed there.

The Sacred Formulas were suspended.

*Suspended were the Divine Formulas; the lighted brightness petered out; silence prevailed. In space, the Igigi were dumbfounded; The sanctuary brilliance was taken off. *etched in stone.

Enlil was speechless and overwhelmed by Anzu's treachery. He blamed Enki for this by sending Anzu to Nibiru-Ki. The men of Earth got together and declared the culprit must be taken down, but by whom?

Who must the rebel face? Ninmah went to her son, Ninurta and told him he was the only one who could stand up against him. She gave him her craft. It was taken to counsel mand all agreed.

Ninurta hitched to his chariot seven weapons and then attached the whirlwind that stirs up dust and set out against Anzu to launch a fierce battle. Anzu saw Ninurta approach. Ninurta spotted him and dove down to show himself. Anzu made a mocking gesture and raised his voice screaming, "The Tablets of Destinies are in my protection, invincible am I."

Ninurta saw the Igigi and knew he was in trouble if they attacked, but they saw the fury in his movements and no one wished to die so they hid behind Anzu's shield.

Ninurta stirred up dust so Anzu could not see his challenger. Anzu spoke through a loudspeaker, "I have carried off all authority, the decrees of the gods. Who art thou to come fight me?"

"I am Ninurta and have been designed by King Anu to restore what you have stolen."

Anzu cut off the brightness and the mountain was in total darkness. Unafraid, Ninurta entered the gloom. He let loose a missile, but the shot hit the shield of protection and returned. More missiles he directed, but they returned. No lightning bolt could penetrate his body. On and on it went.

*Etched in stone. Anzu and Ninurta met at the mountain side. When Anzu perceived him, he broke out in a rage. With his brilliance he made the mountain bright as daylight. He let loose rays in a rage.

Ninurta directed more bolts and they returned. He had to do clever maneuvering to escape them. While on the ground, Anzu was screaming with laughter like a madman. He raised his fists, jumping and screaming, "You are foolish, you can never win over me." The battle ceased. Ninurta headed for Nibiru-Ki to receive instructions as he could not win against Anzu and the great power of the shields.

His father took him a missile to attach to the shooter and gave him instructions of the battle. Ninurta soared to Anzu. Wing to wing they went, back and forth and the other stayed close. Over the mountains to areas all over the Mediterranean. Anzu would swoop down, soar upward and shoot weapons at Ninurta who would maneuver feverously to avoid being struck.

Then Ninurta saw the opportunity to follow his father's advice, "Wing to wing, shoot the missile at his pinions. The craft your mother gave you has seven whirlwinds/blades. Place dust in its compartments, go to the front of Anu's craft, release the dust at the right moment, the wind from the blades will shoot the dust and cover his face. Anzu will hold the steering to keep control of the craft. Go side by side and when you see his pinions exposed fire the missiles."

Like a butterfly, his wings began to flutter to the ground and his craft crashed. The earth shook and the skies darkened. Ninurta quickly ran to a dazed and confused Anzu, took him captive and retrieved the Tablets.

From the mountain top, the Igigi were waiting in dread. When Ninurta approached with Anzu, they came to Ninurta and kissed his feet. Kumarbi fled and Ninurta set free captive Abgal and a few Anunnaki. He then returned to Nibiru-Ki with his captive and the Tablets of Destinies which he installed.

Before the Seven Judges, Anzu was taken. Present were the royals and their children, some were there to judge. Ninurta spoke of his evil deeds, "There was no justification for what he has done. He was always treated well. Let death be his punishment. What say you, Anzu?" There was no comment.

Marduk spoke out, "Give the Igigi a resting place on Earth. Do not hold this to their charge."

Enlil said, "Anzu, you endangered all the Anunnaki and the Igigi, you must be punished." All agreed.

The Seven Judges held council and returned with their verdict. "The punishment is death by execution. Let him be executed by laser."

Ninurta stepped forth and walked toward Anzu who raised his hand and pleaded for his life.

"Spare me. Please spare me." But with no mercy, Ninurta touched Anzu's chest with his laser and shot a killing ray into his body. Anzu's life breath was extinguished.

"Let his body be eaten by the vultures," said Ninurta.

Enki looked at the fallen body of Anzu and said, "Let him on Mars be buried, in a cave next to Alalu and be laid to rest. From the same ancestral seed the two of them were. Let my son, Marduk carry Anzu's body to Mars. Carve his face on a burial stone. Let him rest with his kin, Alalu. Let Marduk remain on Mars as commander there."

"Let it so be," said Enlil.

Another Face was Carved on a rock on Mars.

Time passed, toil continued, the Anunnaki children were growing and so was unrest, now among the Anunnaki in Africa. Enki and Enlil decided to fly to Shurubak to talk this over with Ninmah. When they arrived, both men were shocked at her appearance. It had been a long time since they had seen her. "What has happened to her?" whispered Enlil. Enki, mouth ajar, "It must be the effects of Earth's gravity. The same thing must be happening to us. We must send for the 'Tree of Life', whispered Enki. Enlil nodded.

They told her of the unrest of the Anunnaki in Africa and they couldn't afford to let that happen. Gold must be sent faster to Nibiru, this must be our first priority. Ninurta is well learned about the Earth's inners. He said metal city must be built where gold ores can be smelted and refined for less weighty cargo to make room for the tired miners to return to Nibiru for a rest. It was agreed and commenced. It was called Bad-Tibira.

This flight plan was drawn on a ceramic object and unearthed about 3,200 B.C. from the chronicles:

> ***#2 Built about 351, 400 years ago. The everlasting ground plan, that which for all time the construction has determined. It is the one which bears the drawings from the olden times and the writing of the upper heaven. The cities are: 1. Eridu, 2. Larsa, 3. Nibiru-Ki, 4. Bad-Tibira, 5. Larak, 6. Sippar, 7. Shurubak, 8. Lagash.**

Enki made submersible boats/**submarines** to hasten the shipments. Gold flowed more quickly from Africa to Eden's Bad-Tibira, the refining city where the golden nuggets would be taken from Abzu's furnace of Gibil to where the two rivers branch in from the Zambuzi Basin. From here, the golden nuggets would be shipped north past the Red Sea to the Persian Gulf. Then by land the nuggets would be transported to Bad-Tibira where they would be smelted and refined to gold dust. The gold would be refined to gold dust and by rocket ships were sent to Mars in celestial chariots. The pure gold was shipped from Mars to Nibiru.

This allowed more room in the craft to make room for the tired Anunnaki to return to Nibiru for a rest. New men would come to Earth gung-ho for a time. When the excitement wore off, the men would begin to complain. This would go on for a long time with constant complaints of the hard work in the mines. There gold shipments were lessening coming to the Eden and complaints then flowed there.

Enki was so captivated about the apes that he ignored the problem of impending mutiny. Secretly, on an island off the southeastern coast of Africa, in his laboratory, 'The House of Life' he had begun experiments with the apes to create a worker to take over the mining. His creations were grotesque and pathetic.

When all this was reported to Enlil, he became furious. Furious over the lack of gold shipments and hearing of the creatures on the island, he immediately left Eden to go to the Abzu mines. He asked Ennugi. chief officer of mining, the whereabouts of Enki.

Ennugi reported that for months he has barely seen him; the men in the mines have been on the verge of mutiny for a long time. "I've tried to calm them with promises of rest, returning to Nibiru and elixir. Nothing is working. This has become dangerous."

Enlil went to the island, confronted his brother and demanded that he get to the mines and do something to stop the mutiny. Enlil then heard the noises of his creations and pushed past Enki to see what it was.

What he saw put him in great shock, distorted, misshapen creatures; half man, half animal, some hermaphrodite, man- chickens, heads on animals, apes singing. "Oh, my Universal God, Enki, what have you done? You are going against the Universal Code. God forgive you. You will have to pay a price for this. Get to the Abzu immediately to settle your men!" In anger did Enlil leave.

Enlil returned to the lodging near the mines to rest before returning to Eden. In the mines, the fever of rebellion was rising. Asunu, the ring leader shouted, "Men, we must put an end to this. We toil for hours, sleep a few hours and do nothing else. Left our comforts in Nibiru to slave here in these holes. The 300 Anunnaki in the Eden do not toil as we do. They work above ground, they work outdoors, they can feel the wind on their faces and see the beautiful skies."

Another man shouted, "Enlil will not help us so we must solve our problems. We must rebel. Let us gain relief with hostilities."

They began rantings and setting their tools on fire and created a large bonfire. There was much hostility and screaming. They set fire to their axes and held them high.; the men were out of control.

Crazed, they ran and seized Ennugi and held him captive. There was no way of stopping the boiling rage of the 150 rushing men. With blazing torches, they rushed to Enlil's dwelling. The gateway guardian bolted the door. Enlil appeared and pleaded with them to release Ennugi, that he is guiltless and Enki and Ninurta are on their way. Ennugi was released.

Enlil approached the rioters. Enki and Ninurta arrived and the three men approached the rioters. Over a loudspeaker Ninurta spoke with authority, "King Anu is sending 350 men to replace you. They will be here in two weeks. The men in the mines will be replaced every six months." The men were delighted and calmed down.

Enki summoned Ningishzidda from 'The House of Life' and told him a solution to the problem of toiling is to hasten the creation of a worker. The way we are doing this will take forever. "There are too many failures; mixing genes of chickens, apes, goats, birds and Anunnaki essence/DNA. We must move all we have on the island here to the Abzu so I will not have to travel and can devote all my time on creation."

Enki smiled. *#3 "Let us create a being in our own image and likeness. Let us create a Lulu, a primitive worker. This being will take over the hardships of the work in the mines. Let this being carry on his back the toil of the Anunnaki. There is only one combination that can produce what we need."

Enki hesitated, looked down and with chin in hand said, "Let this primitive being be of Anunnaki essence and the egg of the female hominid…the ape."

"Let us summon council this very day."

CHAPTER 7

A GRAVE DECISION

301,000 years ago. Council was held in the Abzu, in Enki's abode. Those assembled were: Ningishzidda, Ninmah, Enlil, the Seven Judges and the leaders of the cities of the Eden.

"Please be seated," said Enki. "Isimud, would you and Asuna please serve the food and drinks. It's best all have a full stomach and some elixir for what I'm about to tell you."

After they supped and discussed politics Enki said, "Gentlemen and Ninmah, what I propose will astound you. It has me from the beginning and still does. I was aware of the discontent in the mines for a long time and was always able to appease them with pep talks, promises and elixir. It helped for a long time. I left Ennugi in command of them."

"One day, long ago, after the birth of my first daughter, I saw strange creatures in the jungle walking upright. Fascinated by them, I studied them for many years in between my work in the Abzu and in the Eden. I also studied all my surroundings wishing to pursue and learn of all things of the Earth. When I would go to the Abzu and heard the men complaining of work conditions, my mind struck upon the idea that I could create a being who would toil to relieve my men."

Enki looked around to study their faces. "I've been creating beings on the island with no luck as you will see." Enki looked at Enlil's red angry face, but he went on. "My friends, I did not call this meeting to discuss my failures, but to tell you that I feel in my heart that I've found the perfect solution."

Those present looked at Enki with puzzlement, wondering where he was going with this. Enki told them, "I want to create a primitive worker and by the mark of our essence/DNA fashion him. The being that we need already exists."

"What is he saying, DNA and a primitive worker?"

Thus, did Enki reveal his secret. "Creatures in the Abzu there are, they walk upright on two legs. Their forelegs are shorter and they use them as arms with hands. Their legs seem to be those of a different creature. They live among the steppes with other animals. They know not dressing in garments. They eat plants with their mouths and drink water from the lake and ditch. Their bodies are shaggy with head hair like that of a lion. They jostle with gazelles and delight in teaming with creatures in the water."

Enlil spoke out, "No creature like that has ever been seen in the Eden. They must be indigenous to the Abzu."

Ninmah said, "Eons ago on Nibiru our predecessors might have been like that. We don't know. It's a being not a creature."

Enki took them to the Abzu to the jungles to see the apes and they were astounded, then to the 'House of 'Life' for them to see his creations. Shocked they were at the creatures in the cages, grunting and snorting, no words were spoken. Creatures; half ape-man, half-chicken-man, hemihedrites, two-headed goat, half man-bird. Some were singing. On and on. Pathetic creatures that evoked sympathy.

No words were spoken on the return to Enki's abode. Seated, he said, "What you have seen are failures, but the new creatures will be a success for I have studied DNA We will make a creature in our image and likeness. He will be able to follow instructions. We need workers desperately to relieve our men in the mines."

Debating went back and forth. Enlil became furious. "On our planet slavery was abolished a long time ago. To obtain gold was our purpose; not to replace the Father of all beginning."

Heated arguments ensued, Enlil was becoming angrier. On and on went the discussions. It was decided to radio Anu for his opinion. The elders of Nibiru were present and told of the shocking proposition. Back and forth went the arguments. They were told of the mutiny of the miners; gold could have been stopped. Long and bitter were the discussions. Those on Nibiru decided that the survival of Nibiru was at stake and they finally consented to the creation of the being.

Anu beamed the decision, "Men of Earth, the gold must be obtained. It means the salvation of Nibiru. Let the being be fashioned. Great god of Nibiru has spoken. Let the being be fashioned."

The following day found Enki elated; his beloved Ninmah would be by his side. He knew they would never be intimate again, but she would be with him in his creation project. He also chose his son, Ningishzidda to work with them. So to the 'House of Life' they went.

The task of creation began. Enki said, "We must try to combine the two strands of essences. The strands of essences from the female ape must not be harmed and it must be combined with essences (DNAs) of the male Anunnaki. In graduations they must be shaped. In a crystal vessel."

Ninmah prepared the admixture. She gently placed the oval of the two-legged female with the Anunnaki DNA and fertilized the oval, there was a conceiving, a birth was forthcoming. The allotted time of nine months occurred.

Wait, there was something wrong, in desperation, Ninmah performed a caesarian and drew out a living being. The new born was shaggy with hair all over. His foreparts are those of the Earth creature. Its hind parts were those of the Anunnaki. She took the newborn to the ape to suckle. He grew fast, but his hands were not suited for the use of tools and only grunting sounds came from him. His senses were deficient, he could not hear and his eye sight was deficient.

Again they tried. # 2. He looked more like the Anunnaki, but his hands could not hold tools and his senses were deficient. # 3. He had paralyzed feet. # 4. His semen dripped. # 5. He had trembling hands. # 6. Had a malfunctioning liver. # 7. His hands were too short to reach his mouth. # 8. Once more, the new born was deficient.

Enki said, "Perchance the fault is not in the admixture, nor the female's oval, nor the essences, perhaps it is the use of the crystal vessel. Perhaps we should use a clay vessel, the clay of the earth, the earth's own admixture of gold and copper is required." Ninmah made a vessel from the clay of the Abzu.

Into the clay vessel was placed the ape's oval. Then the essence from the Anunnaki's blood was placed in. The fertilized oval was placed into the womb of the Earth female. There was conception. At birth time, Ninmah extracted the newborn with her hands. His image was perfect. He grew, but he could not speak, he grunted and snorted. The three leaders were very disappointed.

For a long time, Enki pondered the matter. He said to Ninmah, "Of all we have tried and changed, one thing was never altered. Into the womb of the Earth female the fertilized oval was inserted. Perchance this is the remaining obstruction."

Ninmah gazed at him and beheld him with bewilderment, "What are you saying?"

He responded, "Of the birth-giving womb I am speaking. The womb that nurtures the fertilized oval gives life and likeness."

Stunned was Ninmah. In the 'House of Life' there was silence. Enki was uttering word that were never heard before. They gazed at each other and wondered what the other was thinking. Finally, Ninmah said, "Wise are your words, my brother. Perchance the right admixture was being inserted into the wrong womb."

"Where is the female among the Anunnaki who will offer her womb?" said Ninmah with a trace of disbelief in her voice.

"Perchance in her womb she will not carry the perfect worker, perchance she will carry a monster in her belly."

Enki said he would ask his wife, Ninki. As he went to leave, Ninmah put her hand on his shoulder and said, "No, no Enki. The admixtures were made by me, reward and endangerment should be mine. I shall be the one to provide the Anunnaki womb, for good or evil to face."

She made the admixture in a clay vessel and Enki inserted it into her womb. She conceived and they waited to see a monster or perfection. Longer than on Earth, quicker than on Nibiru, travail came and Enki assisted her in delivery.

A male child was born. Enki held high the child. "He is the image of perfection," he cried. He slapped the newborn on the hind parts and the proper sounds let out a loud cry. He handed the child to Ninmah and she cried in joy. She placed him to her breasts to suckle.

They called him Adamu; he was the first test tube baby born on Earth. perfect in all parts and beautiful. His hair was black and the color of his skin was a dark blood red like the clay of the Abzu was its hue. Amazed they were at his penis for it had an odd shape, a skin was hanging from its forepart. "Let the Earthling be distinguished from the Anunnaki by his foreskin."

Ninmah called forth the nurses from the Medical Center and asked for seven women to produce seven males and a short time later to produce seven females. She showed them her beautiful son, Adamu. There was a stirring among them, then one by one seven nurses stepped forward.

Delighted, Enki said, "To you, we are grateful. Your names will go down in history." He read their names aloud: "Ninimma, Shuzianna, Ninmada, Ninbara, Ninmug, Musardu and Ningunna." And it was done; seven perfect males were born and let them suckle.

Then Ninki volunteered to give birth to a female. The admixture was made in a clay vessel with the oval of the female ape, fertilized by female Anunnaki DNA. Enki placed it into his wife's womb. She conceived and a beautiful female was born. She had sandy colored hair and blue eyes. They called her Tiamat after old planet Tiamat. Once again, they called upon the seven nurses and they gave their wombs. They delivered seven beautiful females and let them suckle.

When the fourteen infants were old enough, they were placed in a cage so as not to let them wonder away. Ningishzidda was told to watch them, study them and keep a report.

Time passed. So pleased was Enki with Adamu and Tiamat that he decided to take them to Eden to show off his creation. There, they were put in an enclosure All the Royals came to see them also people from the cities, men from Mars and Igigi from Phobos and Deimos were shuttled down. All were agog at what they saw; naked they were. Enlil grew to like them.

When it came time for them to return home, Enlil told Enki that he wanted them to stay. "I need someone to care for the garden to feed my men."

Enki was broken-hearted and told Ninmah of the situation. She convinced him it would be better for them as it would be cooler in the Eden than in Africa. Reluctantly, he agreed. On the way back, they grieved over letting their prized possession in the Eden.

Time passed and in the Abzu's excavations, the Anunnaki miners were grumbling, patience gave way to impatience. They inquired of Enki as to when the Earthlings would relieve them of their labor. The years passed and no young were produced. Ningishzidda made himself a couch of grass and watched them. He noticed they were mating, conceiving there was not. "What is wrong?" wondered he and Enki.

Ningishzidda said, "Let us go to the Medical Center and there to examine afresh the essences of Adamu and Tiamat, and we will take essences of Anunnaki. It must be done on a day that Enlil is not in the Eden." So on a day that Enlil left, they took Adamu and Tiamat from Eden to Shurubak.

Ningishzidda took samples of DNA from them. He studied them under a microscope and compared them to the DNA of male and female Anunnaki. Arranged like twenty-two branches of a Tree of

Life were the essences of the Earthlings. Unlike the Anunnaki's DNA that had twenty-three chromosomes. **"Eureka, I have found it, father!"** They are hybrids. They can't procreate, they are hybrids.'

Enki very distraught, called Ninmah and related the findings to her. She told him that was bad news as the clamor in the Abzu is terrible. Mutiny is in the making. Primitive workers must be procured or the gold extracting will cease. At that time, Ningishzidda told his father to have her come to Shurubak immediately, she is needed. And it must be done before Enlil returns.

Ningishzidda told his father and aunt what must be done. They agreed and he prepared what was needed. He placed Enki, Ninmah, Adamu and Tiamat on an operating table. He administered an anesthetic to each one and they fell into a deep sleep,

From the rib of Enki he extracted the life essence and put it in the body of Adamu. From the rib of Ninmah, he extracted the life essence. Into the body of Tiamat, he inserted the life essence of Ninmah.

Where the incisions were made, he closed up. When the four of them awakened, Ningishzidda declared, "It is done. To their Tree of Life, two branches have been added with procreating powers, their life essences are now entwined."

Enki and Ninmah departed to Abzu. Adamu and Tiamat were taken to Eden by Ningishzidda to 'know' each other. They became aware of their nakedness and Tiamat made aprons of leaves to cover themselves to be distinguished from the wild beasts.

Enlil returned from Bad-Tibira and strolled through the orchid to enjoy the shade. He encountered the couple and noticed the aprons on their loins. He summoned Enki to come to Eden and explain what happened.

Enki not thinking much of it was pleased to explain the matter to him. The chromosomes activated the hormones of the brain and the hormones of the sex glands of their bodies. This made them aware of their genitals. (Gen. 3: 16). In pain will you bring forth children, and thy desire shall be to thy husband.) Large Anunnaki, small ape;

pain in childbirth and oxytocin (love hormone) produced in the brain in the female in sex. (Knowledge brought forth by receiving the 23rd chromosome; knowledge of good and evil).

Enlil's rage could be seen in his blood pressure rising causing his face to redden. He screamed that this whole creation was a terrible mistake. "You took Anunnaki essence, Anunnaki blood, now you have taken from our very Tree of Life, our DNA. Now you have made them like us. Perchance our life cycles you have bestowed upon them. What have you done?"

Ninmah and Ningishzidda came to pacify him. They explained the Anunnaki in the mines are on the verge of mutiny. The workers are needed. Still enraged, he summoned Mushdammu to come quickly to the Garden. He shouted out what happened, "Adamu and Tiamat have become like one of us, they have eaten of the Tree of Knowledge of Good and Evil. Perhaps he will take of the Tree of Life and live forever. Quickly go to the east of the Garden, place the cherubim and the flaming sword (video camera with a laser beam) which turns every way to guard the Tree of Life."

Enlil said in an angry tone, "Adamu, "You had everything you needed in this Garden. Now you must leave and by the sweat of your brow you must till the soil for your own food all the days of your life. Tiamat, for what you have done, now you will bear children in pain and you will forever long for your husband."

Ninmah said, "Enlil, don't be so harsh. They will produce the Earthlings we need."

Enlil screamed in anger, "Let them go where they are needed. Back to where they came from in the Abzu. Away from the Eden. Let them be expelled." (Gen. 3: 23.).

There in the Abzu did Enki place them in an enclosure to "Know" each other. "Multiply, multiply," Enki whispered as he locked the gate.

Days past, weeks past, during which Enki would go there to check on them. Today was different. Today joy struck him, Tiamat was with child, her belly was bulging as she frolicked in the cage.

Enki notified all on Earth, Nibiru and Mars. "Our salvation is at hand, Tiamat is with child."

The time for birth arrived. Ninmah and others arrived to watch the birth-giving. To everyone's astonishment, she delivered twins. The son was named Ayam and the girl, Ede. There was much celebration and happiness. This meant the Anunnaki's freedom. Freedom to have leisure and enjoy life on Earth.

281,400 years ago, the Anunnaki lived on Earth for 183,600 years. The sons of Enki and Enlil married their sisters, half-sisters and nurses from the Medical Center. Their sons and daughters were born with the genes of long-life and they would live for thousands of years. The royals and offspring living on Earth at this time were:

Enlil, his son, 1. Ninurta, born on Nibiru by Ninmah. Enlil and his wife, Ninlil had 2: Nannar and 3. Ishkur.

Enki with his wife, Damkina had Marduk, born on Nibiru. Enki had 2. Ningishzidda by a concubine. 3. Nisaba and 4. Geshtinanna by his half-sister, Ninmah. Number 5. and 6, daughters born by his daughters Nisaba and Geshtinanna. 7. Nergal. 8. Gibil by a concubine. Later, Enki would sire 9. Dumuzi and 10. Ninagal by concubines, 11. Noah by Batanash, 12. and 13. Adam and Eve by Dawn and Dusk.

The ape lived about 35 years. The Anunnaki lived about 600,000 years. The first fourteen Earthlings born of the DNA essence of the Anunnaki and the ape's oval lived to be about 45,000 years old. Their offspring lived to be about 800 years old.

Toiling continued on Earth, thousands of workers labored in the gold mines of Abzu. Gold flowed freely to Bad-Tibira which caused extreme toiling for the Anunnaki in the Eden. They had smelted the gold ore to gold dust to allow more room in the craft for the tired Anunnaki to return to Nibiru for a rest. So work was tripled for them.

Those of the Eden complained about it for a long time, "The Anunnaki of Abzu have it easy while we have to work by the sweat of our brow herein the Eden. We can't go on like this." Enki would smile when he thought of how Enlil was handling this. Especially after the hateful things he said about his creation and furiously casting Adamu and Tiamat out of the Eden. Ninurta suggested that gold dust must be shipped to Bad-Tibira rather than the gold ore. This would lessen the work in the smelting plant in the Eden. So it was done.

About 193,000 years ago, people were running to and fro on Earth. Every now and then Enki could be seen flying over the Eden. He would look down at his beautiful homes and over the thousands of his creation, some playing, many toiling and very pleased was he. "You are my creation, my beings. In my image and like ness did I create you." He laughed and laughed.

157,000 years ago, disaster struck. Global warming was occurring. All over the globe vegetation was flourishing, wild creatures overran the land, rains were heavier, rivers were gushing and the abode needed repair. Volcanoes were erupting. Enki's son, Nergal, who was in charge if the southern tip of Africa, called Enki to tell him that the southern tip (Antarctica) was melting to water and the bars of the seas are not containing oceans and the Earth was trembling.

Enlil reported from the Eden to tell that all is worse than yesterday. "Even the abodes are shaking. From the observatory there is turmoil in the heavens."

Marduk radioed from Mars. "Father, what is going on? Strong winds are raising dust storms, Mars is shaking."

Enki replied that he did not know. He radioed King Anu and told him of the havoc "Just now, all over, thunder and lightning, fire and turmoil in the Asteroid Belt. The asteroids are turning into brimstone and falling on us. They are striking Earth, Mars and the Moon."

Anu immediately consulted the savants. "Enki, it is not good. Nibiru is nearing and the eight planets are now aligned. Mercury and Venus are grouching, the pull is causing Venus to leave her place, she is pulled toward Nibiru, every planet is shaking. Gather all near their radios for now Nibiru is drawing a monster toward us, it is approaching from the celestial deep. Nibiru is drawing it."

One savant screamed, "It is one of the satellites that belonged to Tiamat before North Wind struck her 4.5 billion years ago. Dear God, it is a monster; one league is its head (3 miles) and fifty leagues is its tail (150 miles), and it's approaching fast. No one can stop it and it's heading toward Earth. No, it's heading for the Moon. This monster has darkened the skies of Earth. The Moon is in its way. Its speed is unbelievable, the Moon will surely be destroyed. It is too frightening to watch. Oh my God, it's going to strike."

Fierce was the encounter, a tempest of clouds was raised upon the Moon. The Moon did shake almost as if it would be blown to kingdom come. But the Moon pulled itself upright and remained in its dwelling place. Everything remained intact, except on Mars. Marduk reported that he must return to Earth as there is six feet of dust, and now Mars is uninhabitable. The Igigi remained on Phobos and Deimos.

Things went back to normal, but now Marduk began to complain that he had no position on Earth. He said, "Enlil has taken from us on Nibiru and now on Earth; he has taken all the high positions for himself and his sons."

Enki decided that he and Marduk needed a vacation, so he took him to the Moon. He taught him just about everything he knew about the history of Nibiru, Earth and its history, planets and cycles, etc. There, they stayed for one Earth year.

King Anu informed Enlil that because Mars can no longer be used as a way-station, a place for chariots must be established on Earth so the gold can be rocket directly from Earth to Nibiru. Sippar/Bird City was chosen, and placed under the command of Utu, Enlil's grandson. He was the third generation.

When completed, King Anu came to Earth to celebrate and was entertained by Inanna, Utu's twin sister, children of Ninurta.

Marduk was ignored, as usual and that broke his heart. He left to roam the skies for a long time, in hurt and anger and rightfully so.

Gold flowed freely and so did the tempers of the overworked men in the Eden. Ninurta tired of the moaning and disturbed over Enki not sharing the thousands of workers in the Abzu, took fifty armed men from Eden went to the Abzu. They chased and caught Earthlings in the forests and steppes, male and female and took them to the Eden to work. Upon hearing this, Enki was furious.

Time passed. The Earthlings greatly diminished the toil of the Anunnaki in Eden. However as the Earthlings grew in number, food became scarce and they were constantly foraging for food. The Anunnaki were no longer satiated.

There was a lack of food for a long time and now of the fish and fowl, there was a shortage. Enki came to a point where something must be done. He was scheming a new understanding of how to create civilized man. Men who were smart enough to sow grains and cultivate them. How to attain this? What have I not combined in their life essence? Why is their intelligence limited? He was also worrying over what he had been noticing for many years something he could tell no one except his vizier, Isimud.

"My God in heaven, Isimud, my creation is regressing, they are looking strange. They are producing too many offspring and are degrading back to their wild forebearers. They are becoming half human and half ape (Neanderthals)."

For a long time, Enki devised a plan to solve both problems, ewes and grains must be brought from Nibiru and I must upgrade my creatures to learn to cultivate the soil, till the land, plant seed and shepherd the ewes that become sheep.

"Isimud, help me in my quest. This must be done and no one must ever know. Look over every female to see if she is healthy and beautiful to bear my children."

They looked over all the females of the Abzu, in the Eden, the orchards, marshlands, on the coastlands and islands as they sailed the rivers.

On day as they were boating, Enki noticed two females wild with beauty, frolicking and bathing on the river bank. "Look there,

Isimud, shall I not kiss the one young ones? Drive to shore." Enki got on shore and beckoned to the one closest. She followed him as he stepped backward toward a wooded area. She plucked an apple and offered it to Enki.

He took the apple, bent down and kissed her on the lips. Firm were her breasts. Into her womb he poured his holy semen. By the Lord Enki, she was impregnated. Enki called the second female to him. Berries from the field she offered him. Sweet were her lips, firm were her breasts. Into her womb he poured his semen. She took the holy semen of the Lord Enki and she was impregnated.

Enki waved good0bye to them and slowly walked away from them. "Isimud, stay with the young ones to ascertain pregnancies." And so he did, by the young ones he sat down. By the fourth month, their bulges appeared, By the tenth month, at dawn the first one squatted and gave birth to a male child. At dusk, the second one squatted and gave birth to a female child. Thus, the mothers were called Dawn and Dusk.

Isimud rushed to Enki to tell him the great news. "Isimud, you must forever keep my deed a secret. Let the newborns be suckled by their mothers. Thereafter, bring them to my household in the Eden. Tell all that you found them in the bulrushes in a reed basket."

Time passed and obedient Isimud did as he was told, to Eden he went to tell of what he found. Ninki, Enki's wife, was there. "Ninki, look what I have found among the bulrushes."

She took a liking to the two foundlings and raised them as her own. "I will call the boy Adapa and the girl, I will call Titi." (Adam and Eve, parents of Cain and Abel). So, about **108,400 years ago, civilized man was born.**

They were unlike all other Earthlings, slower to grow, quicker to understanding, with intelligence they were endowed and capable of speaking. Titi was beautiful, pleasant and dexterous with her hands. Ninki took a great liking to her and taught her all manner of crafts.

Enki taught Adapa how to keep records. "Isimud," said the proud father, "See how well Adapa is learning? A civilized man I have brought forth. A new kind of Earthling from my own seed has been created...in my own image and after my own like ness. From the seed they will grow food and from sheep they will shepherd. Anunnaki and Earthling will henceforth be satiated." Enki sent word to Enlil, "A new Earthling, a civilized being has been born in the wilderness."

Enlil flew to Eridu to see and hear more. "Enlil, see how beautiful they are? They are quick to learn. They can be taught knowledge and craft work. Let us have seeds sent from Nibiru that can be sown here. Let them send ewes that become sheep so we can deliver Earth from hunger. Let the new breed of Earthlings be taught farming and shepherding. Let the Earthlings and the Anunnaki together be satiated."

Enlil asked, "They are akin to the Anunnaki. A wonder of wonder that came about in the wilderness by themselves. Call for Isimud." "Isimud, tell me where you found the Earthlings?"

Isimud did so. "Isimud, they are a wonder of wonders, a new breed of Earthling has the Earth itself brought forth. Farming, shepherding, crafts and tool making he can be taught. A wonder of wonders," said Enlil.

King Anu was beamed of the marvel. He was amazed of the fast evolution of man, unheard of in such a short time on Earth. "Yes, I will send you seeds, plants, ewes. For sowing and planting great numbers of men will be needed. We hope they are able to procreate."

Shortly after Titi did give birth to twins, Cain and Abel. As time passed, Adapa grew and King Anu requested that he come to Nibiru as he wished to see the new civilized man. Enk consented and told Adapa not to eat or drink while on the planet. He thought that King Anu may kill him figuring out that he, an Earthling, may have Anunnaki blood.

So did Adapa leave in the spacecraft with Enki's sons, Ningishzidda and Dumuzi. Adapa screamed in terror over the sound of the rockets blasting as it lifted up. The entire trip and seeing all the people of Nibiru was a disaster for him. He also feared he may be killed by the warning of Enki not to drink nor eat while there.

"What is this strange behavior? He neither eats nor drinks?" Anu asked of Ningishzidda. Ningishzidda replied that he had a note given to him by Enki. King Anu went to is chambers to read the message which read, "Adapa was born to an Earthling woman by my seed. Likewise was Titi (Eve) born to an Earthling woman by my seed. They are endowed with wisdom and speech, but not with Nibiru's long life time, the bread of life. This he should not eat. The elixir he should not drink. Adapa must return to Earth to live and die on Earth. His lot must be mortality. His offspring must sow and shepherd on Earth so that the Anunnaki and earthlings may eat."

King Anu smiled and thought that Enki had not mended his free ways with women. He summoned Ilabrat, vizier of the King. "Bring Ningishzidda to me."

He asked Ningishzidda if he knew what was in the message. He answered that he had because he tested the essence of Adapa and found it to match Enki's. He told Ningishzidda that he must return to Earth to be by his father's side to become a teacher of civilized man. Dumuzi will remain here.

At the appointed time, Ningishzidda and Adapa boarded the sky ship and bid farewell. They soared into the heavens. On the trip to Earth, Ningishzidda explained to him the planets, their cycles and gave him lessons about the Sun, Earth and the Moon. Also how the months chase one another and how Earth years are counted.

Ninmah, Enki and Enlil were called to be told of their trip: Dumuzi would stay another shar. King Anu will send ewes to Earth the next shar. He will send medicines and all that was requested. Enlil, still furious that Adapa, an Earthling, went to Nibiru was further enraged when he learned that Enki cohabitated with Earthlings. Enki replied that he broke no rules but insured the satiation of all.

Enlil screamed, "No rules have you broken! You determined the fates of the Anunnaki and Earthlings by a rash deed." He left in a fury.

Marduk was not told how Adapa was conceived and he was impressed by the twin sons. He asked if he could take Abel to teach him shepherding. He took him to the meadows and taught him how to build stalls and how to shepherd. Ninurta took Cain to Bad-Tibira and taught him to build canals for watering and how to sow and reap. He made a plow from a tree so he could be tiller of the soil.

Enki, Ninmah and Ningishzidda decided to build a 'Creation Chamber', a House of Fashioning in anticipation for the arrival of the ewes to be dropped down from Nibiru on the next nearness to the Sun. Here, they would be able to create many sheep from their essence DNA of the ewes.

It was built upon a pure mound near the Landing Platform, Sippar.

The following shar, ewes were dropped off and all that the Anunnaki on Earth requested. After a time of successful multiplying of grains and lamb, Enlil proclaimed a decree, "Let there be a celebration of the "First Fruits."

Before the assembled Anunnaki, the first grains and the first lambs were to be placed at the feet of Enlil and Enki. Marduk led Abel to lay his offering of the lamb at the feet of the brothers. Enlil gave a joyful blessing to both brothers and extolled their labors.

Enki embraced Abel and raised the lamb for all to see, "Meat for eating and wool for wearing has come to Earth from Nibiru." So happy was Enki. This was new to Earth. Grains had been on Earth for many years. Little did Enki realize the results of his praises.

After the celebration of the first fruits was over, Cain was sullen. He was grieved over the lack of Enki's blessing. When the brothers returned to their tasks, Abel began bragging to his brother, "I am the one who brings abundance. It is I who satiate the Anunnaki. I give strength to the heroes and it is I who provides wool for their clothing."

Cain was very offended by his words and he replied, "It is I who luxuriates the plains and makes the furrows with grains. It is in my fields the birds multiply and my canals where the fish become abundant, it is I who produces the sustaining bread and variate the Anunnaki's diet with fish and fowl."

On and on the brothers disputed, through the winter they argued. When Summer began there was no rain. The meadows were dry and the pastures dwindled. Abel drove his flock into the fields of his brother to drink the waters from the furrows and canals. This angered Cain and he ordered his brother to move his flock from the fields. This started an argument and angry words were exchanged.

Farmer and shepherd, brothers uttered words of accusations. They spat on each other and fought with their fists. Greatly enraged, Cain picked up a stone and struck Abel on the head. Again and again, he struck him. He struck him until Abel fell and blood gushed from his mouth. When Cain saw the blood, he shouted, "Abel, Abel, my brother." Abel remained motionless, his soul had departed. Cain remained by his brother for a long time. He sat crying.

Titi (Eve) lay asleep and had a dream. She saw Cain and Abel fighting. She saw Abel's blood in the hand of Cain. "Adapa, get awake, please. It is Abel, I had a dream. I see his blood in the hand of Cain. A heavy sorrow fills my heart. Did something terrible happen to Abel? I am frightened!"

The next morning they awakened, departed Eridu and went to the wear-abouts of the brothers. They found Cain still seated by his dead brother. Titi let out a scream and a great cry of agony, "What have you done, Cain? What have you done?" He was silent, then threw himself on the ground and wept.

Adapa in a state of shock, disbelieving what he was looking upon said, "Titi, remain here. I must go tell Lord Enki what has happened."

Enki accompanied Adapa to the field of Cain. With fury, Enki confronted him, "Accursed you shall be, from the Eden you must depart. You shall not stay with the Anunnaki nor civilized man. As for Abel, his body can't remain in the open for animals to devour." He put him in a grave and piled stones upon it. For thirty days and thirty nights, they mourned the death of their son.

Cain was brought to Eridu for judgment; Enki pronounced exile. Enlil pronounced death. Ninurta said to let the Seven Judges decide.

Back and forth did the arguments go. Enki asked for permission to talk with Marduk in private.

Enki said to Marduk, "My son, my son, your agony is felt. Let us not compound agony with agony. Let me tell you a secret that has heavily burdened my heart. Once upon a time as I was by a river, two Earthling maidens, Dawn and Dusk, took my fancy. For one thing I needed to improve on primitive man as he was regressing to his original ape being. I needed a way to make our beings more intelligent so they could learn sowing and shepherding to satiate our men. These two females were so beautiful I had to impregnate them for the good of our future. Adapa and Titi were conceived by my seed, they conceived civilized Earthlings. Cain, my grandson is your nephew."

Marduk's mouth was ajar, so in awe to what he was hearing. He was in disbelief. For a while he was in shock. He thought about it and then went into a deep laughter. "Much was rumored of your love making prowess, now I am convinced of it. Let Cain's life be spared. Let him be banished to the ends of the Earth."

In Eridu, judgment was pronounced, "You, Cain, for your murderous deed, the killing of Abel, you must depart eastward to the land of wandering/Iran. Your life will be spared, but you and your generations will be known as murders. You will be given a mark so that all will know. Upon your face and the faces of your generations, no beard will grow. Ningishzidda, who knows of DNA altering, will genetically manipulate the proper genes. This is your sentence." (Gen. 4: 15.). And the Lord set a mark upon Cain).

Cain took his sister, Aswan from Eden and they departed to the 'Land of Wandering'. Now the question arose, "Now that our shepherd and tiller are gone who will sow seeds and shepherd the land?"

Adapa and Titi had many children, all girls, finally 103,000 years ago, Adapa and Titi had a son, they called him Sati/Seth which means 'he who binds again'. All together Adapa and Titi had sixty children, thirty boys and thirty girls.

About 95, 800 years ago, Seth and his wife bore a son, Enshi (Master of Humanity). Adapa taught him writing numbers. The sons of Enlil took Enshi to Nibiru-Ki to teach him secrets of the Anunnaki; how to make perfume for anointing and to prepare fruits to make elixir. It was since then that by Civilized Man the Anunnaki were called lords.

Enshi marries his sister, Noam. In the 98th. Shar, he was taken to Bad-Tibira to learn how to furnace and kiln. They bore a son, Kunin in the 99th shar.

The generations of Adapa after Cain were:

In the 99th shar Kunin and his wife Mualit bore a son, Malalu who played music.

In the 100th shar, Malalu wed Dunna and bore a son, Irid (sweet waters). Dumuzi taught him how to dig wells. By the wells in the meadows, shepherds and maidens met to espouse and thus bear children. The Igigi saw this and they desired wives.

The conclusion of the 102nd shar, Here, at the well, Irid met his wife Baraka. A son, Enki-Me (Enoch, meaning understanding), was born. Enki taught him secrets of the Sun, Moon and the planets. Enki-Me/ Enoch, eager to learn the heavens was taken to the Moon by Marduk. Upon his return, he and his wife, Edinni were taken to Sippar and he was taught much; the functions of the priesthood.

In the 104th shar, a son, Matushal/Matheusalah, was born to Enoch and Edinni. After that, Enoch made his second journey to the heavens. Marduk took him to Mars. The Igigi took a liking to him and so on Mars he stayed until the day he died. His records of learning were given to his son.

Matushal wed Ednat and they bore a son, Lu-mach (mighty man). In these days, conditions on Earth became harsher and complaints came from the toilers. Lu-Mach was appointed work master.

During this time Adapa was dying, he summoned his sons to bless them. When Sati/Seth gathered, he asked for Cain. Ninurta flew to the 'Place of Wandering' and brought Cain to his father. Adapa, because of failing eyesight, asked for Cain, the first born to be at his right side and Sati to the left. He touched the face of Cain to see if he was beardless and then he felt the face of his son, Sati, to the left and with beard it was.

Adapa put his right hand on the head of Sati and blessed him, "Of your seed shall the Earth be filled. Your seed shall survive a great calamity (the Great Flood)."

He put his left hand on the head of Cain and said, "For your sin of your birth right you are deprived, but of your seed seven nations shall come, in a realm set apart they shall thrive, distant lands they shall inhabit, but having killed your brother with a stone, by a stone will be your end."

Finishing these words, his hand dropped, he sighed and said, "Summon my spouse Titi and all the children. And after my spirit leaves me; to my birth place by the river carry me. And with my face toward the Sun, there bury me."

Like a wounded beast, Titi cried out and fell to her knees by Adapa's side. They wrapped his body in a cloth. In a cave by the river, he was buried. In the midst of the 93rd. shar he was born and by the end of the 108th shar he died. Adapa was about 54,000 years old.

Cain bade farewell to his mother and siblings. Ninurta, in his Bird of Heaven, returned him to the Land of Wandering. And in a distant land, Cain had sons and daughters. He built them a city and while building, he was killed by a falling stone.

Cain would become the ancestors of the Incas; CA-IN/IN-Ca and other Indian tribes in South and North America, Asia and islands.

CHAPTER 8

THE IGIGI SAW THAT THE DAUGHTERS OF MEN WERE FAIR

In the days of Lu-Mach, hardships on Earth were increasing. On Mars, dryness and dust enveloped the planet. On both planets, conditions were altering, their net forces were disrupted. The Sun was flaring. Instruments were placed in the Abzu at the tips of the Whiteland facing. These instruments were put in the charge of Nergal, Enki's son and his wife Ereshkigal.

In South America, Ninurta was assigned to establish a Bond Heaven-Earth. On Mars, Marduk was given the task to pacify the Igigi. The way-station on Mars must be kept until it can be figured out what is causing the disturbances.

During this time, Enki, Enlil and Ninmah were noticing a drastic change in their looks. Enki, grieving said, "More than 100 shars since my arrival. I was then a dashing leader; now bearded, tired and old am I."

Enlil spoke up, "An enthusiastic hero I was, ready for command and adventure. Now I have children who have children, all born on Earth. Old on Earth we became. But those born on Earth are even older sooner."

Ninmah said, "As for me, they call me an old sheep. While the others have been coming and going, taking turns on Earth. We leaders stayed. Perhaps it is time for us to leave."

"We could leave if we wish. Is it a thing on Nibiru, a thing on Earth? Perchance the life cycles that differ it concerns," said Ninmah.

Thereafter, Marduk told his father that a matter of gravity must be discussed. "The three sons of Enlil have chosen mates. I am your first born and as it is tradition, I was the first one to marry, but Nergal did not wait. The other four sons are waiting for me to marry. Father, I have chosen a bride. A descendant of Adapa, she is of Earth. I have chosen Sarpanit, the daughter of Enoch."

Stunned was Enki as he took him to Ninki to relate the news to his mother. Stunned was his mother, "Does she appreciate your gaze?" Yes, was his reply.

Enki in anger said, "Your princely rights on Nibiru will be forsaken forever!"

Marduk said, "My rights on Nibiru? My rights on Earth have been trampled. This is my decision." Mathusula, the bride's brother was summoned. Humbled, but joyful was he. Ninmah was deeply disappointed. Enlil was furious, he beamed King Anu likewise was furious. The savants also agreed, but said he could marry, but he could never bring her to Nibiru.

About 56,000 years ago. It was announced by his mother, "There will be a wedding in Eridu."

Enlil, the commander announced that Marduk and his bride can't stay in the Eden. Enki gave them a gift, a domain above the Abzu, Egypt. In Eridu, Ninki arranged a wedding celebration for Marduk and Sarpanit.

It was a beautiful wedding. Her people played copper drums to announce the ceremony. Her sisters played seven tambourines to present the bride to her spouse. A great multitude of Civilized Earthlings assembled. It was a coronation. Young Anunnaki attended.

Igigi from Mars came in great numbers, two hundred, and said, "We came to celebrate our leader's wedding. We came to witness a wedding of Nibiru and Earth union."

So did they say, but they had a secret plan. Unbeknown to Enki and Enlil, their secret was to abduct women to have conjugation was the plot. On Mars, they plotted, "What to Marduk is permitted, why should we be deprived? Enough suffering and loneliness of not ever having offspring."

For many, many years during their coming and going between Mars and Earth, they lusted after the daughters of the Earthlings (they called them Adapite Females). So, they plotted to take a wife immediately after the wedding of Marduk.

After the ceremony, a sign was given by Shamgaz. Each Igigi immediately seized by force an Earthling female. They took them to the Landing Place in the Cedar Mountains. They waited there to be challenged by the leaders.

The Igigi, by loudspeaker said loudly, "Enough of deprivation and not having offspring. We wish to marry the Adapite daughters. Your blessing to this you must give or by fire we will destroy Earth."

They told Marduk he must stop this. He told them he agreed for the Igigi.

All shook their heads with begrudging agreement. All, except Enlil enraged without pacification, "One evil deed followed by another evil deed; fornication from Enki and Marduk have been adopted by the Igigi. The planet will be overrun by the Earthlings." In his heart, he plotted evil things against Marduk and the Earthlings.

Upon the Landing Place in the Cedar Mountains the Igigi and females secluded. Children born to them there were called the Rocket Children.

Marduk and Sarpanit had two sons, Asar/ Sirius and Satu/Seth and they dwelt in the domain above the Abzu. Marduk invited the Igigi from the Landing Place to live there; some came, some remained with Shamgaz. To the far east stands some of their offspring went. Ninurta observed the Earthlings increasing rapidly in number. Troubled, he told his father, Enlil. He worried that Enki and Marduk were planning to overtake the Earth.

Enlil said, "Ninurta, go to the other side of Earth, find the descendants of Cain and prepare a domain of your own, build your own army." Ninurta found Cain's descendants on the other side of the Earth. He taught them to make tools to make and play music. He taught them mining, how to smelt and refine ores, how to build rafts out of balsam trees and to cross the great sea.

Ninurta took the descendants to a land beyond the sea, South America. In the domain, they established a new city with twin towers.

In the Eden, Lu-Mach was the work master; his job was to enforce quotas and to reduce the Earthling's rations. His spouse was Batanash, the daughter of Lu-Mach's father. She was of great beauty and her beauty charmed Enki. He wished to be with her so he asked Marduk to send for Lu-Mach to work there.

When Lu-Mach went to Eridu to work he took Batanash to Shurubak, the Haven City. There she would be protected from the angry masses. Enki went quickly to visit his sister, Ninmah. On the roof of the dwelling, while Batanash was bathing Enki slipped in with her. He took her by her loins, he kissed her and into her womb he poured his semen.

In the 110th Shar, **49,000 years ago**. Batanash's belly was bulging. When the time came, a son was born. In the Eden, Lu-Mach was summoned to go to his wife as she had a son. When he looked at the child, shocked was he. White as the snow was his skin. The color of wool was his hair. Blue as the skies were his eyes and shinning like brilliance /Albino. Amazed and frightened he was, to his father, Methuselah, he hurried. He told his father that his son is unlike an Earthling and that he was very puzzled by his birth.

Methuselah came to Batanash and was amazed at his looks. "Is one of the Igigi the boy's father? I demand the truth. Is Lu-Mach the boy's father, you must tell the truth."

Batanash replied, "None of the Igigi is the boy's father, upon my life I swear."

Methuselah told his son, as he placed his arm on Lu-Mech's shoulder, "The boy is a mystery, his oddness is an omen, unique he is, for a task unique, by destiny he was chosen. What that task is, I know not, but at the appropriate time, it will be known."

In those days, the suffering on Earth was increasing. The days grew colder, the skies held back the rain, in the fields, the crops diminished and the sheep were few. So did Methuselah say to Lu-Mach, "Let Respite be his name." Batanash kept her secret.

Enki greatly adored the child. He taught him the writings of Adapa and priestly rites. He grew up in Shurubak and married Emzara. In these days the sufferings on Earth intensified.

And the Lord (Enki) said, "My spirit shall not always strive with man, for that he also is of flesh: yet his days shall be one hundred twenty years." (Gen. 6: 3.).

Enki meant that with each generation the length of life essence of the Anunnaki that was contributed 252,000years earlier will decrease over years.

Enlil was increasingly disturbed by the conjugations of the Earthlings. In his eyes, the mission on Earth had been perverted. The shouting and howling of the Earthling masses were anathema to him.

He shouted to them, "Your conjugations are depriving me of my sleep. The stench of your orgies reaches my nostrils."

In the days of Noah plagues and pestilences affected Earth. There were: aches, dizziness, chills, fevers that overwhelmed the people. In their lands, water from their sources did not rise, the earth shut up its womb and vegetation did not sprout.

Ninmah asked that the Earthlings be taught how to cure diseases. Enlil screamed out, "No." Enki said to teach the Earthlings pond and canal building and let them fish. Enlil screamed out "No, by decree I forbid it. Let the Earthlings perish by hunger and pestilence."

For a shar, 3,600 years, the Earthlings ate grasses of the field. For the second and third shar, they suffered the vengeance of Enlil.

In Shurubak, Noah's city that the suffering was unbearable. Noah went to Eridu to plead with Enki for help and salvation. But Enki was bound to the decrees of Enlil.

On Earth and Mars, the seasons lost their regularity. For two shars, from Nibiru the heavenly circuits were studied. They noticed the oddities in the planetary destinies; black spots were appearing on the surface of the Sun and flames were shot up. Jupiter was misbehaving with dizzying circuits. The Asteroid Belt was pulled and pushed by unseen forces. The Sun and its family were upsetting.

On Nibiru, the savants were alarmed. The people gathered in the public square to get an answer; there was none. On Earth, the tribulations were increasing. For four shars the instruments in the Whiteland/Antarctica were observed. Nergal recorded the rumblings in the snows. The snow-ice that covers the Whiteland was sliding. In the Land Beyond the Sea/South America, Ninurta's instruments reported quakes and jitters.

In the 5th and 6th shars, the phenomena, global warming, gained strength. On Nibiru, the savants raised the alarm of calamities to come, "When Nibiru nears the Sun: the eight planets will be aligned, Mars will be on the other side of the Sun. The Earth will not be protected from the net force of Nibiru, Jupiter will be agitated, Mars shall shake and wobble. The snow-ice of the Whiteland's/ Earth's/ Antarctica shall come down sliding. All this will cause a great flooding. By a huge wave/Tsunami, the Earth will be overwhelmed."

The King and counselors beamed Earth, "Men of Earth and Mars, you must prepare to evacuate. A tsunami will be the result."

In the Abzu, the mines were closed. The Anunnaki there went to Eden. In Bad-Tibira, smelting and refining ceased; all gold to Nibiru was lofted. For evacuating, a fleet of fast celestial chariots were returned to Earth. From one of the celestial chariots a white-haired Anunnaki stepped off. Galzu, Great Knower, was his name. (the first emissary sent from Central Universal Intelligence).

He walked majestically to Enlil. He presented a sealed message from Anu. "I am Galzu, emissary plenipotentiary and Council."

Enlil was surprised as he received no word of his arrival. The seal was authentic and unbroken. It was found to be trustworthy. "For King and counsel Galzu speaks, his words are our command."

Galzu summoned Ninmah and Enki. He smiled at Ninmah and said, "From the same school and age are we." Ninmah could not recall him he was as young looking as a son and she was as his older mother. Galzu explained that is caused by Nibiru's slumbered life cycles.

"Indeed, this matter is part of my mission. Those who stay on Earth the longest are affected more, their bodies are no longer accustomed to Nibiru's cycles. Their sleep is disturbed, their eyesight failing and the net force of Nibiru weighted their walk. Their minds are affected, the sons are older than their parents they had left. Death to the returnees comes more quickly."

Enlil said in anger, "Before, the Earthlings were becoming like us. Now, we as Earthlings become imprisoned on this planet. The whole mission is a failure, we are now as slaves."

"The three of you must remain on Earth. You will stay in celestial chariots during the flood to outwait the calamity. The other Anunnaki have a choice to leave or outwait the calamity in chariots circling the Earth. The Igigi and Marduk, who married the Earthlings must choose to return alone to Nibiru or remain hovering in celestial chariots. For all others, they must be ready to depart for Nibiru."

Enlil summoned a meeting; the leaders, their children. He told them that all who wish to leave must be ready to evacuate. All those who married Earthlings must leave without them or hover during the calamity. The Igigi with their Earthling spouses may head for the highest peaks.

Nannar, Enlil's earth first born said he will outwait the calamity with his family on the Moon. The other royalty decided to hover in craft with their parents. Ninmah will circle the Earth in a chariot.

Enlil angrily said, "Let the Earthlings for their abominations perish. Enki, because of your creation, there has been murder, intermarriage, fornications and starvation. These abominations can't go on. I insist that each one present must take an oath to let the Earthlings perish. They must not be told of the coming deluge, it must be kept a secret. I command you to take the oath now."

Enki, heartbroken and with tears in his eyes, took the pledge. He thought about son, Noah, and all his grandchildren. Ninmah was in tears and whispered the oath. Enki and Marduk departed. Enlil and the others planned on the departure, who will stay, how the grouping to arrange. ; equipment and food. With much embracing and sorrow, the celestial boats were boarded and sent aloft.

Marduk and his family left for Mars. Ninurta went to the mountain lands in South America to report rumblings there. Nergal to watch the Whiteland of Antarctica. Ishkur was to keep the Earthlings from onrushing the craft. Enlil took the Tablets of Destinies to Sippar which became a temporary radio station and there buried them deeply in the earth. Enki placed the Mes in a golden box and took them to Sippar where he buried them deeply.

Enki said to Ninmah, "Other living creatures we must save, some originated on Earth, some from Nibiru. Let us preserve their seed of life, their essences DNA extract for safe-keeping."

Ninmah responded, "I shall do it in Shurubak, you do so with the Abzu's living creatures."

She went quickly to Shurubak with the assistance of her nurses. In the Abzu, Enki and Ningishzidda went to the Olden House of Life, they collected male and female essences and life-eggs. Of each kind two by two for safe keeping they took them to the celestial chariot to hide them while in Earth cycle.

At that time, word from Ninurta, Earth's ramblings are ominous. From Southern Africa, word came from Nergal the White lands are shaking. In Sippar all the Anunnaki gathered for **The Day of the Deluge they Awaited.**

CHAPTER 9

THE GREAT DELUGE/ TSUNAMI

In Sippar/Bird City, the Anunnaki gathered, awaiting the Day of the Deluge. The tensions of waiting were mounting. Lord Enki asleep in his quarters had a dream vision. There appeared the image of a man, bright and shinning like the heavens. The man approached Enki. He saw that it was the white-haired emissary Galzu from CUI. In his right hand, there was an engraver's stylus; in his left hand, he held a shiny smooth lapis lazuli.

He spoke to Enki, "Enlil spoke the truth. The decision he spoke of will be known as 'Enlil's decision', not yours but destiny so decreed. Now into your hands take fate for the Earthlings will inherit the Earth. Summon your son, Noah and without breaking the oath of not telling the humans of the flood, reveal to him the coming calamity. Tell him to build a boat that can withstand the watery avalanche; a submersible one."

Galzu continued, "Build the boat as to the likes of one I am showing you on the tablet. Let him save himself and his kin folk. Also take the seed of all that is useful, be it plant or animal. **This is the will of the Creator of All.**" He drew an image on the tablet and he placed it by Enki's head. The Image faded and the dream, vision ended. He awoke in a shudder and pondered the dream. What omen did it hold?

He arose and there was the tablet by his bedside. There was the design of a boat with Galzu's markings indicating the boat's measurements. Enki called for his men and asked them to find Galzu. By sundown, they reported he could not be found and that he left for Nibiru a long time ago. Enki greatly baffled could not unravel the mystery, but the message was clear.

That night, Enki went to Shurubak where Noah lived and to his reed hut where Noah lay asleep. So as not to break the oath, Enki called to him and spoke to him from the reed wall. From behind the reed screen he spoke, "Wake up, wake up. Reed hut....reed hut, pay attention to my words; a calamitous storm will sweep havoc, destroying mankind; this is the ruling of Enlil. Heed my words, abandon your home."

Enki kept talking to the reed hut's wall, "You will build a boat by measurements shown on the tablet: 350 ft. length by 75 ft width by 50 ft. high. Make sure the boat will be roofed throughout. The sun must not be seen from the inside; the tackle must be strong and tight to ward off the water."

"The boat must tumble and turn to survive the watery avalanche. Noah, you must build the boat in seven days (Gen. 7: 4.). For yet seven days, I will cause it to rain upon the earth forty days and forty nights . . . You must get the entire towns people to help. Tell them you must get away from Enlil as he is angry with your Lord Enki and you are sailing to his abode in the Abzu. Tell them if they stay behind, Enlil will give them all they ask for."

"Gather you family in the boat, heap up food and water, bring household animals....Then on the appointed day, I will send Ninagal to navigate the boat. When you see the rockets blast off from Sippar button up the hatch."

Noah agog said, "My Lord!" he shouted "Your voice I hear. Let me see your face!" Enki replied, "Not to you, Noah, have I spoken. I spoke to the reed wall. By Enlil's decision, by an oath I am bound. All the Anunnaki swore also so if my face you see, surely like all the other Earthlings you will surely die. Now reed wall to my words pay heed."

Noah came from behind the reed wall and saw the tablet and saw the drawing of the boat. He read and understood the building and the measurements.

In the morning, Noah announced to the townspeople, "Lord Enlil is angry with my Lord Enki. The Lord Enlil has been hostile to me. I can no longer stay in this city (Shurubak). I can't set foot in the Eden. To the Abzu, to Enki's domain. I must build a boat quickly so I can depart from here. I need the help of all the townspeople. Thereby, the Lord Enlil's anger will subside and your hardships will end, Therefore, Lord Enlil will shower you with abundance.".

The townspeople gathered about Noah to speedily build the boat. The elders hauled timbers of boat wood. The little ones carried bitumen from the marshes, the wood workers hammered the planks together. Noah melted the bitumen in a cauldron with which he waterproofed the boat inside and out.

On the fifth day the boat was completed. The townspeople were happy to see Noah depart; they brought him food and water. They took food from themselves to appease Enlil.; in a hurry, they drove four-legged animals into the boat, birds from the fields flew in by themselves.

Noah made his wife and sons embark. Their wives and their children also entered. Noah called aloud, "Anyone who wishes to come with us can do so. Come aboard."

But the people envisioned the abundance from Enlil and all that he would give them. Only a few of the craftsmen heeded the call and entered.

On the sixth day, Ninagal, son of Enki, entered the boat. He was to navigate the ark. He was known as 'Lord of the Great Waters'. He boarded the ark with a box of cedar wood in his hand. By his side in the boat, he kept it. In this box was the life essence (DNA) and life eggs of living creatures which had been collected by Enki and

Ninmah with the hopes that these would be used for insemination after the flood. They were to be hidden from the wrath of Enlil to be resurrected if and when the earth was willing.

Enki instructed Ninagal to meet on Mount Ararat when the flood subsided enough to land on Ararat. Ninagal explained to Noah, "All the beasts by two are hidden in this box." Noah and Ninagal with all secure, awaited the seventh day. The day when Nibiru would be closest to Earth.

About 13,000 years ago, in the 120th shar of Anunnaki living here, under the Constellation of Leo, was the flood. Noah was in the 10th shar of his life (36,000 years old).

In the days before the flood, the Earth was rumbling. It groaned and grumbled from within as with pain. Nibiru could be seen as a glowing star in the heavens. There was darkness in the daytime and at night, the Moon could not be seen, it was if it had been swallowed up. The Earth began to shake; by a great force it was agitated. The planets were aligned and Nibiru was approaching the Earth. In the dawn, a black cloud arose from the horizon; the morning's light turned into darkness.

"Noah," said Ninagal. "When the day of horror strikes, those in Sippar will take off in their craft. We will see the fiery rockets of their engines. Here in Shurubak when we see the bright eruptions, this is our signal to button up the hatch."

The Earth tumbled and shook; the sound of the rolling thunder boomed. Lightening lit up the sky over and over. In Sippar, there was much excitement. "Depart! Depart," screamed Utu, commander of Sippar. With a wide sweep of a lighted flag, he gave the command to depart to the Anunnaki. Crouched in their space craft, the Anunnaki were lofted heavenward.

In Shurubak, Ninagal saw the bright eruptions. "Button up! Button up the hatch, Noah." Together they pulled down the hatch that concealed the trap door. Water tight, the boat was completely enclosed. Not a ray of light penetrated the inside.

On that day, that awful day, that unforgettable day, the deluge with a roar began. In the Whitelands/ Antarctica at the bottom of the Earth, the Earth's foundations shook. Then with the roar equal to thousands of thunders, the ice sheet slipped off its foundations. It was pulled away by Nibiru's net pull and it came crashing into the south seas; one sheet after another was smashing into another.

The Antarctica Whitelands surface was crumbling like a broken egg shell. All at once, a huge tidal wave arose/Tsunami. The wall of waters was reaching the skies. A storm with a velocity never before seen began to howl. The Earth's bottom, it winds were driving the tsunami northward.

Northward, the onrushing wall of waters reached the Abzu lands, toward the settled lands it rushed and to all the Eden. When the tidal wave reached Shurubak, it lifted Noh's boat from its moorings, tossed it about and swallowed the boat. It became completely submerged and held firm.

Outside, the storm's wave overtook the people like a killing battle; no man could see another. The ground was totally covered with water. All that once stood mighty was swept away. At the end of the day, the waters covered the mountains. Circling the Earth, the Anunnaki crowding and crouching in their compartments strained to see what was happening on Earth.

In her craft, Ninmah wailed like a woman in travail. She cried and cried. "My created, my people, my children. Look at them. They are like drowned dragonflies in a pond. My creation. All life by the rolling sea has been taken away. The little children. Many people that I have loved are gone…gone."

Those in the sky ships could see all that lived had turned to clay. They were humbled by the sight of the unbridled fury. A power greater than theirs they witnessed with awe. As days went on, they hungered for the fruits of the Earth and thirsted for the fermented elixir. On manna they must survive.

After the tidal wave, the sluices of the heaven opened and a downpour from the skies was unleashed over the Earth for seven days.

The waters from above mingled with the waters of the great below. The mountain peaks looked like islands. Then the waters gathered in their basins, waving back and forth, the water level came lower every day.

Forty days after the tsunami swept the Earth, the rain stopped. Noah opened the hatch and there was no sign of life. A gentle breeze was blowing. Ninagal then set course for Mount Ararat. Noah set forth birds and they returned. He then sent out a dove and it returned with a twig. Land had appeared.

A few more days and the boat rested on Ararat; how very happy they were. Delighted, Noah opened the hatch; the Sun was shining, the sky was clear and there was a gentle wind. "Come out. Let us build an altar, set a fire and offer a lamb to Lord Enki."

Enlil radioed Enki to fly his helicopter and meet him on Mount Ararat. When they landed, they locked arms, but Enlil was puzzled by the smell of roasting meat, "What is that smell, Enki? Has anyone survived the deluge? Let us see."

On the other side of the mountain, Enlil spots Noah and screams in anger. His fury knew no bounds. He lunged at Enki. He was ready to kill him with his bare hands.

Enki screamed, "He is no mortal, he is my own son, your nephew. The creator of all told me to save Noah." He explained it all.

Ninurta said to Enlil, "The survival of mankind must be the will of the Creator of all."

Ninmah said, "On my oath, the annihilation of mankind shall never be repeated." Relenting, Enlil took the hands of Noah and Emzara, his spouse and blessed him saying. **"Be fruitful and multiply…replenish the Earth."**

CHAPTER 10

GONE ARE THE OLDEN TIMES

About 13,000 years ago the Anunnaki had lived on Earth for 120 shars,(432,000), the olden times ended with much sorrow, but life must go on. The waters of the deluge continued to recede; the face of the Earth began to show. The mountain lands were unscathed, but the valleys were buried under mud and silt.

The Anunnaki surveyed the landscapes from Mother ships and helicopters. Ninurta radioed from his helicopter that the Eden and Abzu were still buried under mud and silt. All the cities in the Eden were gone. He reported good news that the Great Stone Platform, the landing place, was still standing so all the ships including those on Mars and those on the Moon could now land. The first to land must clear the debris.

Marduk reported that Nibiru had totally sucked out the atmosphere of Mars, its waters totally evaporated. It is now a place of dust storms. Nannar reported that the Moon could no longer sustain life. The domes have been pulled off the cities. Enlil said that they must now be concerned with their survival on Earth and to examine the sealed creation chamber in hopes of finding seeds from Nibiru.

Happily, they found the diorite chests and the grains were secure. Ninurta planted the seeds in the mountain side terrace. Ninurta then dammed up the waterfalls in the Cedar mountains and other mountains. Noah's oldest son, Shem, was taught how to raise crops. Ishkur found the remaining fruit-bearing trees. Japheth, Noah's youngest son became the fruit cultivator. He found the first fruits that Ninmah had planted 412,000 years ago that made the elixir to appease the toilers.

The elixir was made and Noah became drunk and fell asleep. Then a great gift was given by Enki…The Chest of Life, the chest he guarded during the deluge. He held high the chest and declared, "Look here, the Chest of Life which holds surprising contents. Herein is the life essence/DNA and live eggs that we can place in the wombs of the four-legged animals from Noah's boat. We will have sheep for wool and meat and cattle for milk and hides. Then, with other living creatures, the earth we will replenish."

Enki told Dumuzi that he is to take responsibility of the shepherding task. To Marduk, he gave him his old domain; the lands between the Abzu and the Great Sea. Enki raised an island from the waters by drainage.

In the bowels of the island he carved twin caverns, above them he fashioned stone sluices. From there he cut two channels in the rocks and for the water, he fashioned two narrows for the waters to flow. Thus, he could slow or hasten the flowing water from the highlands. He regulated the water with dams and sluices and the two narrows (the Nile).

From the cavern island of Abzu, Enki raised the rivers of Serpentine Valley from under the waters. In this land of the two narrows/Egypt he fashioned a habitation for Dumuzi and the shepherds.

Ninurta called his father to report an astounding find. "Father, In South America, I have found descendants of Cain. Four brothers and four sisters who are the leaders. They took charge of others. They saved themselves on rafts and survived on a tall mountain."

Enlil radioed King Anu on Nibiru to report their success that they are on their way to a new Earth. But the King radioed that they were not as fortunate because the close passage to Earth and Mars caused much damage to their atmosphere. "Our shield of gold dust has been torn. The atmosphere has dwindled away again. New supplies of gold are quickly needed."

Upon hearing, Enki went to the Abzu with his son, Gibil to survey and search for gold. All the gold mines were gone; buried under the avalanche of water and this sickened Enki's heart. Gone, gone were the mines and Bad-Tibira where hundreds of Anunnaki toiled for many years. In the Eden, also where hundreds of Earthlings toiled and in the Abzu; gold…all gone. All this was radioed to Anu.

Then, a surprise call from Ninurta in South America to Enki. "Father, are you sitting down? Are you ready for good news? The water avalanche of water forged deep cuts into the mountainsides. GOLD, GOLD, uncounted gold nuggets, large and small have fallen into the river. Come see."

Enki and Enlil hurried to the distant mountain. They saw unbelievable amounts of gold that needed no smelting or refining. It was a miracle. Ninurta said that they could use the descendants of Cain to work with the gold as he taught them a long time ago the handling of metals. After the wedding of Marduk and the Igigi, he had brought them to South America.

Now, they must search for dry land to establish a new place for celestial chariots to send the gold to Nibiru. Enlil chose a place precisely on the 30th parallel to locate the new place for the chariots. Enlil said to let the heart of the plain reflect the heavens. Enlil took measurements of distances from the skies. On a tablet, he marked out a grand design. He had the landing place of Sippar in the cedar Mountains be a part of the facilities.

Enlil then measured the distance between the landing place and the chariot place. In the midst he designed a place for MISSION CONTROL CENTER/Jerusalem. There he selected a suitable mount/ Mount Moriah (mount of showing the way). A platform of stones was like those of the/landing Place in Sippar. In the midst, there was a great rock (now inside the Dome of the Rock).

The rock was carved inside and out to place control instruments to radio, guide and control messages and flights to Nibiru. It became the new naval of the Earth to replace the role of mission control center of Nibiru-Ki before the deluge.

The new Landing Place was anchored on the twin peaks of 'Ararat' to demarcate the landing corridor. Enlil said there would be needed two other sets of twin peaks in the southern boundary (the pyramids) to delimit the boundary of the landing corridor. They were needed as beacons to secure the ascent and descent. These would replace the beacon cities of Larsa and Lagash of the olden times.

Enlil selected the location of the twin adjoining peaks to anchor them on the southern delimit. There were no mountains, only flat land protruded above the clogged valley.

Ningishzidda told his father and Uncle Enlil that he could build artificial peaks on the land. On a tablet he drew two smooth-sided skyward rising peaks/pyramids. He built a scale model. On the flat land above the river's valley. He perfected it with rising angles and four smooth sides (the smaller pyramid). Next to it he placed a larger pyramid. He set its sides to the four corners.

The Anunnaki cut the stones with their tools of power (laser beams) and directed them with an anti-gravitational system from their flying craft. The same for the larger pyramid, except within this one, Ningishzidda designed it with galleries and chambers for pulsating.

When these artificial peaks rose to the heavens, the leaders and the Anunnaki were invited to witness the placing of the capstone which was fashioned with an admixture of electrum made by Gibil. It reflected the sunlight to the horizon. By night, it looked like a pillar of fire. The power of all the pyramids crystals focused in a beam to the heavens, a beautiful sight to behold.

Then when Ningishzidda completed the pyramids, the Anunnaki leaders were called in to see the inside of the large one with its crystals pulsating, an astoundingly beautiful marvel. They named this pyramid, Ekur (house that is like a mountain). "It is like a mountain. "It is a beacon to the heavens. Let it proclaim forever that the Anunnaki survived the deluge."

A Song of praise to; *#5 THE NEW FLIGHT PATTERN:

The Anunnaki continued marveling, "From the pyramids to the East where the Sun on the designated day rises, they will ascend toward the pyramids from the southwest where the sun rises on the designated day, they will descend."

Then Enlil, shown by his own hand, activated the Nibiruan crystals inside. Eerie lights began to flicker and an enchanting hum broke the silence. Outside, all at once, the capstone shone brighter than the Sun. The multitude of assembled Anunnaki uttered a great cry of joy. Ninmah, so impressed with the occasion recited and sang a song of praise to the pyramids.

Enki said, "When in future days it will be asked when and by whom has this marvel been fashioned? We must tell them with a monument. Let us create beside the twin peaks, a sphinx. Let it announce the AGE OF THE LION. This will tell future generations that the flood came during the age of the Lion. It will have a lion's body and the face on the monument will be that of Nngishzidda, the peaks designer. Let it gaze precisely toward the place of the celestial chariots. Let the sphinx reveal to future generations when and what purpose."

Constellation of Virgo ...... 12,900 B.C.
Constellation of Leo .... 10, 860 B.C... Flood occurred.
                              Pyramids and sphinx were made.
Constellation of Cancer ..... 8,700 B.C.

And so it was under the constellation of Leo, about 10,860 years before Christ that the great flood, the building of the Great Pyramids and the Sphinx occurred.

Now, the new place of the chariots, Mount Mashu (Mount Sinai) is the instrument-equipped mount at the post diluvial Sinai spaceport can receive gold shipped from across the seas (South America) to Ararat and the chariots can carry the gold to Nibiru.

The new flight pattern. From the pyramids (the new beacon lights) straight to Jerusalem and the new landing place on Mount Ararat. The old landing place became an important part of the new flight pattern and is north west of Jerusalem.

Utu was once again put in command of the place of chariots. And again, Marduk was left out of any command. During the work of cutting the shape of the lion, he in aggrievement said to his father, "To dominate the whole Earth you promised me. Now command and glory you gave to others. I am left again, without task or dominion. In my erstwhile domain are the artificial mountains/ pyramids. On the lion the image must be mine. My face must be on it." So Marduk placed his name on the sphinx 'RA', but it is not his face.

Ningishzidda was angered by Marduk's words. His other brothers were also annoyed by the clamors over domains and his cousins were also aroused. Everyone was now demanding lands for themselves including the Earthlings.

Enlil suggested that for peace to prevail, the habitable lands between us should be set apart.

It was agreed the peninsula was an uncontested divider, it was allotted to Ninmah. Tilman, near Mount Sinai, the land of the missiles was out of bounds for the Earthlings. The habitable lands to the East were given to Enlil and his offspring. The two sons of Noah, Shem and Japheth therein to also dwell.

The dark-hued land mass of the Abzu (central Africa) was granted to Enki and his clan. Noah and his son, Ham and his people were chosen to inhabit. "Let Marduk be their Lord, the Master of the Dark-Hued Abzu. We need to appease Marduk."

In Tilman, in the mountainous south in a verdant valley, Ninurta built a home for his mother, Ninmah. It is located near a spring with date trees and he planted a fragrant garden for his mother.

When all locations were settled, a signal to all outposts on Earth was given to begin the shipment of gold. From the mountain lands across the ocean/South America, helicopters brought in the golden nuggets to the Place of Chariots. And then to Nibiru. On that memorable day, praises were given to all those who worked so hard.

Enlil found a dry spot, Jerusalem for Mission Control Center to replace Nibiru-Ki. He drew up the dimensions and designed a platform of stones/Mount Moriah. There was a great rock in the midst. Enlil had the insides carved out and these openings were for placing the instruments of control...This is the Rock of Testing of Abraham's faith in the Lord to sacrifice his son, Isaac.

The levelness of the platform was achieved by massive land hills and floors resting on archways in the Southern part. These were kept from collapsing by retaining walls on four sides of the platform. The Western side extends for about 1,600 feet. The Eastern side is shorter by about 970 feet. The total is close to 1,500 square feet. The Western wall is the Wailing Wall of the Jews.

There is nothing to compare to it in the ancient past except for Enlil's master piece of the larger platform of Sippar/Baalbek, Lebanon. He had built that 411,000 years ago. This old facility was used as part of the new flight plan.

Ningishzidda built the pyramids around 10,095 B.C. Estimated time to build the pyramids around 765 years. Marduk's The face on the sphinx is not that of Ningishzidda. It is the face of Asar/Osiris, Marduk's son.

THE FIRST PYRAMID WAR

About 10,000 years ago, Nibiru was still demanding gold for their atmosphere. Rivalries were paramount on Earth. However, slowly the Earth returned to life with the seeds of life that had been preserved by Enki. What had survived by itself was augmented on land, in the air and in the waters. The most precious gift of all was mankind, the descendants of Cain found in the South America. The few Anunnaki clamored for the civilized worker.

The peaceful truce was shattered by a dispute between Asar/Osiris and his brother, Sati/Seth. These gods abetted by the Igigi broke the tranquility. During the Deluge, Marduk's sons married the daughters of Shamgaz, Asta and Nebat. Shamgaz was the leader of the Igigi.

Asar and Asta settled in the dark-hued lands of Africa with his father, Marduk. Satu and Nebat settled in the Landing Place in the Cedar Mountains with Shamgaz, his father-in-law. He became very jealous of Asar residing in the rich lands, he wondered which lands the Igigi would rule.

Every day, over and over, Shamgaz would incite the Igigi, Satu and Nebat about Asar inheriting the rich lands of Africa. Day after day he talked of being cheated until he had them worked into a frenzy of jealousy. Shamgaz decided to hold a banquet and invite all the Anunnaki and the Igigi. He told Nebat that we will plot her brother-in-law's demise. The three of them plot Asar's death.

On that terrible day, Asar and Asta came to the celebration. Nebat had everything beautifully set and she herself beautified. With lyre in hand, she sang a song to mighty Asar. Satu placed before his brother a choice cut of roasted meat. As he cut it with a salted knife, he bowed before his brother. Shamgaz offered Asar new wine in a large vessel that contained poison.

Asar drank. He rose, sang and danced with symbols in his hand. Then he was overcome by the poison and fell. Shamgaz said loudly to Satu, "Let us take him to a chamber for a sound sleep." In the chamber, they lay him in a wooden coffin. They closed the coffin with tight seals and threw it into the sea.

When word of their deed reached Asta, she went screaming and wailing to her father-in-law, Marduk. She told him Asar was brutally thrown to his death into the sea. She said the coffin must be found quickly and to please hurry.

Marduk gathered a search team and into their helicopters they flew to search the sea. By the shores of the dark-hued land (Africa) it was found. Inside, lay the stiff body of Asar. Marduk screamed out, tore off his clothing and put ashes on his forehead. Enki cried out.

Asta screamed out to her father-in-law that he must copulate with her to give her a son and said that Satu must die. Enki said that this could not be done. That the brother who killed the brother, Satu must give her a son. Asta puzzled by this law would never consent to have sex with her husband's murderer. Secretly she went into the shrine where Asar's body lay, she extracted from his penis the seed of life. Quickly she went to her chamber and injected the sperm into her womb and she conceived.

Satu soon delivered word to Enki and his sons also to Marduk and his brothers that he is the sole heir and Marduk's successor. He announced that he would be master of the two narrows/upper Egypt.

Asta called forth the Anunnaki council and refuted his claim with, "With Asar's heir, I am with child."

Council and Satu had to wait out the gestation period and for the child to reach the age of rulership. Asta hid her child among the rivers bulrushes to avoid the wrath of Satu. She called her son Horon/Horus and raised him to be his father's avenger.

From earth year to earth year, the Igigi and their offspring spread over land, from the landing place to the borders, to the land that was off limits to Earthlings. They threatened to overrun the landing place of celestial chariots/Tilmun/Mt. Sinai.

In the dark-hued lands, Horon grew to be a hero. He was adopted and raised by his Uncle Gibil, Enki's son. He trained and instructed him to fly like a falcon and fashioned winged sandals for soaring. He made Horon a divine harpoon; its arrows were bolts of missiles.

Gibil had taught him arts of metals and smithing. He revealed the secret of the metal called iron from which he armed his army of loyal Earthlings. They marched across land and river to challenge Satu and the Igigi.

When Horon and his earthly army had reached the border of Tilman, the land of missiles, Horon sent words of challenge to Satu, his uncle, "I am Horon, son of Asar, between us alone is the conflict. Let one on one meet in contest."

In the skies above Tilman/Sinai, Satu in his helicopter awaited Horon for combat. When Horon soared toward him like a dragon, Satu shot a poisoned dart at him and like a scorpion's sting, it felled Horon. All were watching. With his medical skills, Ningishzidda rushed to Horon's side and converted the poisoned blood to benevolent blood/dialysis.

By morning, Horon was healed and he returned to his deed. Then Ningishzidda provided him with a fiery pillar, a heavenly fish with wings and fiery tail. It's eyes/lights changed color from blue to red to blue.

Toward Satu, Horon soared in the fiery pillar far and wide the chased each other, fierce and deadly was the battle. Horon's fiery pillar was hit. Then with his harpoon, he smote Satu who came crashing down to the ground. Horon bound him in tethers. He brought his captive uncle before the council. They saw that he was blinded and that his testicles were squashed. He stood like a discarded jar.

"Let Satu live. Let him end his days as a mortal among the Igigi," so said the council.

Horon was declared triumphant to inhabit his father's throne and they placed it in the Hall of Records.

Troubled by events, Enlil summoned his three sons: Ninurta, Nannar and Ishkur. He said that in the beginning, Anunnaki gods made man in their image, now the Anunnaki are becoming like Earthlings. Cain killed his brother, now Marduk's son kills his own brother, Horon raised an army from Earthlings and used our secret metal weapons. He went on to tell them that now the Igigi are advancing toward our place of chariots, Tilman and soon they will lay claim to all heaven and Earth facilities. And we must take counter steps.

He told Ninurta that he must build a Heaven-Earth facility in South America. Ninurta there, chose mountain lands beside a great lake/ Lake Titicaca to build post-diluvial Mission Control Center and a space port to ship gold to Nibiru.

Soon a horrible incident would happen; Dumuzi, Enki's son, fell in love with Inanna Ishtar/Aphrodite, Enlil's granddaughter at the celebration of the Pyramids. The love grew deeper and knew no bounds; a passion enflamed their hearts. A wedding was planned. Enki gave Dumuzi a large domain above the Abzu (Meluhha) the black land. It was a beautiful rich area; highland trees, abundant waters, large bulls roamed, cattle, copper from the mountains glittered like gold.

Marduk was very jealous of his brother Dumuzi. He felt he had to take a back seat to everyone and now for his youngest brother. It was more than he could bear.

Inanna was deeply loved by her family. She was beautiful, expert in martial arts and flying the heavens. She was presented with her own sky-ships. The deep passionate love was welcomed by both families so as to bring peace between the clans. A wedding gift of an olden bed, blue hued lapis stones and sweet dates, her favored fruit... Marduk was furious.

Inanna told Geshtinanna, Dumuzi's sister, of her passionate love for Dumuizi. She told her that she and Dumuzi will rise to a great nation and he will rise to be a great Anunnaki. His name will be exalted above all others. Jealous, she rushed to tell Marduk and he devised a plan of what she must do.

And she did, she rushed to the herder's dwelling where Dumuzi worked. She was lovely, dressed and perfumed, she seduced him to bed her. He fell asleep and dreamed a vision that the Master sent seven men and they took from him his sheep, ewes, headdress, his royal robe and his staff of shepherding. They seized him naked and bound his hands in fetters. They left him to die.

He told Geshtinanna that Marduk will accuse him of raping her. Emissaries will arrest me. The trial will disgrace me. He realized then that she and Marduk plotted this against him. Like a wounded beast, he screamed out, "Betrayal, how could you?"

He escaped through the desert and ran to the mighty waterfalls to hide. Dumuzi fell, hit his head and the gushing waters s wept away his lifeless body in white froth.

Ninagal retrieved his lifeless body and took him to the abode of Nergal and Ereshkigal in the lower Abzu and placed his dead body on a stone slab. When Enki heard of his son's death, he screamed in pained agony. "What have I sinned? Water…water. My name means 'whose home is water'. I splashed down on Earth in water. The water of the deluge killed my creation and by water has my son died," he bewailed. Enki further bewailed to hear of Marduk's evil plan.

Geshtinanna told of his evil plots. When Enki heard of the plot, greater was his agony for he said that now, Marduk, his first-born will also suffer for this evil deed.

Inanna grieved, hurried to lower Africa to retrieve Dumuzi's body. When her sister-in-law Ereshkigal, heard that Inanna was coming, she was at the first of seven gates. Knowing of Inanna's evil reputation, ordered that she must leave one of her accoutrement and one of her weapons at each gate. She arrived before Ereshkigal, naked and powerless.

"Inanna, you are scheming to have an heir by my husband." She ordered her vizier, Namtar, to let loose the sixty diseases upon Inanna. When her family did not hear from her, Enlil begged Enki to find her. He beamed Nergal to learn what his wife had done to Inanna and that something had to be done immediately.

From the clay of the Abzu, Enki made two emissaries **(GREYS/ETs)** without blood and they could withstand death rays/radiation. To the lower Abzu he sent them in a small craft; they were to bring Inanna back dead or alive.

Ereshkigal looked at these strange skinny, rubbery creatures, about 4 feet tall, large heads, and large, dark, almond eyes. Shocked and puzzled by their appearance, she asked, "Are you Anunnaki?" They did not answer. "Are you Earthlings?" They did not answer.

"We have come for Inanna, dead or alive." They sent the messages by 'mental telepathy'. She directed Namtar to use the weapons of magical power against them. They remained unharmed. He took them to the lifeless body of Inanna hanging on a stake.

The clay emissaries took her down and placed her on a slab. They directed on her, a pulsar and an emitter. They scrubbed upon her the Water of Life, and in her mouth they placed the plant of life. Inanna stirred, she opened her eyes and arose from the dead. When the emissaries were ready to return to the upper world, they demanded to leave with Inanna and the lifeless body of Dumuzi. Enki ordered the greys to take them to upper Egypt, Dumuzi's land.

She washed his body with pure water, anointed him with sweet oil, clothed him in a red shroud and lay him upon a slab of lapis. In a rock she carved out a rest place for him and there to **await the Day of Rising**.

In great anger, she went to the abode of Enki, "I want retribution for the death of my beloved Dumuzi. I demand the death of Marduk, the culprit." She demanded.

Enki replied, "There has been enough death. Marduk was an instigator, but a murderer he is not." She went to her parents wailing to high heavens, "Justice, revenge, death to Marduk. He has killed my lover."

Council was held at Enlil's abode, all of his children were present. It was a council of war. Ninurta asked for strong measures. Utu, Inanna's twin said, "Marduk has exchanged secret words with the Igigi."

Enlil agreed, "The Earth must be rid of the serpent, Marduk. I will radio Enki now and demand that Marduk surrenders."

Enki summoned his sons and told them that he was still grieving Dumuzi, but he must defend Marduk's rights. He said that Marduk instigated evil, but by fate did Dumuzi die. He must be protected from Ninurta's gang and protected by all of this. Gibil and Ninagal agreed, Ningishzidda opposed and Nergal said he would aid only if Marduk were in mortal danger.

The Second Pyramid War, about 9,400 years ago

The death of Dumuzi caused a war of ferocity unknown before to erupt between the two clans: The Enlilites and the Enkiites. This was a battle between Anunnaki loosed upon another planet. Some of the Anunnaki were Nibiruan born.

Inanna began the warfare. In her sky ship, she flew over the domains of Enki, his sons and Marduk. Over a loud speaker she called, "Marduk, I, Inanna, challenge you. You killed my Dumuzi and I want justice."

Marduk took flight to the land of Ninagal and Gibil. Inanna followed him there. She screamed to Marduk and made daring maneuvers, showing her power and to evoke fear. Ninurta assisted her, he shot withering beams at the enemy's stronghold. Ishkur, Enlil's son, attacked from the skies, scorching lightnings and smashing thunders. He attacked with missiles and killed the fish of the rivers. He dispersed the cattle in the fields.

Marduk retreated to the north, the land of the pyramids. Ninurta followed and rained poison missiles on the land. His weapons that tear apart the people, robbed them of their senses. The canals turned red from their blood. Ishkur's brilliant weapons turned the night into flaming days. As the devastating battles continued, Marduk ensconced himself in the large pyramid.

Gibil, Enki's son, devised an unseen shield to hide the pyramid. His brother, Nergal, raised an all-seeing eye to the heavens. Inanna directed by a horn, attacked their hiding place with a weapon of brilliance.

Horon came to defend his grandfather, Marduk, but Inanna's weapon damaged his right eye. As this was happening, Utu, Inanna's twin held off the hordes of Earthlings beyond Tilman. At the foot of the pyramid, the two clans of Anunnaki clashed in battle. It was horrific. Enlil screamed out to Enki to tell Marduk to surrender and let the bloodshed end. Ninmah messaged that brother should talk to brother and let the fighting stop. In his hiding spot in the pyramid, Marduk defied the enemy and made his final stand. Inanna could not surmount the stone structure; its smooth sides deflected her weapons.

Ninurta learned of the secret entrance, he found the swivel stone on the north side. Through a dark corridor he went until he reached the grand gallery. Its vault was aglitter like a rainbow by the many hued emissions of the crystals. Marduk was aware of his intrusion and awaited with many weapons. Ninurta responded with weapons, smashing the wonder crystals as he kept going up the gallery.

Marduk retreated to the upper chamber, the place of the pulsating stone. At the entrance, he lowered the sliding stone blocks. This barred all from admission into the pyramid. Inanna and Ishkur followed Ninurta.

Ishkur said, "The chamber in which Marduk is hiding, let this encased chamber be his stone coffin. Look, these three blocking stones are ready for down sliding."

"Yes," said Inanna. "Let his death be a slow one by being buried alive. Let this be Marduk's sentence."

They let loose the three blocking stones for plugging. Now Marduk was sealed alive in his own dark tomb with no sun light, air, water or food.

Marduk's spouse, Sarpanit saw the incident, wailed and screamed of the injustice. With her son, Nabu, she hurried to her father-in-law, Enki. "Marduk has been imprisoned without a trial. He must be returned to the living." She went to Inanna and pleaded for his life, but Inanna was not appeased and said Marduk must die. Ninmah was called and she said to let him live in exile. It was agreed to let him live in exile.

They summoned Ningishzidda to rescue Marduk since he constructed the Ekur, he would know how to circumvent the blockings. He had the men chisel a doorway, they bored a twisting passageway upward creating a rescue shaft, an opening, and cut a doorway in the stones. The workers continued through hidden hollowings to the pyramid's midst. At the vortex of the hollowings they will break through the stones. They blew open a doorway to the insides, circumventing the blockings and continued up the grand gallery and then raised the three stone bars. They then reached the uppermost chambers…Marduk's death prison.

They found Marduk laying on the floor. He was dying from lack of air. They carefully lowered the Lord Marduk through the twisting shaft and brought him t into the fresh air. All were waiting for him and much gratitude was given Ningishzidda for the rescue.

Enki said aloud to Marduk that his life has been spared, but all agreed that he must forfeit his birth right and go into exile in the land of the bisons. Marduk, in disbelief said that he would rather die than forfeit his birthright, "Over and over, what was mine was stolen and now, my birthright?"

Sarpanit thrust Nabu into his arms and softly said, "We are part of your future." Marduk, angry and humbled inaudibly said, "To fate I yield." So to a place where horned beasts are hunted, Marduk with his wife and son went to North America.

Ninurta entered the pyramid with destruction in mind. Through the shaft, then through a horizontal corridor to the pyramids vulva he went. On its east wall in a niche was an artificial Destiny Stone emitting a red radiance. It was a tracking power/laser beam that strikes to kill. Fearful he shouted to his lieutenants to take it away and destroy it to obliteration.

Retracing his steps through the grand gallery to the topmost chamber, Ninurta entered and saw a hollowed out chest within was the pulsating heart. Its net force was enhanced by five compartments. * #6 and #7 With his baton/laser he struck the stone chest and it responded with a resonating sound. Its gug stone that determines directions he ordered it taken to a place of his choice.

Coming down the Grand Gallery, Ninurta examined the twenty-seven pairs of Nibiruan crystals; many had been damaged in his fight with Marduk; some survived the struggle. He ordered that the whole ones be removed from their grooves. He pulverized the others with his beam.

Once outside the pyramid, he soared in his blackbird and turned his attention toward the Apex Stone atop the pyramid. To him, it represented his enemy's (Marduk) epitome. With his weapons he shook it loose and it toppled to the ground. Over his loudspeaker in his craft, Ninurta declared victoriously, "By this, the fear of Marduk is forever ended."

To replace the incapacitated beacon (pyramid top) a mount near the place of celestial chariots was chosen Within its inners, the salvaged crystals were rearranged. Upon its peak, the gug stone for directing was installed. The mount was Mount Mashu/Mount Sinai. The Mount of Supreme Baroque.

Enlil summoned his clan to confirm commands over olden lands and to assign lordships over new lands: To Ninurta, Enlilship powers were granted; to be surrogate to his father's lands.

To Ishkur he granted lordship in Sippar, over the Landing Place in the Cedar Mountains. Also the domain northward; south and east where the Igigi and their offspring had settled.

To Nannar was given the peninsula where the place of the chariots was. To Utu, commander of the Place and the Naval of the Earth.

To Ningishzidda was given lordship to the Land of the Two Narrows; Egypt. To this Enki's other sons and Inanna objected, she lay claim to it as this land which was given to her and Dumuzi as a wedding gift. Since she couldn't have it she demanded a domain of her own.

Two shars 7,200 years have passed since the Great Deluge. It was now, 4,000 B.C. 6,000 years ago. The Earthlings had proliferated from the mountain lands to dried lowland. Many civilized mankind of Noah, born of Anunnaki seed had proliferated. Offspring of Igigi who intermarried roamed about. In the distant land, Cain's kinfolk survived.

Few and lofty were the Anunnaki who came from Nibiru and few were their perfect descendants. They wondered how to establish settlements for themselves and the Earthlings. They wondered how they could remain lofty over mankind; how to make the many **obey** and **serve** the few.

These concerns were beamed to King Anu. He radioed that he would return to Earth one more time to solve these concerns which would be;

"RELIGION"

CHAPTER 11

KING ANU'S LAST VISIT TO EARTH

About 6,000 years ago, the Anunnaki had lived on Earth for 439,200 years. While the Anunnaki awaited the King, they reestablished the abodes in the Eden. The Earthlings settled in the mountain lands where the descendants of Shem dwelt, in Africa. The leaders let them settle upon the newly dried soil.

Upon Enki's old city, Eridu, in the center of the raised platform, a new house was built. It was called The House of the Lord Whose Return is Triumphant. It was adorned with gold and silver and precious metals provided by Enki's sons.

Above the abode, the twelve Zodiac signs of the Constellations were marked out in a circle pointing skyward. Below waters were running where swimming fish flow. In the sanctuary where no one could enter, Enki kept the formulas.

Where Enlil's Nibiru-Ki stood before the flood, a new city, Nibiru-Ki was built. This sacred precinct was walled off from the Earthlings quarters. A stairway rose to the heavens, led to the top platform. There, Enlil kept the Tablets of Destiny and they were protected by his weapons which were the 'lifted eye'/camera that scans all and the 'lifted beam'/ laser that penetrates all. In the courtyard, Enlil's jet sky bird was kept on a pad in its own enclosure.

It was decided that King Anu and Anti would not stay with Enki or Enlil, but in a pure white structure called Unug-Ki which was erected in the midst of Eden. Shade trees were placed throughout. Its exterior rose in seven stages; the interior was regal. When the celestial chariots approached Earth, Anunnaki sky ships soared toward it, maneuvering as to greet them. They guided the guests to a safe landing in Tilman, the Place of the Chariots.

Utu, Enlil's grandson was commander of Tilman. He greeted his grandparents to Earth. So pleased they were to meet. So happy was Utu to meet his grandparents for the first time. The leaders came to greet their parents; they hugged and kissed, laughed and cried. They were ecstatic.

The grandchildren looked at their grandparents in awe. The three children, Enki, Enlil and Ninmah looked at Anu and Antu and noticed to their horror that they looked older than their parents. Enlil and Enki were old and bearded. Ninmah, once a raving beauty was bent and wrinkled. Anu and Antu were as shocked as the three children's visage.

In sky ships, the royalty were taken to Eden and landed in a prepared place near their abode. All the Anunnaki were there to greet them, as an honor guard they stood. They were praised and taken in to bathe, rest.

In the evening, seated in an open courtyard, an evening breeze rustled the trees. All of their children surrounded them. A bull and a ram were roasting on a fire. A great banquet was prepared for the royal couple awaiting an astonishing event…The arrival of Nibiru's passing!

Zumul learned in the matter of stars and planets awaited Enlil's instructions. In the evening, Enlil signaled Zumul. He ascended near the steps of the house of Anu (Unug-Ki) to announce the arrival of their home planet.

Zumul stepped on the first step to announce the appearance of Jupiter. On the second step, he announced that Venus was seen. Mercury was announced on the third step. Anshar on the fourth step. Mars on the fifth step. The Moon was announced on the sixth step.

Then on a signal from Zumul, the hymn, "The Planet of Anu in the Skies Rises' began to be sung from the top most step, the seventh. At that time, the **'RED-HALOED NIBIRU CAME INTO VIEW.** What a joy, the Anunnaki clapped, sang, danced to music. They sang, "To the one who glows bright, the heavenly planet of Lord Anu."

On a signal, a bon fire was lit; from place to place the whole land of Eden was lit with bon fires. Food of all kinds were served accompanied with wine and beer. All over the Eden there was joyful dancing, clapping, eating and drinking.

Their King was truly on Earth. They could see the red planet in the heavens. The planet from where their ancestors came; ancestors to even the naked black-haired Earthlings What an occasion and what a sight to behold.

At the end of the festivities the royal couple slept for several Earth days. On the sixth day of their visit, Anu summoned his sons and Ninmah. At this time, he learned of all the happenings on Earth; flood clean up, wars, peace. He learned of Enlil's dislike for the Earthlings and that he wanted them dead in the flood, the survival of Cain's descendants and the Land in South America. And the discovery of gold there.

Enki revealed to his father the visit of Galzu, the emissary he sent who had his seal and told him to save Noah by an ark. He said that Enlil and Ninmah could not return to Nibiru for they would die.

Shocked was Anu, "My son, I am deeply puzzled. A secret emissary by that name was never sent by me. It is not true that you would die. Truly, Earth's cycles wreak havoc on their bodies. But this was all cured by elixirs on Nibiru."

Shocked, Enlil and Enki said at the same time, "Whose emissary is Galzu if not yours? Who wanted to save the Earthlings? Who made us stay on Earth? If not your seal…whose?"

Ninmah answered, "For the Creator of all did Galzu appear. Was the creation of Earthlings also destined?" The four sat silent for a long time…wondering.

Anu said, "And now for the matter of which I have come. The will of the Creator of all is clear to see. We are only emissaries on Earth for the Earthlings. The Earth belongs to the Earthlings. We are intended to preserve and advance them. Cities must be established for man. You must set aside from them sacred precincts for you, the Anunnaki. Kingship must be established on Earth as we do on Nibiru. Give crown and scepter to a chosen man and through him convey words of the Anunnaki to the people to enforce work and dexterity."

Enlil said, "We will establish a priesthood in the sacred precincts. The Earthlings will serve and worship the Anunnaki as lofty lords. Secret knowledge will be taught to them, and they can convey civilization to mankind."

"We will create four regions, three for mankind and one which will be restricted from them. The first region will be in the Olden Eden, established for Enlil and his sons to dominate. The second region will be in the Land of the Two Narrows/ Egypt; for Enki and his sons to lord over. The third region, not mingled with the other two, in a distant land (Indus Valley) grant to Inanna. The fourth region, the peninsula will be consecrated to the Anunnaki alone. It will be 'The Place of chariots, Tilman."

Anu's visit to South America. He felt it was time for him to see the progress of the land across the seas. But before he left, he discussed the sorrow in his heart for Marduk and that he may forgive him when he sees him and release him from exile. Enki said he would radio Marduk of his grandfather's arrival and tell him where to meet you.

Anu and Antu surveyed the Eden and all its lands of the olden times and shown the areas where the new cities are being built. He was shown all the regions.

On the morning of their eighteenth day at departure, all the Anunnaki came to say good-bye. The King blessed the young Anunnaki and told Inanna that he is giving her the temporary beautiful abode that he and Antu stayed in.

He said to the congregation, "Let all here heed my words. This home Unug-Ki is given to Inanna and also the sky ship in which we surveyed the lands be hers. Call her Anunitu/Beloved of Anu."

There were many tears shed as their king and queen departed. It would be his last visit to Earth.

And off to South America they went with Enlil, Enki, Ninurta and Ishkur. There in the lands of Ninurta where he governed over the descendants of Cain, they arrived. To impress his grandfather, he built him an abode by the shore of the great mountain lake, Lake Titicaca, it was made of great golden riches. Its great stone blocks had been cut to perfection. The inside was covered with pure gold. There was a golden enclosure covered with flowers of carnelian.

After they ate and rested, Ninurta took the entire group to survey the lands. He showed them how the golden nuggets are collected. Anu so amazed at all the gold he saw stated that there is enough gold here to serve the needs of Nibiru many years. So pleased and proud of Ninurta was he.

"Come," said Ninurta. "I want to show you the artificial mountain/pyramid." To a pyramid. he took them and showed them the Inners that had a place for smelting and refining metals. "We have discovered a new metal by extracting it from the stones and combining it with the abundant copper. A strong metal it is and we call it anak/tin."

Ninurta took them to the great lake from whose shores come the metal. "Have you named the lake, Ninurta?"

"No," he replied.

"Well, from henceforth call it the Lake of Anak/tin."

"Agreed. Now, let us go to the land of Marduk up north. We radioed him the time and place to meet us where horned beasts are hunted." On top of a mountain they landed. Marduk was there with his son, Nabu. He came to stand before his grandfather.

"Aah, Marduk, my grandson. It has been such a long time since we have seen you….too long. I have missed you. I had to see you before we leave for Nibiru. So, this is my great grandson, Nabu? What a handsome lad he is." He embraced him. "Where is Sarpanit?"

Marduk, through tears replied. "My wife is dead. My Sarpanit is gone. Now Nabu alone resides with me. It has been sad and lonely for us here in this God forsaken land."

Anu pressed Marduk to his chest and said, "Enough, enough, you have been punished and suffered enough." He placed his right hand on Marduk's head and said, "Marduk, from this day forth, you are forgiven by my blessing. You may return to the Eden."

From North America, they returned to the high mountain of South America. All who went there went below to Ninurta's new place for the chariots, its running (Nasca flight strip) stretched to the horizons. The royal couple's celestial chariot stood, prepared and waiting. It was loaded to the brim with gold. The silver craft glistened in the sunlight.

At departure time, Anu said, "My children, I am so proud of what you have accomplished here on Earth. Your beautiful children and your beautiful cities. I am extremely proud of your loyalty to your home planet, Nibiru, your dedication. We would have perished a long time ago. There are no words to express our gratitude for your saving our lives."

He wiped tears from his eyes. Antu was crying. "Whatever destiny has intended for the Earth and the Earthlings, let it be so. If man, not Anunnaki is destined to inherit the Earth, let us help destiny. Give mankind knowledge and teach him secrets of Heaven and Earth. Teach them laws of justice and righteousness. Then depart and leave. I, your father, God Anu and Nibiru have spoken. I have given you my fatherly instructions."

So after eighteen days on Earth, the grandparents hugged and kissed their children and departed into the craft. Many tears were shed as they watched the beautiful craft ascend straight upward, and continued slowly upward, high in the sky. The craft dipped downward and tilted its sides to say good-bye. Then with unbelievable speed, it disappeared out of sight.

There was a long silence and tears from those on the ground. The silence was broken by an angry Marduk, "What is this place of celestial chariots? Who built it? Who is charge of it and what else has transpired in my absence" He screamed in rage, his face reddened and eyes bulging as he related the pain of his exile that his wife lived a sad and lonely life without her loved ones. She died suffering loneliness. While he was imprisoned to die in the pyramid and then put in exile all because Dumuzi died an accidental death.

Enki approached his son and told him that he had been in exile for about 3,400 years and much has happened. He told him of the dividing of the lands and that Inanna was given the third region to the East (Indus Valley) and Anu's sky ship and his city of Unug-Ki by Anu. Enraged, Marduk screamed. "Inanna, who is just a granddaughter, the woman who lays with many men and murders many of them."

Enlil sensing trouble told Ishkur to remain behind to protect the gold and the area. Enlil tried to appease Marduk as they left for the Eden.

He would not be appeased. He thought to himself that he had dreams of his own and by god he would see to it to get what is due him. To the Eden they departed. They must make changes.

Earth is turned over to man, so Earth must now be ruled by Earth Time. 6,000 years ago.

A council meeting was held to set up new rules. Enki said that all are sorrowful to see King Anu depart. He told them that in South America, King Anu forgave Marduk and to welcome him back. There was applause. And then he gave them a shocking announcement. "King Anu has turned Earth over to the Earthlings. We will use Earth time, not Anunnaki shars. We will teach Earthlings all they need to know to govern, to build, to grow food, livestock, make bricks, refine gold, etc. We will begin to build."

There was stirring and anger as the Anunnaki shouted that this has been their home for thousands of years. On went the arguments. Enki appeased them by the thought that all who wished could return home one day and young Anunnaki will always be glad to come to Earth.

"I will begin a new calendar. **The Age of the Bull, 4,200 B.C. to 2,000 B.C. Dedicated to Enlil, The Age of the Bull.**" The beginning of the new calendar count was 5,780.

All agreed except Marduk who was fuming but kept quiet.

The Earthlings were taught all matters of living. Earthlings and Anunnaki lived side by side.

Cities were erected of the old sites: In Lagash, a precinct was built for Ninurta. Utu lived in a new Sippar on top of the old. Ninmah got a new medical center. Nannar was given Urum/Ur. Ishkur returned to mountain lands of the North. Inanna stayed in Unug-Ki. Marduk and son stayed in Eridu. The region called Ki-Engi was given to the Igigi/land of the watchers. The black-haired people were given a land of their own called **Kishi, the first city of man. Here Enki planted 'The heavenly bright object in consecrated soil. Ninurta was appointed the first King of Kishi.**

Ninurta journeyed from Kishi to Eridu to obtain the Mes, laws of governing for kingship, from Enki. Enki went to the sacred place and brought the 50 Mes for governing.

In Kishi the black-haired people were taught to calculate with numbers. Ninsaba, Enki's daughter, taught them writing. Ninkashi taught them beer-making.

Ninurta taught them kiln work and smelting and how to make wheeled wagons and how to harness asses. The laws of justice and righteousness behavior promulgated Kishi. He also taught them how to mix tin with copper. He was held in high esteem by the black-haired people. What a glorious time for him. He was honored with the constellation of the archer, Sagittarius.

Inanna demanded a domain from her grandfather, Enlil. He said the day will come. She became angry and devised a plan to get the Mes from Enki. She went to his abode, gave him much drink and seduced him to bring the Mes to her. While he slept, she took the 94 Mes These discs contained all the information of the universe and everything in it and on the planets. She escaped with them.

Enlil permitted her to keep them. Humiliated by his deed, Enki was furious and screamed at her, "Because of the way you have attained them, you will never have good luck…Karma."

Marduk/Nimrod was furious because he had been given nothing and now, Inanna has a city of her own and the power of the Mes. "Enough of this humiliation. I will build my own city. Enough, you just wait and see. "He screamed…

So Marduk/Nimrod built **The Tower of Babel, 3,453. B.C.** He chose to build his city, Babylon, a place previously selected, Unug-Ki (Uruk), the city of the temporary abode for King Anu during his last visit on Earth.

Marduk summoned his son, Nabu, the Igigi and their offspring to the site chosen for his sacred city. It was a few miles north east of Nibiru-Ki, the olden Mission Control Center of Enlil. He gathered them at this land and explained they will build a sacred city, Babylon and a place for sky ships. "Let us make a **shem** (rocket) for ourselves." There were no stones to build the city or rocket launcher/biblical ziggurat.

He taught them to make bricks, burn them by fire so they could build the city, and the tower to rocket to reach the heavens/Mars where he was commander for thousands of years. They began building the tower and quickly was it rising. Enlil heard of this and rushed to talk him out of it; he would give him other locations, etc. It did not work.

Fearing that Marduk may surpass his power, he called a meeting with his sons and told them he must be stopped. It was held in

Nibiru-Ki a short distance from Marduk's site. He said Marduk can't be permitted to build this gateway to heaven which he is entrusting to Earthlings. There will be no stopping mankind in any endeavor. His sons agreed and determined Enki should not know "We will leave at dark and attack them from the air as soon as we see the tower." When they saw the tower from their aircraft, they rained fire and brimstone upon the tower. Upon their encampment, they dropped missiles.

Enlil said, "I must scatter the leaders and the followers, I will confuse their counsels to scatter their unity. The Earthlings spoke only one language (Anunnaki). I will confound them so they will not understand each other." Thus, Enlil manipulated the left side of their brain, they were confused and they scattered. Marduk departed to the skies.

3355 B.C. Twenty-three kings had reigned in Kishi. Enlil decreed kingship be turned over to Unug-Ki. The bright heavenly object was transferred to Unug-Ki's soil and songs of praise went to the ruler, Inanna who had guardianship over the Mes.

Marduk, after a long absence returned to upper Africa. He expected to become master here as this was the land his father gave him. Shocked and furious he was to find his brother, Ningishzidda master. He had used the offspring of the Igigi/Earthlings, oversee this lush land.

"Ningishzidda, What have you done in my land during my absence? Why was my grandson, Horon, sent to a desert place, a place that has no water, a boundless place where no sexual pleasures are enjoyed? My brother, I am here in my proper place, from now on you will be a deputy of mine. You will not be in charge. If you are inclined to rebel, to another land you must go."

The two brothers embarked on a bitter quarrel that lasted 350 years. **3113 B.C.** Finally, Enki went to Ningishzidda, "My Universal God. I can't take any more of this quarrelling. The people are being ruined by the trouble you and Marduk are causing. It has to stop for the sake of peace. You must depart to other lands."

Ningishzidda said, "Father, I have built the pyramids with power tools and aircraft. I built the powerful sphinx as you directed in the image of the lion to signify to future generations they were built under the Constellation Leo. I have worked hard. This lush land is my love. Marduk was gone for a long time. What of the sphinx, it has my face on it?"

Enki replied. "I'm sorry. He is the eldest son born on Nibiru. Please, son, you must leave here us in peace You must relinquish your power here. Please, you must go and leave us in peace."

Ningishzidda, cried, bowed his head and said, "Very well, father, I will go to the land beyond the ocean/Mesa America in the south west of Mexico The land of the Mayas. The land above Ninurta's. I will take with me Olmecs from Africa."

Today, there are giant stones of them found in Mesa America. These Olmecs look similar to Nigeria's leader, General Bangda.

Ningishzidda took his band of men and set his domain in Mesa, America. Here, Chichenitza was part of his domain. He wrote the Mayan Calendar which he started 3113 B.C. and has it ended December 21, 2012 A.D. He was known in Egypt as Thoth, Tehuti. He became known as the Winged Serpent and Quetzalcoatl in the new land.

In the annals of the First Region, Enlil's land was given the name Magan, land of the cascading River. In the Second Region upper Egypt/ Land of the Two Narrows, Marduk's lordship was established. Here, also resides the people's whose language was confounded. They lived in Inhem-la/ the dark-brown land.

Neteru, guardian of the watchers was the name given to the Anunnaki who were to teach these confounded people a new language.

Marduk was worshiped in this region and given the name Ra/ the Bright One. Enki was given the name Ptah/The Developer. When he heard that Marduk was going to remove Ningishzidda's face from the sphinx, he was furious. He shouted to Marduk that his brother built the pyramids, years of expert work and toil in the land. His face belongs there.

Marduk screamed, "No, father, this is my land I've been pushed aside for thousands of years. I was ignored, exiled for Inanna's sins and abused by my own cousins. No, no. Ningishzidda's face is coming off. And on goes the face of my son, Asar/Osiris."

Marduk wanted total control, he changed the calendar to count by tens, not sixty, he divided the year by tens and replaced the watching of the Sun to the watching of the Moon. He combined the north and south into one crowned city and appointed a man called Mena as king. He gave the Igigi a new name . . . **Nefilim**. He built a new city on land between the great rivers of the Nile and called it Mena Nefer/Mena's Beauty.

He built a city called Annu to honor his grandfather. On a platform he built a temple for Enki. Here, a rocket-launcher was erected. It rose like a sharp rocket. In its shrine he placed the nose of the rocket/ben-ben. It was the rocket ship Enki had used for countless years. Enki gave all matters of Mes to Marduk.

Marduk asked his father what he gave Ningishzidda that he did not receive. His father replied that he got everything Ningishzidda was given, except the knowledge of reviving the dead. Marduk's land grew prosperous.

2903 B.C. Inanna was given the Third Region. She was allotted the zodiac sign of Virgo.

Far away in the eastern lands beyond the seven mountains was her domain, Zamush. In the valleys beneath Mount Ararat was a city called Aratta. The people cultivated grains and horned cattle. Decreed by Enlil, Enki devised a new language and a new kind of writing for Aratta. Enki gave the Mes to Aratta, not to Inanna's civilized world to punish her for stealing them.

Inanna flew from Unug-Ki to Aratta., she carried the precious stones of Zamush to Unug-Ki. Enmerkar(grandfather of Gilgamesh) reigned as second king, replacing Inanna, He coveted the wealth of Aratta and schemed to reign there. He sent an emissary to Aratta demanding riches, but the king of Aratta could not understand the language. He sent him back with a message inscribed on the wooden scepter to share the Mes.

The king of Unug-Ki and all did not understand the new language, the message inscribed on the wooden scepter. The king ordered the wood be planted in the garden. Ten years passed and the wooden scepter grew into a shade tree. In frustration, Enmerkar went to his grandfather Utu, and asked him what he should do. He told him to bring Nisaba, Enki's daughter, mistress of scribes and writing and she will translate.

Nisaba smiled, "It is the tongue of Aratta. Here, I'll write it down for you.", "The King of Aratta requests that you share the Mes with him."

Furious, Enmerkar summoned his son, Banda to deliver his reply to Aratta, "Submission or die." Banda fell ill on the journey and died.

Throughout the years since Dumuzi's death, Inanna/ Aphrodite still longed for her lover, she dreamed of him. He told her he would return and they would love again. She traveled much between Unug-Ki and Aratta, restless and ungratified. To ease the pain of his absence, she established a 'House of Pleasure called Gigunu. Here, in this sacred precinct of Unug-Ki, she would lure the young Anunnaki bride grooms to her bed with sweet words on their wedding night. They would always be found dead the next morning.

It was at this time, Banda left for dead, searched for and found by his grandfather. He was brought to Unug-Ki and when she saw him, she thought it was Dumuzi. She bathed him in her abode. "Dumuzi, my beloved. She bedded him and when he awoke the next morning and found he was alive, she shouted for joy, "The power of not dying was placed in my hands, immortality is granted me." She called herself Mardul, a goddess.

Word spread and when Marduk heard, he grew jealous.

Banda succeeded his father, High Priest, Enme-Kay. He married, Enlil's granddaughter, Ninsun. 2,900 B.C. They bore a son, Gilgamesh. He succeeded Banda on the throne. As he grew older, he worried about death. He was aware that the Anunnaki lived a long time and the Earthlings died much earlier. He questioned his mother, "Shall I, too, though I am two-thirds god?"

"Divine, must I as a mortal Earthling, climb over the wall (die)?" His mother replied that as long as he lived on Earth, the death of an Earthling he must experience. She told him to go to his grandfather, Utu, son of Enlil, to plead with Enlil for him to go to Nibiru. He refused, but his mother returned many times to plead for him.

Finally, Utu agreed and told Gilgamesh that he must leave Unug-Ki to go to Tilman, the Landing Place to board for Nibiru. Ninmah, hearing of this felt it was too dangerous for him to go alone. She made a double of Gilgamesh she named Enkidu. He was not born of a womb, he had no blood in his veins.

The Epic of Gilgamesh. 2,737 B. C. Gilgamesh and comrade, Enkidu, journeyed to the Landing Place. Utu with his oracles: tracking devices, cameras, heat sensors and lasers oversaw them. At the entrance to the Cedar Forest, their way was blocked by a fire-eating monster (robot)/ With trickery, they confused the robot's sensory mechanism and broke it to pieces.

When they found the secret entrance of the Anunnaki, they were challenged with the deadly snorts of the 'Bull of Heaven' a robotic craft of Enlil. This monster chased them back to the gates of Unug-Ki. At the cities ramparts, Enkidu smote the monster robot.

When Enlil heard of this, he wailed to the high heavens in agony. He said since Enkidu had slain the Bull of Heaven, he must perish in the waters and so it was...Enkidu drowned. Gilgamesh was absolved of the slaying of the Bull because he was instructed to go to Tilman by Utu and Ninsun.

Yet, seeking the long life, Gilgamesh was permitted to proceed to Tilman, the place of the chariots. He went through the subterranean tunnels and cane upon a beautiful garden called Garden of Precious Stones. There, he met Noah, now 47,000years old.

Noah and Gilgamesh had long talks. He revealed the events of the Great Flood that occurred 7,837 years earlier. He told Gilgamesh he had been given an off-shoot from the 'Tree of Life' from Nibiru. He said it prevents him and his wife from growing old. A man can regain full vigor by eating of it; a man of old age can be young again. It was given to me by Enki when we rested the ark on Mount Ararat right after the flood.

He got an evil thought, 'I must have that plant.' When Noah and his wife were asleep, he went to the well. He tied stones to his feet and dove into the well. He grabbed the plant and uprooted it. With the plant in his satchel, he hurried through the tunnels and reaching Unug-Ki (biblical (Erech) he laid down to sleep. While asleep, a snake was attracted to the fragrance and snatched the plant and vanished with it.

Upon awakening, Gilgamesh pleased with his catch, reached into his satchel to find it gone. He cried out, "Oh no, my 'Plant of Life' is gone, to die, I am destined." He wept. He returned to Unug-Ki and therein he died as a mortal. (Casket of Gilgamesh found in Iraq 2003. States (Gilgamesh King of Uruk).

Kingship of the First Region (Eden) the city of Nannar and Ningal was transferred to Urim- (Ur).

Marduk, angered hearing that Gilgamesh, a demigod, was given permission to live on Nibiru and hearing of Inanna declaring herself a goddess. Stating that she was able to resurrect the dead and of her desires and intentions to take back Dumuzi's domain of Upper Egypt that was a wedding gift, troubled and angered. He set out to counteract Inanna's schemes. A clever scheme He thought up... **RELIGION...RELIGION...RELIGION,**" he shouted aloud." The thought of divine godship greatly appeals to me I will announce myself as a GREAT GOD."

He went on, looking at himself in the mirror, posing, he said, "I will announce myself as God. I must find a way to keep the loyalty of my masses. To promise them resurrection and immortality on Nibiru, this will gain following and loyalty."

So, he went everyplace proclaiming himself God, RA. He said he would give them resurrection, immortality on Nibiru, build tombs facing eastward so when called forth from the gave you will be facing your way to your journey. On and on, he went, ranting and screaming promises. He promised the 'Tree of Life', the 'Waters of 'Youth'. There will be the coming of the gods to planet Earth. Gold is the flesh of the gods.

Marduk got the men stirred with his promise of power, so with weapons, the kings ordered the men to invade the lands of Abzu and lower Africa. These were the lands of Marduk's brothers and they were furious and their anger grew.

"What is Marduk up to that he tramples over his own brothers?" said Nergal. "We've done him no harm and defended him in his wrongdoings." The brothers went to Marduk and asked him to stop the invasions. They appealed to Enki to have him stop.

"No Father, I will not stop. I've waited for thousands of years for what is rightfully mine. Inanna has sinned against you and me over and over. I hear she wants my lands. Never, never. I will get her first. I will capture the adjoining lands of Magan and Meluhha. To be master of the Third Region is my plan. It will be so and no one is going to stop me. The Earth is mine to rule."

Enki walked away shaking his head…Marduk followed him screaming, **"THE EARTH IS MINE TO RULE…MINE… FATHER, MINE!"**

CHAPTER 12

THE BOMBING OF MOUNT SINAI/SODOM AND GOMORRAH

Marduk made himself supreme God and declares Babel will be built. He gathered more and more followers and gave more and more speeches on his godship, resurrection and immortality.

After kingship was transferred from Unug-Ki to Urim (Ur), Nannar and Ningal smiled on the people. Nannar was worshiped as god of the Moon. He decreed the count of the Moon as twelve cycles and twelve festivals of the year to each of the twelve Anunnaki gods. He would one day replace Anu on the throne of Nibiru.

Throughout the First Region, Eden shrines and sanctuaries were built to Anunnaki gods. In these temples, people could go to their gods and pray directly to them. **Thus, religion was started**. In the cities of man, local rules were designated to righteous shepherds, artisans and farmers; they exchanged their products far and wide. Laws of justice were decreed; contracts of trade and divorce were honored.

In school, the young ones were taught by Scribes; subjects of recorded hymns, proverbs, wisdom and happiness. There were unfortunately, quarrels and many encroachments. Inanna and her brother in their sky ships roamed from land to lands. The people of the Upper Plain of the two rivers/ Nile took a great liking to Inanna. She found the sound of their language pleasant and she learned to speak it. They called her Inanna Ishtar.

They called: her Uncle Ishkur/Adad. They called the city Unug-Ki,/ Uruk. They called Urim/Ur. They called her father Nannar/Sin, Lord of the Oracles. They called her brother Utu/Shamash. They called Enlil/Elil. They called Nibiru-Ki/Nippur. They called Ki-Engi. Land of the Lofty Watchers.

Marduk wanted to be known by the priests as the Eldest of Heaven, first born on Heaven and now on Earth. He had hymns written about his greatness, Lord of Eternity, Everlasting over all gods, the one with no equal. He placed himself above all gods. His brothers and cousins were alarmed at what he was saying and felt great danger.

Enki went to him and asked him the meaning of his proclamations. He answered, "Father, the Heavens bespeak of my greatness. The Bull of Heaven, Enlil's constellation sign was slain by his own offspring, Gilgamesh. In the Heavens, the Age of the Ram…my age is coming. These are unmistakable omens."

Enki went immediately to his abode in Eridu and examined the twelve constellations on the first day of spring in the beginning of the year. He carefully observed sunrise in the Constellation of the Bull.

In Nibiru-Ki and Urim, Enlil and Nannar made observations in the Lower World where the instruments station had been, Nergal attested the results, it was still the Age of the Bull and that the Age of the Ram was remote. Both clans fearful of the dangerous madness of Marduk, notified him and told him the Age of the Ram was a long time away.

Marduk refused to relent and was assisted by his son, Nabu. He sent emissaries to all domains all over the world that his time had come, the Age of the Ram. The Anunnaki leaders appealed to Ningishzidda to stop Ningishzidda in his pursuit of power.

"Ningishzidda, you must go to 'all parts of the world' where there are inhabitants and teach the people how to observe the skies. This way, they will know that Marduk's time has not yet come."

In his wisdom, Ningishzidda devised stone structures to act as observatories. Ninurta and Ishkur, Enlil's sons helped him erect them. At Stonehenge, Chi-chichenitza, Africa, South America, North America, in the settled lands, far and wide they taught the people far and wide to observe the skies through these stone structures.

They showed the people how to read the sun rising and the stars and constellations. The showed them that the Constellation of the Bull was still rising. They told the people not to believe Marduk.

Enki watched these goings on in much sorrow. He wondered how fate twisted the original order. After we declared ourselves gods, now we are dependent on mankind's support. The Anunnaki decided one leader was needed and went to Inanna. She told them there is a strong man, Arbakad, his father is commander of four garrisons and his mother is a high priestess. He is wonderful.

Enlil gave him a scepter and crown and appointed him 'Righteous Regent'. A new land not far from Kishi was unified called Agade. Sharru-Kin ruled the city. With Inanna's troops, combined with his, they ruled all the lands from the upper sea to the lower sea. The troops were stationed to protect all borders of Inanna's Fourth Region and Tilman on Mount Sinai.

Marduk was apprehensive of the troops there. He gazed at them constantly and all knew that like a falcon, he would pounce on his prey.

To the place in the First Region where Marduk attempted to build a rocket launcher did Sharru-Kin move there and implanted the Heavenly Object so now it was sacred soil. From there to Agade.

Marduk was enraged and rushed to the tower's place and screamed, "How dare you. I am the possessor of this sacred soil.

I will establish a gateway to the gods How dare you sit where I built the tower!"

He told his followers to go to the river to divert the attention of his enemy's troops that protected the border of the Fourth Region. Marduk's men raised dikes and walls in place of his felled tower. They built him an abode, Esagil. Nabu called it Babel, Gateway of the gods, in honor of his father.

In the heart of Eden, Marduk established himself there. This area Enlil had decreed for himself and his descendants. When Inanna heard of this in Aratta, in fury did she and her men soar in their sky ships. Inanna with the fiery weapons inflicted death on Marduk's followers. The battle was horrendous, never before on Earth did the blood of the people flow like rivers.

Nergal, left his area in lower Africa to plead with his brother, "Marduk, for the sake of the people, please leave the Eden. Let us peacefully wait for the Sign of the Ram to come into existence. It is not time now."

Marduk reasoned this would be the right thing to do; they withdrew. Marduk again traveled from land to land to watch from the skies. Because of his absence from the Second Region (Upper Africa) that was granted to him, he became known as Amun. 'The Unseen One'.

Inanna was appeased because Sharru-Kin succeeded Arbakad to the throne of Agade. Enlil and Ninurta had gone to South America. Marduk was still traveling. Inanna saw this and decided to seize all the lands.

She ordered Narram-Sin to march against Magan/Africa and Meluhha, Marduk's domains. She commanded him to commit a sacrilege to march his army through the Fourth Region to Sinai, the sacred Tilman. He then invaded Magan (Upper Africa). He attempted to enter the sealed pyramid, sealed since the War of 8,763 B.C.

Enlil so furious over Narram-Sin's transgressions that he put a curse on him and his city, Agade. He died of a scorpion's sting. Enlil commanded that Agade be wiped out.

After Marduk became the 'Unseen god', his Second Region disintegrated. All over, there was disorder and confusion. Enlil radioed King Anu to get his advice. Anu told him to deposit kingship in the hands of Nannar and he's to rule from Urum where the heavenly object remained in the soil. Ur-Nammu, a righteous shepherd was appointed in charge; he put an end to all violence and strife in the lands. Prosperity was abundant.

Around this time about 2, 800. B.C., Enlil had a night-time vision. The image of a man, bright and shiny like the heavens, stood at his bed. He recognized him as white-haired Galzu (Gabriel). He was holding a tablet of lapis lazul. On it there were the twelve constellations. He pointed with his left hand three times to the Bull Constellation and to the Constellation if the Ram.

Galzu spoke to Enlil, "The righteous time of benevolence and peace will be followed by evil doing and bloodshed in three celestial portions. The Ram of Marduk will replace Enlil's Bull."

"Marduk has declared himself Supreme God; he will seize Earth. A calamity that has never occurred on Earth before will happen as decreed by fate. As at the time of the Great Flood a righteous and worthy man, Noah, was chosen, so it must be again. A new man will be chosen and by the seed of this new man, civilization will be preserved as intended by the Creator of All."

So for the third time did Galzu, the Divine Emissary from Central Universe Intelligence, appear to beings on Earth. Enlil told no one, but in the temple of Nibiru-Ki he asked among the priests who are the celestial savants are.

The High Priest said, "There is an oracle priest, Tirhu (Terah, father of Abraham). He is a descendant of Ibru, Arpakshad, Shem and the great, great grandson of Noah. He is the sixth generation of Nibiru-Ki priest's." They intermarried with the royal daughters of Urim's Kings.

The High Priests continued advising Enlil, "Get yourself to Nannar's temple in Urum in time to observe the heavens for celestial time; seventy-two years is the count of a celestial portion. Carefully record the passage of three which is two hundred sixteen years. Enlil arrived in Urum and said to Tirhu, "Count the prophesied time."

In the meantime, Marduk went from land to land all over the world to tell them how great he was and spoke of his supremacy. He did this to gain followers for his purpose to gain control over the whole world. Nabu, his son, was inciting the people in the lands of the upper seas and lands bordering Ki-Engi. His purpose was to seize the Fourth Region, the Sacred Area.

Clashes were occurring between the dwellers of the east and west. Kings formed warriors, caravans ceased traveling and the cities raised walls for protection. Enlil thought that what Galzu had told him is indeed happening.

Enlil set his attention on Terhu and his sons. This is the man to choose; the man chosen by Galzu.

2113 B.C. Enlil told his son, Nannar to establish a city, Harran, in the land of Arbakad and appoint Tirhu as High Priest there. His son Abraham was ten years old.

2095 B.C. Two of the three prophesied portions were completed. Abraham was twenty-eight years old and married. At that time, Ur-Nammu died from a fall off a horse. His son, Shulgi succeeded him and anointed himself high priest of Nibiru-Ki. His lusts centered on the joys of Inanna's vulva.

Ur launched military expeditions against Canaanite provinces. Nannar ordered Shulgi to send Elamite troops to suppress the unrest in the Canaanite cities. Elamites reached the gateway to the Sinai Peninsula and its spaceport.

In the mountain lands, not belonging to Nannar, Shulgi enlisted in his army. With their help he overran the western lands ignoring the sanctuary of Mission Control Center (Jerusalem), Shulgi set foot in the Sacred Fourth Region (Sinai Peninsula). That was taboo to enter and he declared himself King of the Fourth Region. Anu and Enlil ordered the death of Shulgi.

2048 B.C. Enlil was furious about these defilements. He spoke to Enki of this, "The rulers of your region have exceeded all bounds. Marduk is the fountainhead of all our troubles. He must be stopped."

Enlil told Enki nothing of the visitation of Galzu's warning of the evil caused by Marduk. Instead he turned to Tirhu in Harran. He turned to Ibru-um (Abraham) who he saw as a princely offering, valiant and acquainted him with priestly secrets.

Enlil said to Abraham, "I command you to go to the sacred place of the chariots, Tilman, in the Sinai. You must protect this sacred place so the chariots can ascend and descend; they must be able to carry the gold by rockets to Nibiru."

Abraham was now seventy-five years old. Abraham left Harran and Marduk arrived. He, too, had observed the defilements of Shulgi. "See these are the birth pangs of the **New Order**." He said to Nabu. "From Harran on to the threshold of Sumer, I plan my final thrust. I will direct the raising of the army from Harran which is situated on the edge of Ishkur's domain, but I will wait out my time; my time of the Ram."

2048 B.C. When Abraham was seventy- five years old, God (Enlil) said to him, "Get out of thy country, leave behind Sumer, Nippur and Harran and go to the land which I will show thee." A long text known as 'Marduk's Prophesy' he addressed the people of Harran on a clay tablet, gives the clue confirming the fact and the time of his move to Harran, 2048 B.C. This was also the year that the Enlilite gods decided to kill Shugi ordering "Death of a Sinner."

Abraham traveled swiftly southward to the destination Negev, the dry region bordering the Sinai Peninsula. He took troops with him and stationed themselves at the gateway of the Sinai. He did not stay there long. As soon as Shulgi's successor, Amar-Sin, was enthroned in Ur in 2047 B.C. Abraham was ordered to go to Egypt. He met the Pharaoh and gave him many gifts. He stayed for seven years.

2041 B.C. Amar-Sin launched his last and greatest military expedition against the west and were overtaken by Marduk's spell. It was a great war whereby cities of men and strongholds of gods and their offspring were attacked.

2041 B.C. Theban princes of upper Egypt defeated the lower Egyptian dynasty launching Egypt's unified kingdom lasted until 1790 B.

Abraham returned to Negev. He was trained in warfare by the Hittites and with swift camel- riding cavalry men he arrived in the nick of time. Legions of an alliance of Enlilite kings were on the Sinai space port.

2040 B.C. The War of the Kings. (Gen.14). Where the kings of the East and the Kings of the West culminated in a remarkable military feat by Abraham's swift cavalry men, Abraham was eighty-eight years old.

The invaders marched along the Eastern side of the Jordon River. The Enlilites wanted to settle the age-old account of the intermarrying of the Igigi/Nefilim with Earthling women, but the Sinai spaceport was their main concern; to keep it out of the hands of Marduk.

The invading forces came by way of the King's Highway. Running north and south of the eastern side of the Jordon. But when they turned westward toward the gateway of the Sinai, they met the blocking forces of Abraham. The Bible records the feat as the Smiting of Khedorla, Omer and the kings who were with him.

Preventing entering the Sinai Peninsula, the army of the East turned northward, the Dead Sea was shorter then and the area was very fertile. There were five cities including Sodom and Gomorrah. Here, the four kings fought and defeated the five kings. Looting the cities and taking captives, including Lot, Abraham's nephew who resided in Sodom. They then turned back; this time on the Western side of the Jordon.

A refugee from Sodom told Abraham that his nephew, Lot had been taken captive, Abraham armed three hundred eighteen men and gave chase. They caught up with the invaders north near Damascus. Lot was freed sand the booty was recovered.

OH, LUCIFER, FALLEN, FALLEN, FALLEN

2024 B.C. The last Pharaoh of the 10th Dynasty was overthrown by the princes of Thebes.

2024 B.C. When twenty-four Earth years of Marduk's sojourn in Harran had passed, he tearfully made an appeal to the gods and whomever descended from them.

"I confess my transgressions and for these, I am sorry. Oh gods of Harran, great gods who judge, learn my secrets. I remember my memories as I girdle my belt. I was born on Nibiru, the first grandson of our god, Anu. I came to Earth and never received my rightful place here."

He went on and on of the injustices he received; exile for Inanna's evil, "I wandered the Earth, never belonging… Let me establish my city ad my temple, Esagil as an everlasting abode, to install a king in Abil. In my temple house let all the Anunnaki gods assemble to accept my covenant." Not one person showed any sympathy.

Enlil summoned a great assembly to take counsel in Nibiru-Ki. All the Anunnaki were there. They opposed Marduk's recent wishes and were opposed to him and Nabu. Accusations and recriminations filled the chamber.

Enki said, "What is coming no one can prevent. Let us accept Marduk's supremacy."

Enlil said angrily, "If the Time of the Ram is coming, let us deprive Marduk of the Bond of Heaven and Earth (Jerusalem… and the instruments of Mission Control. Also let us obliterate the place of the chariots (Mount Sinai, Tilman) so he can't control the restricted area."

Enki's son, Nergal spoke out, "Let us use the weapons of terror."

Enki opposed. Enlil radioed King Anu on Nibiru. "Father, Marduk is trying to gain control of Earth. We can't let him take control of Mission Control Center and Tilman, the place of chariots on Mount Sinai. He is of violent nature. We have decided to bomb Mount Sinai to prevent him from taking control of this sacred site. All has agreed to bomb. You need to know and give us your approval."

King Anu from Nibiru beamed back the message to Earth, "So be it!"

Upon hearing this, Enki shouted as he departed, "What is destined to be will be. Your decision to undo Marduk's ruling will fail." Enki smiled as he left feeling that no one knew where the bombs were hidden, safe in a cave in Africa. It was he, with Abgal, who put the weapons there about 437,000 years ago. Enki did not know that Abgal revealed the location of the bombs when he was sent to exile for the rape charge.

Enlil stood up and said, "Let's select two men to carry out the bombing. Who shall it be?" An Anunnaki god stood up and said, "It is wise to choose a man from each family. This way there can't be hatred over members from one clan doing the devastation. I suggest Ninurta and Nergal."

Now this is the account of how fate led to destiny…the great calamity did occur. Let it be recorded for all time.

2024 B.C. When the decision to bomb, to use the weapons of terror was made, Enlil kept two secrets. He told no one of this dream vision of Galzu's appearance. He told no one where the weapons were hidden. Despite all the protests of using the weapons of terror the council voted for their use.

When Enki heard of this, he knew the weapons were very old so he hoped that after such a long sojourn the weapon's terror had evaporated. Little did he know or expect that after such a long time, the missiles still had the power to cause a horrible calamity as never before known on Earth. Enki comforted himself knowing that a code was needed to unclad their terror.

However, Enlil revealed to Ninurta and Nergal how to awaken the missiles from their deep sleep. He said, "As a forewarning, if the weapons are used, the chariot place on Mount Sinai must be vacated by the Anunnaki. The citizens must be spared and the people must not perish. This was done on Nibiru many thousands of years ago and the devastation was terrible."

Nergal in his sky ship soared to the hiding place. Then did Enlil tell Ninurta of the vision of Galzu and him revealing that he told him to choose Abraham to take over Noah's role in the survival of Earthlings. He told him the sign of the Ram was coming and Marduk was to rule and will cause much evil and bloodshed. He will seize supremacy on Earth and then a terrible calamity will occur. By the seed of Abraham will the seed of mankind be preserved. He must be chosen to take the place of Noah to be the leader of men.

Enlil continued, "Nergal is hot headed, make sure he does not go crazy on this objective. Make sure the cities are spared and that Abraham is forewarned. I will signal to you when Marduk returns so he will perish in the bombing. I love, you my son." As he hugged him.

Ninurta radioed the Anunnaki and said, "Send two emissaries (Anunnaki) to go to Sodom and warn Abraham and his family to leave the area immediately because Mount Sinai is to be bombed. Because of their close proximity these two Sodom and Gomorrah they will also perish."

He continued, "Tell the family of Abraham that upon the signal; they must go quickly and not look back. They must seek the shelter behind the mountain to avoid radiation from the weapons of terror. If they don' listen they'll be turned to vapor."

While the two Anunnaki men were warning Lot, the men of Sodom asked to lay with the Anunnaki. They began to surround them and the Anunnaki lasered their eyes blinding them.

When Ninurta arrived at the weapons place, Nergal had already brought the weapons out of the cave. Ninurta gave Nergal the code to awaken the seven weapons from their long slumber.

For seven days and nights, the two cousins awaited the signal from Enlil when Marduk return to Babel so they can strike him. Marduk announced to his followers, "Our weapons are armed. I declare my supremacy my time has come. The Sign of the Ram is declaring that it is my time!"

At the signal, Ninurta departed for Mount Sinai, Nergal followed. Soaring in the skies, the two cousins surveyed the land, knowing what they must do, but never knowing the horror it would bring. Ninurta looked behind and saw Nergal keeping up with him. With a squeezing in his heart, Ninurta gave the thumbs up signal to "Keep Off", meaning to let loose.

At that, Ninurta let loose the first terror weapon from the skies over Mount Mashu/Mount Sinai. With a flash it sliced off the top of the mountain. In an instant, it melted the mountain's innards as well as the controls within that were taken from the pyramid's inners, including the Nibiruan crystals.

It was at this time that Lot and his family rushed to depart and hid behind the mountain. Lot's wife delayed to look back at the destruction. She was vaporized. (Salt and vapor had the same word). Gen. 10: 26.).

Above the place of celestial chariots, Ninurta unleased the second weapon. With the brilliance of seven Suns, a gushing wound was made in the plain's rocks. The earth shook and crumbled. After the brilliance, the heavens darkened. Burnt and crushed stones covered the plain of the chariots. All the forests that surrounded the plain, only tree stems were left standing.

Ninurta from his sky ship, Blackbird, shouted the words, "It is done!" The control that Marduk and Nabu so coveted, they are deprived of forever." With these words, he soared away.

Nergal desired to emulate Ninurta. His heart urged him to be the annihilator. So, following the King's Highway, he flew to the verdant valley of the five cities. In the verdant valley, Nabu was converting the people to join Marduk. Nergal planned to squash him like a caged bird.

Over each of the five cities, Nergal sent from the sky a terror weapon. He shed off five cities of the valley; they were overturned to desolation with fire and brimstone. They were upheavaled. All that lived there were turned to vapor, including Sodom and Gomorrah.

Mountains were toppled by the awesome weapons. Where the sea waters were barred, the bolt broke open. Down into the valley, the sea water poured and flooded the valley. When the waters poured upon the cities, ashes and steam were rising to the heavens.

"It is done!" Screamed Nergal. "In my heart there is no more vengeance."

The two heroes surveyed their handiwork and they were puzzled by what they saw. There was a darkening of the skies that followed the brilliance. Then a storm began to blow swirling within a dark cloud. An evil wind carried gloom from the skies horizon. As the day wore on, the Sun was obliterated with darkness. At night time, a dreaded brilliance skirted its edges. It made the Moon disappear at its rising.

When the dawn came the next morning, a storm wind began blowing from the West, from the upper sea. A dark brown cloud directed Eastward; the cloud spread toward the settled lands. Wherever it reached, it delivered death and mercilessly to all who lived. From the Valley of No Pity, the five bombed cities toward Shumer by brilliance spawned, the death it carried.

"Dear Almighty God, what is this, Ninurta, what is this?" Cried Nergal. "The people are dropping like flies when the evil wind nears them. The cattle, sheep, dogs are dropping dead. What is this?"

"Quickly, quickly, let's warn them. You call Enki and I'll call my father!" cried out Ninurta.

In a frantic voice and in much panic, Ninurta said, "Father, the weapons of terror have caused an evil wind. The unstoppable evil wind delivers death to all." He was sobbing. "Oh, my God, what is happening? Warn the gods and the people of Shumer that the wind is heading in their direction. It is killing everyone and everything in its path. Tell them to escape immediately." He was sobbing. "Oh, father, it is terrible. Please, hurry."

In shock, Nergal radioed his father and warned him to please alert everyone. Please help the people. Enki could hear the fear in his son's voice Enlil and Enki transmitted the alarm to the gods of

Shumer, "Escape quickly. Sound the alarm. The bombs that were dropped on Sinai and the five cities are continuing to wreak havoc in the wake of the winds. All must leave immediately. Let the people disperse, let them hide. The devastation is terrible."

From their cities the gods did flee. They were like frightened birds escaping from their nests. The people of the land found it futile to run as they were clutched by the hands of the evil wind. Stealthy was the death. The five cities and the fields were attacked like a big ghost. The evil passed over the highest walls.

The thickest walls it went over like flood waters. No door could shut out the evil wind, no bolt could turn it back. Those who hid in their houses behind locked doors were felled like flies. Those who fled unto the streets, in the streets their corpses piled up. Coughs and phlegm filled their chests; spittle and foam filled their mouths as the unseen wind engulfed the people. Their mouths were drenched with blood.

Slowly, over their lands the evil wind blew. From the west to the east, it traveled over the plains and the mountains. Everything that remained behind the evil winds were the dead and dying; people and cattle perished. The waters were poisoned, all vegetation in the fields withered. From Eridu in the south to Sipper in the north, the evil wind overwhelmed the lands.

Babil, where Marduk declared supremacy was spared. The evil wind by-passed the city. All the lands south of Babil were devoured by the evil wind. The heart of the Second Region was destroyed.

After the great calamity, Enlil and Enki met to survey the affects, in shock and dismay they were as they flew over the entire area. Such devastation they could never imagine. They flew to Victoria Falls to review and discuss what they should do. They landed their craft and sat by the beautiful falls.

Enki said that the sparing of Babil is a divine omen that Marduk is destined to supremacy.

Enlil replied, "It must have been the will of the Creator. I must tell you of the visitation I had with Galzu. He told me to choose Abraham and of this great calamity that was to come."

"If you knew of this, why did you not prevent the use of the weapons?"

"My brother, enough is enough. Enough seen was the reason. After your coming to Earth for gold, it was obstructed by an obstacle. The obstacle was we did not have enough man power. We found a way to circumvent this obstacle which was to create Earthlings to relieve our toil. This creation was the greatest solution. Also there were unwanted twists and turns when you have the celestial cycles and the constellations assigned. Who could distinguish between the two?"

Enki nodded as he listened to his brother's words. He said, "The First Region is destroyed. The Second Region, Africa is in confusion. The Third Region, Inanna's Indus Valley is wounded. The equipment taken from the great pyramid that was put in the in the inners of the Mount Sinai has totally melted. This is what happened."

Enlil very saddened said, "If this was the will of the Creator of all, that is what has remained of our mission to Earth. By the ambitions of Marduk were the seeds sown, the crop that results is for him to reap."

Enlil accepted the triumph of Marduk. "Let Marduk declare his supremacy over the desolate regions. As for me and Ninurta, we will no longer stand in the way."

Enki asked, "Would matters have been different if the weapons of terror had not been used?"

Enlil retorted, "Should we have heeded the words of Galzu not to return to Nibiru. Should Earth's mission have stopped when the Anunnaki mutinied? I did what I did and you did what you did. The past can't become undone."

"Is there a not a lesson in that too?" Asked Enki. "Is not what happened on Earth a mirror of what happened on Nibiru? . . . The nuclear bombing on Nibiru a long time ago. Is this not the tale of the past writing the outline of the future? Will mankind, in our image created, repeat our failures and our achievements?"

There was a silence for a long time. Enlil stood up to leave. "I must leave now."

They stood up and locked arms as brothers, as comrades, who together met with and challenged the confrontations on an alien planet.

Enki hugged his brother, "Shall we meet again on Earth or Nibiru?"

Enlil replied, "I will go to South America with Ninurta to continue our quest for gold."

His brother replied, "And I too must remain on Earth to save our planet. I will stay out of sight."

Enki softly said, "Good-bye, my brother." He sat down again near the falls and watched his brother walk away until he could no longer see him. He sat alone with his thoughts for several minutes.

Then Enlil's craft appeared above the falls. It soared upward and then swooped down toward Enki. Enlil tilted his craft from side to side to wave good-bye to his brother and then soared heavenward. Enki wiped away a tear as he watched the craft disappear out of sight. He was left alone with only the thoughts of his heart.

Enki sat and pondered aloud, "Was it all destined or was it by fate that this and that decision was fashioned. If heaven and Earth are regulated by cycles within cycles…Then that which has happened, will occur again? Is the past the future?"

"Will the Earthlings emulate the Anunnaki? Will Earth relive Nibiru with a hole in Earth's atmosphere and nuclear holocausts? Will I, the first to arrive, be the first to leave?"

(Earth emulated Nibiru with two nuclear explosions, both in Japan. And a hole in the atmosphere was discovered in Antarctica by three British Scientists, John Shanklin, Brian Gardener and Joe Forman in 1985).

Besieged by thoughts, Enki decided to write down all the events and decisions, starting with Nibiru to this day on Earth to be put in record, a guide for future generations. Let posterity at a time designated by destiny to read the record. Let the past be remembered as prophecy to understand the future.

He later summoned his scribe, Endubsar. "Endubsar, I want you to write my biography. I want you to tell all that I experienced on Nibiru and on Earth. I will relate to you all that has happened." And so it was. (Page v, Enki's autobiography as told to Endubsar).

And Life Goes On…A few Anunnaki remained on Earth, most of them underground to mine gold for their beloved Nibiru and to build underground cities. They will then call themselves Anunni as they are no longer on Ki/Earth. Many Earthlings, their slaves, will still be desperately needed.

Marduk has now become the sole ruler-god on Earth. His names are: Ra, Amon, Amen, (where Catholic church gets the Amen) and most of all, he wants to be known as 'the Unseen God' whereby he can rule earthlings by "fear".

CHAPTER 13

ALL ROADS LEAD TO ROME

Before the bombing of Mount Sinai, 2024 B.C. Abraham was chosen by the Universal God to take the place of Noah to replenish the Earth. Sarah, his wife gave him no children. She had an Egyptian handmaid named Hagar; she told Abraham to go to her so that she (Sarah) may obtain children by her. He went in unto Hagar and she conceived. Knowing she conceived, she despised her mistress.

Sarah told Abraham to choose between them. He chose his wife and told her to do with Hager whatever she wished. Sarah dealt harshly with Hagar and she fled. An angel told her to return to Sarah and submit herself.

The angel told her he will multiply thy seed so that they will be too numerous to count. You are with child, a son, you shall call him Ishmael. He will be a wild man; every man's hand will be against him. He shall dwell in the presence of all his brethren. Hagar gave Abraham a son and he called him Ishmael. Abraham was fourscore and six years old, (86 years old).

When Abraham was ninety years old, God appeared to him and told him: he will be fruitful, the father of many nations. I make a covenant with you and your future generations I will give your all the land of Canaan. Every man child among you shall be circumcised when he is eight days old. (Vitamin K, blood coagulator, is produced in the body eight days after birth).

God l told him My covenant with you: Sarah will be the mother of all nations, she will bear a son, Isaac. Ishmael, I have blessed, he will be fruitful, a great nation, he will beget twelve princes. Abraham could not believe as Sarah was ninety years old. This very day, Abraham was circumcised and Ishmael circumcised at thirteen years old.

Sarah asked Abraham to cast out Hagar and her son, because she would not permit Ishmael to be heir with Isaac. Abraham took bread and a bottle of water to Hagar and sent her and Ishmael away. She wept. God called to her and told her to lift him up for I will make him a great nation. They dwelt in the wilderness of Paran.

The Lord told Abraham that by his seed all the nations of the Earth will be blessed. Abraham dwelt in Beersheba. Sarah was 127 years old when she died. Abraham buried her in a cave of the field of Machpelah before Mamre. The name is Hebron in the land of Canaan.

Abraham grew old and was stricken in age. He called his eldest servant and made him promise that he would never let his son, Isaac take a wife of the daughters of the Canaanites, among whom he dwells. But go into my country and my kindred and find a wife for my son, Isaac. So his servant went to Mesopotamia unto the city of Nahor. To the well went he and waited. Rebecca came to get water. The servant ran to her and asked her whose daughter was she. She told him she is the daughter of Bethuel, Nahor's son whom Milcan bare unto him. "I put the earring upon her face and the bracelets on her hands."

The Lord spoke, "Take Rebecca and go to your master." When he arrived, Isaac saw her and brought her into his mother's tent and she became his wife.

Abraham married Keturah and she bare him six sons. Abraham gave all that he had to Isaac. He died at a hundred threescore and fifteen years (175 years old).

Ishmael had twelve sons: Nebajoth, Kedar, Adbeel, Mibsam, Mishma, Dumah, Massa, Hadar, Tem and Kedemah. Ishmael died at 137 years.

These are the generations of Isaac who at age sixty, by Rebecca; twins, Esau covered of red hair all over and Jacob. Isaac loved Esau and Rebecca favored Jacob.

There was a famine in the land. The Lord told Isaac not to go to Egypt, but to Gerar. Isaac sowed the land, did well and became very great. He was told to leave and he pitched his tent in the valley of Gerar. He then moved to Beersheba. Esau at forty years old took a wife, Judith.

Isaac grew old and his eyesight dimmed. He summoned Esau at his deathbed to bless him. Rebecca got Jacob and they tricked Isaac into believing he was Esau. He blessed Jacob, giving him Esau's birthright, all that he had.

Before Isaac died he told Jacob not to take a wife from the Canaanites. Jacob went from Beersheba to Haran. He tired on his journey and decided to rest in the city of Luz. He took stones and placed them for his pillows. As he slept, he dreamed he saw a ladder set up on Earth. The top of it reached to heaven and behold the angels of God ascended and descended on it.

Jacob was witnessing the Igigi loading gold. The Lord spoke to him saying that he is the God of Abraham and he is given the land where he rested. Your seed will be numerous and spread all over. Jacob renamed the city Bethel.

Jacob went into the land of the East. He fell in love with Rachel. Due to customs he had to marry the first-born daughter, Leah. He had six sons and a daughter by Leah, and by Rachel's hand maiden, two sons, Dan and Naphtali. And a son by Zilbah, Leah's hand maiden, but none by Rachel. God remembered Rachel, she married Jacob and she gave birth to Joseph.

After twenty-one years of service to Laban for the honor to marry his two daughters, Jacob took his family and animals and left for the land of his fathers. As he entered his home lands, Esau was awaiting him with four hundred men. Jacob, greatly afraid as he had stolen Esau's birthright, sent 470 animals to appease him.

He rose up that night and took his two wives, two servants and eleven sons and sent them over the brook to safety. Jacob was left to sleep alone. Jacob wrestled with a man (Anunnaki) all night. And when the man couldn't prevail against him, he tasered the hollow of the thigh and knocked it out of joint. The angel blessed Jacob and told him from this day forth, you'll be called Israel.

When he met his brother, Esau, Esau embraced him and fell to his knees. Esau returned to Seir and Jacob journeyed to Succoth, and later settled in Canaan. Jacob/Israel loved Joseph more than all his children and made him a coat of many colors. The brothers became jealous. Joseph dreamed a dream that one day he would reign over them and they hated him even more.

The brothers went out to feed the flocks. Israel sent Joseph to go with them. He found them in Dothan and upon seeing him, their jealously raged, and they threw him into a pit to die. The brothers returned with Joseph's coat covered with animal blood and reported to Israel that Joseph was killed by a beast.

Joseph was found and by a captain of the guard, and brought him to Egypt. The master saw that the Lord was with Joseph and made him prosper in all he did. The master's wife asked him to lie with her; he refused, she accused of rape, and had him imprisoned.

While imprisoned, Joseph interpreted dreams. The master asked him to interpret his dream and told him of it. Joseph told him his dream meant there will be seven fruitful years, then with the East wind, there will be seven years of famine. He placed Joseph in charge of preparing for the seven years of famine. Joseph had two sons born of Asenath.

Joseph was thirty-seven years old when the famine struck all over the face of the Earth. Joseph opened up the storehouses. All the countries came to Egypt to buy corn, including his brothers. Joseph made himself known his brothers and they all wept. He told them they were forgiven.

Joseph was summoned from Egypt to come to his father's house as he was dying. Joseph fell upon his father's face and kissed him. They all left to bury him in the field of Machpelah in the land of Canaan. Here in a cave, where Abraham, Sarah, Isaac, Rebecca and Leah are buried, so was Israel buried.

The twelve tribes of Israel; Reuben, Simeon, Levi, Judah, Zebulun, Issachar, Dan, Gad, Naphtali, Benjamin, Asher and Manasess.

Joseph died at one hundred ten years old. He was embalmed and put in a coffin in Egypt.

The Anunnaki/Ananni, living underground still mined the gold for Nibiru. Enki was living under water, residing in their underground cities and became known as Poseidon. Enlil was living with his wife, Ninki, and son, Ninurta, in South America. Ninurta's wife, Bau, had died of radiation poisoning of the evil wind during the bombing of Mount Sinai.

Marduk was now supreme god and controlled the Earth. His city, Shumer, was spared the bombing, so he ruled from there. Twice he had been given rulership of Egypt, and still reigned over it as the unseen god.

1,433 years ago. The twelve tribes of Israel settled in Egypt; every man and his household came with Jacob. The children of Israel were fruitful and increased abundantly and became mighty.

There was a new Egyptian king who did not know Joseph. He said unto the people that the children of Israel are more and mightier than we. We must deal with them wisely They may join our enemies and fight against us. He set taskmasters over them to afflict them with burdens. They built treasure cities.

The more they afflicted them, the more they multiplied. The more they made their lives bitter in hard bondage the stronger they became. In mortar brick service in the field, the rigor and beatings increased. They had their mid wives kill their male children.

A Levite married a daughter of Levi. The woman conceived and bare a son. Fearful that the Egyptians would kill him, hid him for three months. When she could no longer hide him, she made a basket of bulrushes, dubbed it with slime and pitch and placed the child within. And laid it in the flags by the river bank.

The daughter of Pharaoh came to wash herself and saw the basket and the child. The baby's sister asked if she should find a nurse of the Hebrew women to nurse him. Upon consent, she went to her mother and told her to nurse her child. The Pharaoh's daughter called him Moses.

When Moses grew, he saw the abuses of the Egyptians toward the Hebrews. One day, he witnessed an Egyptian smiting one of his own brethren. He killed him and hid him in the sand. When he went out the next day, two men of the Hebrews asked, "Why did you smite thy fellow?" The Pharaoh heard of this and sought to slay Moses. Knowing he had been seen, he fled to the land of Midian.

The priest of Midian had seven daughters and they came to the well and drew water. Shepherds came and chased them away, but Moses stood up and helped them. The priest gave Moses his daughter, Zipporah and she bare him a son, Gershom.

Moses led the flock to the backside of the desert and came to a mountain, even to Horeb. The angel of the Lord appeared to him in a flame of fire out of the midst of a bush, the bush burned with fire and the bush was not consumed (light from the sky ship). "I am the God of Abraham, Isaac and Jacob."

He told Moses that he has seen the afflictions of his people, he hears their cries and knows of their sorrows. "You must go to Pharaoh to bring my people from Egypt. They are to be taken to the land of the Canaanites, etc. unto the land flowing with milk and honey. You must tell Pharaoh either he lets them go or he will suffer my wrath."

Moses went to the Pharaoh and told him these things. The god of the Hebrews has spoken and said to let his people go. The Pharaoh laughed at him and said that he did not know this god. And he will never let the people go.

Moses said to him, "God Jehovah said, "I will smite with my rod and will cause the waters to turn to blood." And so it was done; the fish died, the rivers stunk and they could not drink of the waters and there was blood throughout the land, for seven days.

Moses returned with this message Jehovah said to let them go or he will cover the land with frogs. The frogs came up and covered the land of Egypt. Pharaoh called for Moses and said he will let the people go. God listened to Moses, and the frogs died out of the houses, villages and fields. However, the Pharaoh had a change of heart.

The Lord said to Moses to strike out thy rod onto the dust and millions of lice came forth all over the land; lice in man and beast. And it was done. Terrible it was, but Pharaoh refused.

Moses returned with the offer; release them or the Lord Jehovah will smite thee with flies. It came to be and still. Pharaoh told Moses to stop the flies and your people may leave. Again at the last minute Pharaoh hardened his heart and changed his mind.

Moses returned with a message from Jehovah to either let the people go or tomorrow all of your cattle will die. He did not heed and all his cattle, horses, asses, camels, oxen and sheep died. So the next day it did so happen. He did not let the Hebrews go.

Under the command of the Lord, the next day, Moses in the presence of Pharaoh took a handful of ashes from the furnace and sprinkled it toward heaven, and boils broke forth with blains upon man, beast magicians and all Egyptians. And still was the heart of Pharaoh hardened.

Moses reported that Jehovah will smite thee and thy people with pestilence and be cut off from earth. It happened and Pharaoh would not let the Hebrews go.

God told Moses to rise early, go to Pharaoh to tell him that tomorrow, I will cause it to rain grievous hail such as never been seen before. All your cattle will die. Outside, upon man, beast, and every herb of the field was destroyed. All this came about with thunder, lightning, fire mingled with hail. Still, his heart was hardened.

Moses was again told by the Lord to go to Pharaoh to warn him that if he doesn't let his people go, tomorrow, he will send locusts that will cover the face of the earth. He did not heed the warning.

Moses stretched out his hand and an east wind was upon the land all night and in the morning came the locusts. They went all over the land of Egypt; the land was darkened and they ate all of the lands growth. The Pharaoh told Moses he they could leave. A strong west wind took away all the locusts. But again, he hardened his heart and would not let the Hebrews go.

The Lord said to Moses, "I will bring one more plague upon Pharaoh and upon Egypt. About midnight, I will go out into the midst of Egypt and all the Egyptian first born will die. There will be a great outcry and you will be able to leave." He told Moses to have the Hebrews to mark their doors with lamb's blood so he it will be made known not to kill anyone within.

And so it was done. In a craft, a pillar of fire by night and a cloud by day, God led the people through the way of the wilderness to the Red Sea. Pharaoh in disbelief and anger that they let the Hebrews go, sent six hundred chariots and all the chariots of Egypt and every captain to pursue the children of Israel. They overtook the Hebrews encamping by the sea.

The Egyptians were marching after them and fearful they became. The angel of God, in the craft, which went before the camp of Israel, removed the pillar of the cloud and it went from in front of them and hovered behind them.

It came between the camp of the Egyptians and the camp of Israel. It put forth a cloud of darkness over the Hebrews and gave light to the other so they couldn't be seen. Thus, no one could come near each other all the night.

The Lord told Moses to stretch out his hand over the sea and the 'Lord's craft' caused the sea to go back, make the land dry and the waters divided.

The craft used an antigravity beam to spread the waters and dry the land. They placed a filtering system over the antigravity beam and let a small space on either side of the system to hold the waters up like glass walls on both sides. This permitted the Hebrews to walk on dry land.

The Egyptians in their chariots went in after them, and when they reached the center of the sea, the filtering systems was removed, thus weighing them down with the antigravity beam. The Egyptians took off their chariot wheels because they drove "heavily". They "looked up" at that which was discomforting them.

In a test of faith, the Lord told Moses to stretch his staff out over the sea. Having done that, the waters came upon the Egyptians, their chariots and horsemen. Those in the craft had shut off the antigravity beam and the waters returned; all the Egyptians drowned.

They went into the wilderness of Shur, and could find no water for three days. To Marah where the waters were bitter they went. Then to Elim where there were twelve wells and there they encamped. They journeyed to the wilderness of Sin, between Elim and Sinai.

They murmured that they were hungry so the Lord rained manna from the craft and promised them there would be more manna the next day and flesh to eat. The food was gathered and eaten. For forty years the children of Israel journeyed until they came to borders of Canaan.

There, they cried out for water and the Lord told Moses to go before the people, take the elders of Israel and take his rod.

"I will stand before thee upon the rock in Horeb, thou shall smite the rock, water shall come from it so your people may drink." The place was called Massah.

The lord told Moses to take his men and fight in Rephidim. Moses said to Joshua to choose men to fight Amalek tomorrow and he will stand on top of the hill. Moses by directing his rod, and with the help of Aaron and Hur won the battle. Moses met his father-in-law, Jethro and told him of defeating the Egyptians and freeing the Hebrews.

The Lord appeared unto Moses to tell him he will come to him in a thick cloud in three days to give him laws. The people gathered and Moses was called to come up where he gave him a tablet with ten commandments and sixteen rules, 36 judgments and many laws. God also told them to make an ark to hold the Tablets of Law; to make it of shittim wood; 52", X 31" X 31" and place Testimony within and cover the ark.

"Place the mercy seat above the ark. I will meet with thee, and 'commune' with thee **from above** the mercy seat." Telephone to the Lord and he will commune with them from wherever he is. He instructed that no one touch the ark or they will die. Later, however, the ark was tilting, ready to falls and Uzzah quickly grabbed hold of it, got burned and was electrocuted immediately.

The Israelites remained encamped at Mount Sinai. They were separated into each family clan. Moses died at eighty years old in the land of Maub and was buried in the valley.

1450 B.C. The Lord told Joshua to leave the wilderness and Lebanon, and go unto the great river Euphrates and go over this Jordan thou and all this people. All the land of the Hittites and the Great sea shall be your coast. They traveled to Jordan and lodged there for three days. He said to follow the Ark of the covenant, when you see the priests bearing it, follow it with twelve men out of the twelve tribes. When they reached the Jordan, the waters subsided, and all the Israelites passed over on dry land.

Twelve stones were placed where the feet of the priests stood in the midst of Jordan in Gigal. The Lord told Joshua that he has given them the land of Jericho. "Go ye with the forty thousand men, encompass the city. Go around the city once each day. On the seventh day, you will compass the city seven times and the seven priests shall blow the trumpets. When you hear the sound of the trumpet, all the people shout with a great shout and the wall shall fall." So it was done. From his craft, the Lord observed.

Israel continues to conquer the Canaanites. (Judges.1: 11.). Israel becomes a barbaric nation. God called on Gideon and he defeated the Midianites and brings peace to Israel. But Israel continues the vicious cycle.

In the Book of Judges, the children of Israel departed; every man to his tribe and to his family and they went out from thence, every man to his inheritance. In those days there was no king of Israel.

Samuel, the son of Elkanah and Hannah, faithfully served god and became a prophet. God sent him to anoint Saul who came from the land of Gibean, as the first king of the Israelites.

He ruled well for many years. However, he ran into a lot of problems when he waged war against the Amalekites. God rejected Saul as king. He spent the rest of his days being tormented by evil spirits and tried to kill David who was destined to take over his throne.

1,000 B.C. At this time, the Earth's population was about 54,000,000. The majority were in the mid-east. In Israel there were eight cities south of Damascus, east of the River Jordan: There were fifteen settlements west of the River. A small population in East Asia. Also upper east Africa was populated, and England.

David ruled as an ideal and he was an ancestor of the future Messiah. He conquered Jerusalem, taking the Ark of the Covenant into the city and established the city founded by Saul.

David, arranges the death of Umah the Hittite to cover his adultery with Bathsheba. David's son, Absalom, tries to overthrow him; David flees Jerusalem during Absalom's rebellion and when he dies, David returns to rule Jerusalem. He chose Solomon, his son, as his successor. In 931 B.C., at age eighty, he died a peaceful death.

874 B.C. to 853 B.C. King Ahab, the son of King Omar reigned over the ten tribes of Israel. He built the temple Baal. Many considered him the worst ruler Israel ever had. His wife, Jezebel was so evil she became the symbol of all that can be evil in a woman. King Ahab was killed in battle by an arrow. (Gen.1Kings 22: 34.).

Elijah, the prophet, rebuked King Ahab for his evil. Elijah was highly approved by the followers of Yahweh (1 Kings. 17: i.). His eminence was seen in the religious reformation he brought. Between his first appearance and his final disappearance was a succession of amazing miracles. Elijah was taken to heaven (Mars).

In the year 753 B.C. Rome was founded by twin brothers, Romulus and Remus. It began as an iron Age hut village. Over 450 years from 753 B.C. to 303 B.C. Rome had grown and became an empire in the wake of Julius Caesar.

763 B.C. God sent Jonah to go to Nineveh to preach as the people there were wicked. On the boat, a terrible storm came, and the sailors blamed Jonah, they pushed him overboard. God sent *a big fish (submarine, Enki made the first on 351,000 years earlier). *Read addendum.

Revelation: Ch. 17. V. 18. And the woman which thou sawest is that great city (ROME) which reigneth over the kings of the Earth.

ALL ROADS LEAD TO ROME.

Earthlings are still being used underground as slaves to mine gold, to build and care for the underground cities. To obey, serve and feed the Anunnaki now calling themselves Ariaani.

CHAPTER 14

THE LIFE OF CHRIST

In 606-562 B.C Nebuchadnezzar was king of Babylon. He was the greatest king of Babylon. He succeeded his father, Nabopolassar, in kingship and married Amytes of Media. Nebuchadnezzar defeated the Egyptians and Assyrians with the help of the Medes, liberated Babylon from the Assyrian rule; subdued Palestine and Syria and controlled all the trade routes across Mesopotamia.

King Nabopolassar died three months after Nebuchadnezzar's victorious battle in Egypt. Upon hearing the death of his father, he rushed home to assume the throne in Babylon (634-562 B.C.).

Upon ascending the throne, Nebuchadnezzar spoke to the gods in his inaugural address, "O merciful **Marduk**, may the house that I've built endure forever. May I be satiated with its splendor, attain old age therein with abundant offspring and receive therein tribute of the kings of all regions from all mankind."

Nebuchadnezzar was a powerful leader, but he was soon an enemy of God (Enlil) whom the deity of the Israelites intended to make an example of. He defeated the Egyptian routes across Mesopotamia.

In the third year of the reign of Jerusalem, King of Juda, Nebuchadnezzar came to Jerusalem and besieged it. The King of Judah and some articles of the Temple of God were delivered into the hands of Nebuchadnezzar. He carried them to the temple in Babylon.

King Nebuchadnezzar ordered Ashpenaz, chief of his court officials, to bring into the King's service some royal young Israelites who are handsome, bright and qualified to serve as seers. Among those who were chosen from Judah were Daniel, Hananiah, and Azarrah. In the second year of his reign he had dreams which troubled him. He called forth magicians, astrologers, enchanters and sorcerers. None could answer him. Over and over he asked and still no results. He ordered all his wise men to be put to death.

When Daniel was told of his death sentence. He went to his condemned friends and begged them to plead with God to tell them the secret of Nebuchadnezzar dreams. During the night, in a dream, the mystery was revealed to Daniel.

Daniel sent a messenger to tell the king that he knows the meaning of his dream.

"Your majesty looked and before you stood a large statue. The head of the statue was made of pure gold, its chest and arms of silver, its belly and thighs are bronze, the legs of iron. Its feet partly of iron and partly of baked clay. Thou sawest that a stone was cut without hands, (God) which smote the image upon his feet that were iron and clay (Rome) and broke them to pieces. Now, I will interpret the dream."

"Your majesty, you are the King of Kings. You are the golden head. In your hands he has placed all mankind, beasts and birds. After you another kingdom will come, Medes and Persians, inferior to yours. It is of silver. Next a third kingdom of bronze, Greece, and it will rule the Earth. Finally, there will be a fourth kingdom, Rome, strong as iron for iron breaks and smashes everything and as iron breaks things to pieces, so it will crush and break all the kingdoms."

"The feet and toes are partly of potter's clay and part of iron. This will be a divided kingdom, yet it will have some strength of iron in it, even as you saw iron mixed with clay. So, this kingdom will be partly strong and partly brittle. And just as you saw the iron mixed with baked clay, so the people will be a mixture and will not remain united any more than iron mixes with miry clay."

In the times of these kings, the God of Heaven will set up a kingdom that will never be destroyed nor will it be left for another people. It will crush all those kings down and bring them to an end, but it will itself endure forever. This is the meaning of the rock cut out of the mountain, but not by human hands, a rock that broke the iron, the bronze, the clay, the silver and the gold to pieces.

King Nebuchadnezzar built an image as Daniel described. He then ordered Shadrock, Meshach and Abednego to bow to the image; they refused. He ordered his soldiers to tie the three men and place them in the hot furnace. They did and much to their amazement and the Kings, they looked into the fire and saw the three men untied and with a fourth who looked like a man of God.

The King had a second dream and Daniel interpreted it. His report was not good as Daniel told him that he would lose his power, and live among the animals and lose his power for his disbelief in God. It thus came true.

He had a third dream; "Mene, Mene, Tekel, Parsin."

Daniel for the fourth time, interpreted the King's dream; Mene means God has remembered the days of your reign and brought it to an end. Tekel, you have been weighed on the scales and found wanting. Parsin; Your kingdom is divided and given to the Medes and Persians.

605-562   B.C. His kingdom was divided and given to the Medes and Persians. 509 B.C. Rome was established and gained dominion over western Mediterranean. (The beginning of ruling the world). Greece ruled until 323 B.C.
556 B. C. Nibiru nears Earth. Many Anunnaki leave to their home planet. Nibiru will return in 3,600 years.
530 B.C. Daniel died.
509 B.C. Roman Republic was established and gained dominion over the western Mediterranean. The beginning of Rome ruling the world.

331 B.C.   Marduk died. Alexander rushed to the Esagil ziggurat temple to shake hands with Marduk, but found the great god was dead, lying in a golden coffin.

27 B.C.   Imperial Rome came into being. It lasted 1,500 yrs. until 1473 A.D. Rome continues to rule the world up until the present. (Rev. 17: 18.). The woman which thou sawest is the great city, Rome, which reigneth over the kings of the Earth.

In Daniel's Image of the four nations to rule the world: Nebuchadnezzar, Medes and Persia (kings), Greece and Rome. From out of Rome, a little horn came up (Antichrist). This fourth beast shall be the fourth kingdom and the last upon Earth and diverse from all kingdoms.

And the ten horns out of this kingdom are ten kings that shall rise after them, and another (the 11th nation) shall rise after them; His number is # 666. He is of the prince of the people, a title given to Titus, an Italian, and he shall be diverse from the first, and he shall subdue three kings. (Daniel. 7: 24.). So, he who come in as the eleventh nation (Spain) will be the Antichrist and he must be Italian.

These nations will be the nations of the old Roman Empire. 1. 1958. Belgium, France, Germany, Italy, Luxembourg,. Ireland, United Kingdom, Greece, Portugal, 11.1986 Spain.

In the day of these kings of Daniel, the God of Heaven will set up a kingdom that will never be destroyed nor will it be left for another people. It will crush all those and bring them to an end. But it will itself endure forever. THE KINGDOM OF JESUS CHRIST.

2024 B.C. Enki, the god who created man tells of the coming of the Creator who will judge all. "I did all I could to prevent the great calamity (the bombing of Mount Sinai) I failed. Was it fate or destiny? In the future it shall be judged, for at the end of days a Day of Judgment there shall be. On that day, the Earth shall quake and the rivers shall change course and there shall be darkness at noon and a fire in the heavens in the night. The day of the **returning of the celestial God (Jesus)** it will be. And who shall survive and who shall perish, who shall be rewarded and who will be punished, gods and men alike."

Enki admits there is a celestial God who will judge all and punish or reward each one. 'Lost Book of Enki' Page 12.

There are 365 prophecies in the Old Testament of the Coming of Christ. Here are some of them:

Gen: Ch. 49, V. 10. The scepter shall not depart from Israel.
Micah: Ch. 5. V. 2. Jesus was to be born in Bethlehem.
Isaiah; Ch. 7, V. 14. Jesus was born of a virgin.
Jeremiah: Ch. 31, V. 15. Prophesied slaughter of babies soon after the birth of Christ.
Hosea: Ch. 11, V. 1. When Israel was a child… and called my son out of Egypt.
Isaiah: Ch. 40, V. 3-5. The voice of him that crieth in the wilderness.
Daniel: Ch. 9, V. 25. Prophecy of the beginning of Christ's ministry.
Isaiah: Ch. 56, V. 7. Prophecy of the cleansing of the temple.
Zechariah: Ch. 9, V. 9. Christ's triumphant entry, riding on an ass.
Daniel: Ch. 9, V. 26. The messiah to be cut off, and the destruction of Jerusalem.
Psalms: Ch. 41, V. 9 Judas betrayal.
Zechariah: C. 13, V. 7. The disciples forsake Jesus.
Psalms: Ch. 35, V.11. False witnesses at Jesus's trial.
Psalms: Ch.22, V. 7-8. Jesus scorned and mocked.
Isaiah: Ch 53, V. 4-5. Christ beaten and torture.
Isaiah: Ch. 53, V. 7. Messiah silent when accused.
Psalms: Ch. 22, V. 16. Nailing of Jesus's hands and feet.
Isaiah: Ch. 53, V. 8. Jesus's death foretold.
Psalms: Ch. 22, V. 18. Soldiers gambling for Jesus's coat.
Psalms: Ch. 69, V. 21. Christ to be given vinegar.
Psalms: Ch. 109, V. 4. Jesus lived what he preached.
Isaiah: Ch. 53, V. 12. Jesus crucified with two others.
Zechariah: Ch. 12, V. 10. Jesus died of a broken heart.

Psalms: Ch. 24, V. 20. Not one bone was broken.

Isaiah: Ch. 53, V. 9 Lord placed in a tomb of the rich.

Psalms: Ch. 16, V. 10 Prophesy of resurrection Psalms: Ch. 69, V. 18. Prophecy of Ascension

Psalms: Ch. 110, V. 4. Christ is our high priest.

Another prophecy concerning the coming of Christ: Zachari, a certain priest of the course of Abia, and his wife, Elizabeth, was of the daughters of Aaron. She was barren and they both were well up in years. And it came to pass that while Zachari executed the priest's office before God in the order of his course. V.9. According to the custom of the priest's office, his lot was to burn incense when he went into the temple of the Lord.

The custom was to burn incense in the 'latter part of June'. An angel appeared on the right of the altar of incense. He told Zachari that his wife was pregnant and said to call him John. Isaiah. 40: 3-5). The voice of him that crieth in the wilderness (announcing Christ).

(Luke. 1: 26.). When Elizabeth was six months pregnant (December) an emissary of the Universe was sent to Mary of Nazareth and told; V. 31 "behold thou shalt conceive in thy womb and bring forth a son and call him Jesus." He told her that her cousin, Elizabeth, was six months pregnant. v. 41.

(Matt. 1: 20,). An angel appeared to Joseph and told him his wife, Mary, "that which is conceived in her is of the Holy Ghost. (artificial insemination). V.21. And she shall bring forth a Son and thou shalt call Him Jesus: for He shall 'save' His people from their sins." John was born March 25, 1 A.D.

For millions of years all this while, the loving God, His Son, Jesus, and all the angels of the Universe were witnessing, tracking, recording all the creations, all the works; the results of Lucifer's rebellion. They witnessed the horrors, wars, diseases, mutilations, genetic failures, extreme sadness, extreme sexual, emotional, physical, spiritual, mental pain and abuse; flesh eating flesh, prey and predator in the jungles and in the settlements.

For millions of years they have witnessed his sexual deviations of nature: homosexuals, pedophiles, bi-sexuals, causing suicides, murders and eternal earthly destruction of the psyche until they are in their graves and then eternal damnation.

They witnessed the kidnapping, enslavement of young boys taken to a hell underground to slave in the mines, to dig gold for their masters (Anunnaki/Ananni) work building cities, repairing them and feeding them. They die young from exhaustion and hunger; torn from their parents never to be seen again. (Admiral Byrd's plane was forced down to an underground city.

They saw the imprisonment of souls in a physical body and death on prison planets. To be forever imprisoned on a prison planet unable to escape even after death; their souls to remain forever in torment, never to leave the planet.

Only Jesus Christ, Creator of all, must come to stop one of His once beloved creations, Lucifer, from condemning Earthlings to eternal damnation. He and His Father must have discussed this man times. Christ must come to Earth to shed His Blood to purify man to enter His Kingdom. Just as astronauts are sprayed with a disinfectant before going into a space capsule so as not to infect the Universe, so must we be sprayed with the Blood of Christ.

Everything that occurs in the Universe is planned and timed for reasons known only to God. Now is the time chosen to send Christ to Earth to save man from eternal enslavement of body and soul.

*Christ was born on the Feast of Atonement, September 25, 1 A.D. six months after the birth of John, the Baptist who was born March 25, 1 A.D.

When Herod, the king heard of the wise men inquiring about where Jesus was born, he became angry out of fear that one day Jesus would rule over him. He sent men to Bethlehem to search for the child. He told them to kill all children under two years old. Joseph, Mary and Child fled to Egypt and remained until an angel appeared and told them Herod was dead and to go to the land of Israel.

When he heard that Herod's son reigned there, he turned aside into the parts of Galilee. He came to a city called Nazareth so that the prophecy may be fulfilled that Jesus be called a Nazarene. And here is where Jesus spent His childhood.

Jesus at a young age worked with his father as a carpenter. He must have known what His mission on Earth was, at twelve years old he delayed one day in the temple answering questions of the priests. In panic did His mother search for Him. When she found Him, He answered, "Do you not know that I must be about my Father's business."

It was written that Jesus traveled the world with his wealthy Uncle Josephus who owned a boating business.

At thirty years old, John began preaching in the wilderness of Judaea, "Repent ye for the Kingdom of Heaven is at hand. Prepare ye the way of the Lord, make His path straight." (Luke. 3: 1.). A voice of one crying in the wilderness. John was dressed in clothing of camel's hair and a leather girdle about his loins. His food was locusts and wild honey. He went preaching of the coming of the Savior; traveling Jerusalem, Judaea and all the regions round about Jordon.

When he saw Pharisees and Sadducees come to his baptism, he called them a generation of vipers. He asked them who warned them to flee from the wrath to come. (Matt: 3: 1.) "I indeed baptize you with water unto repentance: but He that cometh after me is mightier than I whose shoes I am not worthy to wear: He shall baptize you with ye Holy Ghost and with fire." Then cometh Jesus from Galilee to Jordon unto John to be baptized of him.

V. 14. But John forbad Him, saying, "I have need to be baptized of Thee and comest to me?"

V. 15. And Jesus answering said unto Him, "Suffer it to be so now for thus it becometh us to fulfill all righteousness." Then he baptized Him.

V. 16. And Jesus, when He was baptized, went up straightway out of the water: and lo the heavens were opened unto Him, and He saw the spirit (craft) of God descending like a dove (gliding) and lighted upon Him. And a voice of heaven saying, "This is my beloved Son in whom I am well pleased."

Then was Jesus led up of the spirit (beamed up into the craft to be carried) into the wilderness to be tempted by the devil. And when He had fasted forty days and forth nights, he was afterward very hungry.

A heaviness came upon the mountain, Christ slowly turned to see Lucifer, His own creation, lurking close by. "Aah, Lieutenant Lucifer we meet again," the Lord must have thought.

The tempter, who was once the most beautiful angel in the Universe, Lieutenant Lucifer, was now an arrogant, distorted, slithering entity. His beauty was gone; replaced with the face of a coldhearted sociopath turned psychopath. He was far removed from the beauty of the all-encompassing Universal Love; his eyes and face were that of a hardened criminal.

He slithered his way toward Christ and in a soft, syrupy tone said, "If thou be the Son of God, command that these stones become bread."

Christ answered, "It is written, man shall not live by bread alone, but by every word that proceedeth out of the mouth of God."

Then the devil took Him up (craft) into the holy city and sitteth him on a pinnacle of the temple. He said unto Him in an evil, "If thou be the Son of God cast thyself down. for it is written. He shall give his angels charge concerning thee, and in their hands they shall bear thee up, lest at any time thou dash thy foot against a stone."

Jesus answered him, "It is written thou shalt not tempt the Lord thy God."

Again, the devil taketh Him up into an exceeding high mountain and showeth Him all the kingdoms of the world and the glory of them. He sayeth unto the Lord, "All these things will I give you if thou wilt fall down and worship me."

Then Jesus said unto him, "Get thee hence, Satan, for it is written, thou shalt worship the Lord thy God and Him only shalt thou serve."

Then the devil leaveth Him and behold, angels came and ministered unto Him. Jesus then heard that John was taken prisoner so he left Nazareth and headed for Galilee. He dwelt in Capernaum, on the sea coast in the borders of Zabulon and Nephthalim, thus fulfilling the prophecy of Isaiah that Jesus would travel by the way of the sea beyond Jordon, Galilee of the Gentiles.

Wherever Jesus went, the people who were in darkness saw great light and those on the verge of death, life sprung up. From that time, Jesus began to preach, "Repent for the kingdom of Heaven is at hand."

As He walked, he chose men from the people, Peter, Andrew, James, John. He went all about Galilee, teaching, preaching and healing all manner of disease among the people.

His fame went throughout Syria: cured many diseases and torments, lunatics and those with palsy. Great multitudes of people followed Him from Galilee, Decapolis, Jerusalem, Judea and beyond Jordon.

And seeing the multitudes, he went up into a mountain: and when He was set, his disciples came unto him. He taught them the Beatitudes. And advice on how to treat your fellow man.

When He came down from the mountain, He looked upon the great multitudes who followed Him. A leper asked Him to cure him and Christ did so. When He entered Capernaum, a centurion asked Him to cure his servant at home who had palsy and was grievously tormented. Jesus said He would go to his home, but the man said he was not worthy for Jesus to enter his home.

Jesus told him because of his great faith to go home and his servant will be healed. Peter's mother was sick with the fever and Jesus touched her hand and she was healed. And people came who were possessed with demons, He cast out the spirits and they were healed.

He then departed to the other side of the mountain and there, a scribe said to Him, "I will follow thee wither so ever thou goest."

Jesus said, "The foxes have holes and the birds of the air have nests, but the Son of man hath nowhere to lay His head."

(Why did Jesus love to be called Son of Man? His blood is AB+; to let the world know He was not of the Anunnaki gods whose blood is O-).

Another disciple said that he must leave to bury his father. Christ answered him, "Follow me; and let the dead bury the dead."

Jesus entered into a boat, followed by His disciples. Later, He was awakened by them pleading that He save them from the tempest as the waves covered the ship. He answered them, "Why are ye fearful O ye of little faith?" He arose, rebuked the winds and the sea; and there was a great calm.

At the other side of the country, two men possessed by devils, and they said to Him that if You cast us out, suffer us to go away into the herd of swine. So it happened, they were cast into the herd of swine and the whole herd ran violently down a steep place into the sea. Those that kept the swine fled into the city to report what Jesus had done. The whole city came out to meet Jesus.

He raised a certain ruler's daughter from the dead. A woman ill with a blood condition, touched his hem and was cured. His fame went abroad into all that land. He then cured two blind men, casting out demons from a dumb man. He went to cities, villages synagogues, teaching the gospel and curing people.

He called unto Himself twelve disciples and gave them powers. He told them to gather the lost sheep of Israel. "Behold, I send you forth as sheep in the midst of wolves". "Not one sparrow falls to the ground that my Father does not see." And "Every hair on your head is numbered." So you will be protected.

He sent two disciples to console John in prison. To tell of the good works being done.

Jesus came upon His own city and a man sick with palsy was brought to Him. Jesus said, "Son, be of good cheer; thy sins are forgiven thee." Thus, he was healed. Certain scribes said to themselves that He blasphemeth. They said that Jesus sits and eats with sinners. He was called a wine jibber(sot), homosexual and mentally ill because He said He was the Son of God.

A woman taken in adultery was brought into the midst of Jesus and the crowd. They said this woman was caught in adultery. Jesus knelt down and wrote something in the sand. Perhaps the name of the man she sinned with. He rose and said, "Let he who is without sin, cast the first stone. Go, and sin no more," said He to the woman.

He saw Matthew there and told him to follow Him, and obediently he did.

Jesus performed many miracles and was followed by multitudes. One time turning five loaves of bread and two fish into enough to feed 5,000. He said, "Suffer little children to come unto Me. If anyone harms one of my little innocent ones, it is better that a millstone be placed around his neck and he be cast into the sea." He loved and smiled at all He met.

He gathered twelve apostles to follow Him to teach them so they may continue on when He's gone. He taught them how to live good lives on Earth, to love and help their fellow man, to believe in Him, to preach to others that He is the King of the Universe in a way to prepare them to one day join Him in His eternal, Heavenly Kingdom.

Jesus asked His disciples not to tell anyone that He was Jesus Christ. He told them He must go into Jerusalem and suffer many things of the elders, chief priests and scribes and then to be killed and be raised up on the third day.

He told them that He, the Son of Man shall come in the glory of His Father with the angels; and then He shall reward every man according to his works. He went into the temple of God and cast out all who bought and sold in the temple. In anger, He overthrew the tables of the money changers.

Matt. 24: 1. Jesus went out from the temple: and His disciples came to Him to show Him the buildings of the temple. 2. Jesus said, "See ye not all these things? Verily I say unto you there shall not be left one stone upon another that shall not be thrown down.

(70 A.D.) Destruction of the temple) by Titus, the prince of the people... Daniel's Italian antichrist, descendant of the prince of

the people, who will come in as the 11th nation and whose number is 666.

V.3. As Jesus sat upon the Mount of Olives, His apostles came to Him saying, "Tell us when these things be? And what shall be the sign of thy coming and the end of the world?" Jesus answered about His coming: V.4. Jesus said, "Take heed that no man deceives you. V.5. For many shall come in my name saying, I am the Christ and shall deceive many. V. 6. And ye shall hear of wars and rumors of wars: see that ye not be troubled: for all these things must pass, but the end is not yet. V.7. For nation will rise against nation and kingdom against kingdom: and there shall be famines, pestilences and earthquakes in diverse places."

V.8. All these are the beginning of sorrows. V.9.Then they shall deliver you up to be afflicted and shall kill you; ye shall be hated for all nations for my name's sake. V.10. Many will be offended and betray one another and hate one another. V.11.many false prophets shall rise and deceive many. V.12. Iniquity will abound and the love of many will wax cold. V.13. He that endures to the end will be saved. V.14. The gospel of the kingdom will be preached in all the world for a witness unto all nations and then shall the 'end times' come. Jesus **commands us** to know about the time of this coming. But not to know when the end will come.

Matt. 24: 32. Now learn a parable of the fig tree; When his branch is yet tender, and putteth forth leaves, ye know that summer is nigh: V. 33. So likewise ye, when ye shall see all these things, know that it is near, even at the doors. V. 34. Verily I say to you, this generation will not pass away, till all these things be fulfilled.

The fig tree is Israel. It came into existence May 14, 1948. A generation is 70 years; from 1948 to 2018 is 70 years. What things must be fulfilled? Earthquakes, kingdom against kingdom, famines, pestilences, people betraying one another, false prophets, iniquity, people waxing cold and the rapture. V. 27. For as light cometh from the east and shinith to the west, so shall be the coming of the Son of man be.

The second question the disciples asked, "What are the signs of the end of the world? He answered, "Heaven (Nibiru) and Earth will pass away, but my words will not pass away. (Matt. 24: 35.)." But of **that day**, knowest no man, not the angels which are in heaven, neither the Son, but the Father."

11Peter 3: 10. But that day, (about 1,000+ years from now when Nibiru nears Earth about 3,000 A.D) the heavens shall pass away with a great noise, and the elements shall melt away with fervent heat, and Earth also and the works that are within shall be burned up; a collision between Earth and Nibiru?

No one can possibly know when Nibiru in its nearness (perigee) to the Sun will cause the disturbance, gravitational pull to create the explosion to melt the elements, so after a 1,000 year reign on Earth, in the new Jerusalem, we must all leave together with Christ to a new location.

The new Jerusalem is 12,000 stadia; 1,400 miles in length, width and breadth (350 miles long on all four sides). It can house 39 billion people, allowing 100 sq. acres for each individual. (Rev. 21: 1-2.).

Jesus is going to return to Earth two more times; like a thief in the night at the translation (rapture) and take his Bride to dinner in the New Jerusalem. The second time in clouds for all eyes to see for the battle of Armageddon.

At this time when Jesus was telling His disciples about the times right before His coming as a thief in the night to take His Bride out of the world. He will take His Bride at this time to have dinner in the New Jerusalem. There are many prophecies concerning the rapture. Then WW 111, a one-day war, between the U. S. and Russia will take place. (Ezek: 38).

Vatican will be bombed by Russia. Catholic prophecy.

Jesus said, "I came into the world and the world received Me not. I came unto My own and my own received Me not. But to as many as received Me, to them do I give the power of becoming Sons of God." I do not believe that Jesus will let His Christian Sons of God go through a 'Jewish Tribulation'.

Then all hell will break loose. "Pray that ye may be found worthy to escape the following Jacob's Tribulation for it will be three and one-half years of slavery and adjusting to the New World Order and then; V. 15. When ye shall therefore shall see the abomination of desolation, spoken of by Daniel the prophet, stand in the holy place, let him understand.

v. 21. For then shall be great tribulation such as was not since the beginning of the world to this time, no, nor ever shall be. For such it will be for three and one-half more years of torture, confusion, betrayals, wars, building up to the Battle of Armageddon. Every nation on Earth will be gathered together for battle in the Valley of Megiddo.

And it came to pass when Jesus had finished telling of the end times, He said, "Ye know that after two days is the Feast of Passover and the Son of man is to be crucified."

Jesus's teachings, miracles and word that He claims to be the Messiah went before Him to reach officials and the high priests. There was much anger, fear and contempt that He dared to call Himself God Matt. 26: 3-5. Then assembled together the chief priests, scribes and the elders of the people unto the palace of the high priest who was called Caiaphas. And consulted that they might take Jesus by subtilty and kill Him. But they said not on the feast day lest there be an uproar among the people.

Six days before the Passover, Jesus came to Bethany where Lazarus was which had been dead, whom He raised from the dead. They made Him supper and Martha served, but Lazarus was one of them that sat at the table with him.

Mary anointed the feet of Jesus with expensive oil. Judas said to her, "Why was not this ointment sold for three hundred pence, and given to the poor?"

Jesus said, "Let her alone; against the day of my burying hath she kept this. For the poor always are with you, but me ye have no always."

Many people of the Jews came to see the risen Lazarus. And because of this miracle they believed in Jesus. The chief priests consulted that they might put Lazarus also to death. On the next day, many people came to the feast of Passover to see Jesus.

They took branches of palm trees and went forth to meet Him. Hosanna: Blessed is the King of Israel that cometh in the name of the Lord. And Jesus when He found a young ass, sat thereon; as it is written. Fear not, daughter of Sion: behold, thy King cometh, sitting on an ass's colt. Many people were there to see Jesus, including Greeks.

They told Phillip they came to see Jesus. Phillip and Andrew conveyed the message. Jesus said, "The hour is come that the Son of man should be glorified. Verily, verily, I say unto you, except a corn of wheat fall into the ground and die, it abidith alone: but if it die, it bringeth forth much fruit. If any man serve Me, let him follow Me, and where I am so also shall my servant be: if any man serve Me, him will My Father honor. Now is my soul troubled; and what shall I say? Father save Me from this hour: but for this cause came I unto this hour. Father, glorify Thy name."

Then came a voice from Heaven, saying, "I have both glorified it, and will glorify it again". The people that heard it, said that it thundered: others said that an angel spoke to them. Then one of the twelve called Judas Iscariot, went unto the chief priests. He said, "What will ye give me, and I will deliver Jesus unto you?" They covenanted with him for thirty pieces of silver.

He sought the opportunity to betray Jesus.

The first day of the Feast of Unleavened Bread the disciples came to Jesus asking Him where to prepare to eat at the Passover. He told them to go into the city to such a man and tell him that the Master said, "My time is at hand. I will keep the Passover at your house."

At about six P.M., the disciples did as Jesus asked, they made ready the Passover. When the time came, He sat down at the table with the twelve. And as they did eat, He said, "Verily I say to you, that one of you shall betray Me."

They were exceedingly sorrowful, and began every one of them to ask, "Lord, is it I?"

Jesus took bread, blest it, broke it and gave it to the disciples. He gave them the cup to drink of it. He answered and said, "He that dippith his hand with me in the dish, the same shall betray Me. The Son of man goeth as it is written of Him, but woe unto that man whom the Son of man is betrayed! It had been good for that man if he had not been born."

V.25. Then Judas answered and said, "Master, is it I?". said unto Him, "Thou hast said." And as they were eating, Jesus took the bread, blessed it, broke it and gave it to the disciples and said, "Take, eat, for this is My Body." V.28 "For this is My Blood of the New Testament which is shed for the many for the remission of sins. But I say unto you, I will not drink henceforth of this fruit of the vine until that day when I drink it new with you in my Father's Kingdom." Then they had sung a hymn.

Then about 8.P.M., they walked an hour to the mount of Olives. Jesus said, "All ye shall be offended because of Me this night: for it is written I will smite the shepherd, and the sheep of the flock shall be scattered abroad. But after I am risen again, I will go before you into Galilee."

Peter told Jesus that he would never be offended of Him. V. 34. Jesus said, "Verily I say to you that this night, before the cock crows, thou shalt deny me thrice."

Then, they went to a place called Gethsemane and He said, "Sit ye here, while I go and pray yonder." He took with him Peter and two sons of Zebedee, and He began to be sorrowful and very heavy. He said, "My soul is exceedingly sorrowful, even unto death: tarry ye here and watch with me." For an hour He prayed.

It was dark now. Jesus went further, fell on His face and prayed saying, "O my Father, if it is possible, let this cup pass from me: nevertheless, not as I will, but as thou will."

He cometh to His disciples and found them asleep. "Peter, "Why could ye not watch with me one hour? Watch and pray that you will not enter into temptation: the spirit indeed is willing, but the flesh is weak."

He went away again the second time, and prayed saying, "O my Father, if this cup may not pass away from me, except I drink it, thy will be done." V. 43 And He came and found them asleep again: for their eyes were heavy.

And He left them and went into the garden again and knelt to pray. So alone, so all alone. Being God, He knew what was ahead of Him. The humiliation and mental torment of the trial, the extreme pain of the beating and the agony of the crucifixion.

He began to tremble knowing every pain that would come upon Him during the beating and crucifixion. Fear, loneliness crept over Him. The sound of His heart was pounding in His head and His heart was pinching. Jesus agonized over the thought of it all, He actually bled through his sweat.

Luke: Ch.22, V. 44. Then being in agony, He prayed more earnestly. Then His sweat became like great drops of blood falling down to the ground. (hematidrosis; blood in sweat caused by extreme anxiety, fear). He prayed saying the same words He said before, "O my Father, if this cup may not pass away from me, except I drink it, thy will be done."

Then cometh He to His disciples, and saith unto them, "Sleep on now and take your rest: behold the hour is at hand and the Son of man is betrayed into the hands of sinners. Rise, let us be going: behold, he is at hand that doth betray Me."

Lo, Judas came and with him a great multitude with swords and staves from the chief priests and the elders of the people. Judas gave a sign, saying, "Whomsoever I shall kiss, that same is He: hold Him fast." He came forth to Jesus and said, "Hail, Master," and kissed Him; 'The Midnight Kiss'.

Jesus said to him, "Friend, wherefore art thou come?"

The soldiers laid hands on Him and took Him. One of Jesus's disciples took a sword and smote the ear of a servant of the high priest. Jesus picked up the ear, placed it and it was healed.

Jesus said, "Put away thy sword: for all that take the sword shall perish from the sword. Thinkest thou that I cannot now pray to my Father and He shall presently give me more than twelve legions of angels." (about 82,000 angels).

They took Jesus to Caiaphas, the high priest where the Scribes and the elders were assembled, "Are ye come out against a thief with swords and staves for to take me? I sat daily with you in the temple and ye laid no hand on me." But all this was done, that the scriptures of the prophets must be fulfilled." Then all the disciples forsook Him and fled.

They that laid hold of Jesus led Him away to Caiaphas, the high priest where the scribes and elders were assembled. They sought false witness against Jesus, to put Him to death and found none though many came. At last, came two false witnesses saying, "This fellow said, "I am able to destroy the temple of God and build it in three days."

Jesus answered not. The high priest said, "I adjure Thee by the living God that Thou tell us whether You are the living God, Christ the Son of God?"

Jesus answered, "Thou hast said: never the less I say unto you, hereafter shall you see the Son of man sitting on the right hand of power and coming in the clouds of Heaven."

The high priest tore off His clothes, saying, "He has spoken blasphemy. We need no further witnesses. What think ye?"

They answered, "He is guilty of death." Then they spit on His face, buffeted Him and others smote Him with the palms of their hands, saying, "Prophecy unto us thou Christ, who is he that smote thee?"

Now Peter sat without in the palace: and a damsel came unto Him saying, "Thou also was with Jesus of Galilee." Peter denied it saying, "I know not this Man." He went out into the porch, another maid said, "This fellow was also with Jesus of Nazareth." Peter denied saying, "I do not know this Man." After a while another said, "Surely thou also art one of them; for thy speech betrayeth thee." Peter began to curse and swear saying, "I know not the Man."

Immediately, the cock crew, at about 4 A.M. Christ turned and looked at Peter. Peter remembered the word of Jesus, "Before the cock crows, you will deny Me thrice." And he went out and wept bitterly.

When the morning had come, all the chief priests and elders of the people took counsel against Jesus to put Him to death. They bound Him and led Him away to be delivered to Pontius Pilate, the governor.

Judas saw He was condemned, repented, returned the thirty pieces of silver and threw them on the temple floor. They bought the potter's field with the money. Thus, fulfilling the prophecy spoken of by Jeremy saying, "And they took the thirty pieces of silver and gave them for the Potter's Field."

Jesus stood before the crowd and the governor who asked, "Art Thou the King of the Jews?' Jesus answered, "Thou sayest." When accused by the chief priests and elders, He answered nothing. Pilot asked Him how many things did they witness against Thee? He answered not.

Now at that Feast, the governor wished to please the people by letting them choose the prisoner whom they wanted. "Whom will ye that I release unto you, Barabbas or Jesus which is called Christ?" Pilate knew Jesus was delivered by the chief priests out of envy. His wife pleaded with him to have nothing to do with Jesus for he is a just man.

The **chief priests** and **elders** called out to release Barabbas, persuading the multitude to follow to release Barabbas. The governor answered them, "Wither of the twain will ye that I release unto you?" They screamed out, "Barabbas."

Pilate then asked, "What shall I do with Jesus which is called Christ?" They all called out, "Let him be crucified!" The governor asked, "Why, what has He done?" They cried out more, "Crucify Him. Crucify Him." Pilate washed his hands and said, "I am innocent of the blood of this just person."

Then answered all the people. "**His blood be on us and on our children.**" Thus, the soon coming tribulation upon the Jews, 'Jacob's Tribulation.' Barabbas was released.

Jesus was taken to the common hall be beaten and then crucified. The Romans perfected the art of the crucifixion as a form of torture that was designed to produce a slow death with maximal pain and suffering. It was a cruel method of execution for the vilest of criminals.

Flogging was a legal preliminary to every Roman execution. The whip was a short strap with three braided leather thongs at the end. On the tip of each thong was an iron ball or sharp pieces of sheep bone. The legal number of lashes were 39, so with 3 iron balls at the tip of the three thongs, the lacerations were 117 cut, open, bleeding gashes.

They gathered to Him a whole band of soldiers. By now, Jesus had no sleep for about 51 hours. He was tired from the trial, the questioning and the emotions of desertion. They platted a crown of thorns and put it upon His head. From each pierce, the blood immediately gushed, ran down into His eyes, face and neck. They took off His clothing and tied Him to an upright post to be beaten. Jesus looked around and saw none of His friends. Heartbroken was He and afraid that He may not be able to stand up under the weight of Sin.

The soldiers began the flogging. With every slash they gave Him, out of jealousy of His beautiful body and Him claiming to be God, they would have used much more strength and force with each slash than on any one else.

With every strike, He would have cried out in pain. One, two, three…He looked over to see His mother watching in extreme agonizing, mental and emotional pain. Four, five, six…blood gushing out of the wounds.

'Dear God, how much longer can I hold up to it all? My dear Mother to witness this.' With every scream of her Son, she put her head down and left out a silent scream. A mother's agony known only to a mother.

Over and over the pain, the shame; 29, 30, 31 lashes; He could hear the people laughing, mocking, "Son of God, set Yourself free." Many people seeing Him naked and being beaten was humiliating. "My Father, please help me to endure this and all that is yet to come." As the soldiers repeatedly struck His back with full force, the iron balls would cause deep contusions, cutting into the subcutaneous tissues.

As they continued the flogging, the lacerations tore into the underlying skeletal muscles which produced quivering ribbons of bleeding flesh. The metal at the end of the whip tore into His sinews, inner veins and the bowels would be exposed. The blood loss would produce circulatory shock. The amount of blood lost would determine how long the victim would survive on the cross; 37, 38, 39 lashes with screams following each whip lash. Blood was now covering most of His body from His head to His feet.

After the scourging, the soldiers taunted Him. "Hail, King of the Jews," and they hit Him and spit on Him.

The soldiers put on Him a purple robe. The weight of the material on the open sores would scrape and burn. "Hail, King of the Jews," said they as they struck Him with their hands. Pilate went forth again and said, "I bring Him forth to you, that ye may know that I find no fault in Him."

Then Jesus, tired and weak, with His head bent low, came forth, wearing the crown of thorns and the purple robe. Pilate saith unto them, "Behold the man!" When the chief **priests** and officers saw Him, they cried out, "Crucify Him, crucify Him!"

Pilate said, "Take Him and crucify Him. I find no fault in Him. Shall I crucify your King?" He wished to release Jesus.

They answered, "We have no king, but Caesar." Then delivered Him therefore unto them to be crucified. They took off the robe and put on His own raiment and led Him away to be crucified. Then they placed a reed in His right hand; bowed the knee before Him and mocked Him saying, "Hail, King of the Jews."

Broken hearted and humiliated, this King of the Universe bowed His head low as they spit on Him. Then took the reed from His hand and struck Him, on the head with it. After that they mocked and spat on Him and put His own raiment on Him and led Him away to be crucified.

Jesus so weakened, bent over as the 80 lb. cross bar was placed on His left shoulder on top of the open wounds. With every step, the cross bar would scrape over the open flesh causing pain. As He walked in the heat, salty perspiration would run into his open sores, burning them.

Miriam approached Jesus and pushed a white cloth to His face to relieve Him. When she took it away, the imprint of Jesus's face was transfixed upon it. Jesus grew faint and He stumbled three times. His scourging was so violent that caused severe blood loss. His blood pressure would have dropped causing fainting and organ failure. The soldiers stopped Simon, a Cyrenian, and laid upon him the cross to bear.

Two criminals were led with Him to be put to death and walked to Calvary to be crucified. Walking together with them was a complete military guard. People and the rulers were walking near Jesus, laughing and mocking, saying, "He saved others, let Him save Himself, if He be the Christ, the chosen God." One of the soldiers carried a sign on which was the condemned man's name and his crime. This would be placed in the center of the top post.

Mary, His mother, following behind in complete emotional and mental pain, seeing her Son being tormented and mocked. They came upon Golgotha. The three heavy wooden posts were already secured in the ground. To prolong the crucifixion process, a horizontal block or plank, serving as a seat was attached mid-way down the post. The soldiers led Jesus to His cross and given a bitter drink of wine mixed with gall. Then Jesus said, "Father, forgive them for they know not what they do."

He was thrown to the ground on His back with His arms outstretched along the crossbar. As His back struck the hard earth, the pain would be excruciating as stones and dirt entered the wounds.

He was put on the crossbar and His wrists were nailed to the cross. The nails were 6" iron spikes. These nails would crush the large median nerve. The damaged nerves would produce excruciating bolts of fiery pains in both arms, and cause the index and middle fingers to shoot outward toward the thumbs.

They lifted Christ and the crossbar onto the post. The soldiers nailed His feet to the front of the post. The nails were pounded into His deep peroneal nerve at the front of the ankles causing more excruciating pain. Also branches to the medial and lateral plantar nerves were injured by the nails driven in His feet. This would cause more excruciating pain. Christ's knees flexed and his bent legs rotated outward.

When they completed the nailing, the sign was attached to the cross just above his head. It read, "Jesus of Nazareth, the King of the Jews." He was hanged at twelve noon. The soldiers taunted Him saying, "Thou that destroyeth the temple, and buildest it in three days, save thyself. If thou be the Son of God, come down from the cross."

Then the soldiers after they crucified Jesus, took His four garments and gave each soldier a part. They cast lots for His coat. Thus the prophecy was fulfilled: "They parted my raiment among them and for my vesture they did cast lots."

Insects would lite upon a burrow, into the open wounds, in the eyes, ears, nose of our dying Jesus. Birds of prey would tear at these sites.

Each minute would seem like an hour as He tried to relieve the pain from His open bleeding gashes in His back rubbing against the rough wooden post. There would be muscle cramps, loss of feelings in both outstretched arms; the uplifted arms would add to discomfort.

Over and over He would slump down in exhaustion, breathing would be difficult. He would have to lift Himself up in order to breath. Each breathing effort would become agonizing and tiring, reducing the oxygen levels in the blood. Over and over until He would become so weak that He could no longer breathe and eventually lead to asphyxiation.

All the while, His mother crying out, not able to help her Son. She and Mary Magdalene were crying at the base of the cross.

The two criminals were on either side of Christ. The one said, "If thou be the Christ, save thyself and us."

The second thief said, "Lord, remember me when thou cometh to thy kingdom." Jesus said, "Today shalt thou be with Me in paradise."

Jesus now knowing that all things were accomplished, that the scripture might be fulfilled saith, "I thirst." A soldier filled a sponge with vinegar, put it in hyssop and put it to His mouth.

At the sixth hour, a darkness came over the land until the ninth hour. At the ninth hour, that which was causing the darkness slowly 'removed' itself. Jesus cried up to Him in a loud voice, "Eli. Eli, la-ma sa-bach-tha-ni?" That is to say, "My God, my God why has Thou forsaken Me?" Jesus said. "Father, unto Thy hands, I commend My Spirit. It is finished." He yielded up His ghost.

And behold, the veil of the temple was rent in twain from the top to the bottom, and the earth did quake and the rocks rent. The graves were opened (rapture) and many of the bodies of the saints which slept arose. And came out of the graves. After His resurrection they went into the holy city and appeared to many. Earthquake chart lists an earthquake occurred April 3, 34 A.D.)

Now the centurion and they that were with Him said, "He is the Son of God."

Bodies were not permitted to remain on the cross during the Sabbath, so came the soldiers and broke the legs of the two criminals so they would die. When they came to Jesus and saw He was dead, a soldier with a spear pierced His side and fore with came there out blood and water. This was because hypovolemic shock, fluid collected in the membranes around His heart and lungs. These things were done, that the scripture should be fulfilled.

While Jesus was still on the cross, the Sudarium (sweat cloth) was wrapped around the face of Jesus and pinned to the back of His head.

Joseph of Arimathaea went to Pilate and begged for the body of Jesus. He wrapped it in a clean linen cloth. The cloth was 14 ft. 5 in. long, 3 ft. 7 in. wide. A long strip 3" by 14 ft, 5 in. was cut off the side to be used to tie the body. The Sudarium (sweat cloth) was folded and placed to the side.

Nicodemus was the first to come to Jesus by night. He brought a hundred pounds of a mixture of myrrh and aloes. They soaked the Shroud in the one hundred pounds of spices.

The long strip of cloth was tied around His feet, and ankles and wrapped upward around the shroud. Jesus was laid into His new tomb.

The chief priests and the Pharisees went to Pilate telling him that Jesus said He would rise on the third day. Pilate told them to go to the tomb and seal it with a stone. Which they did.

At the end of the Sabbath, Jesus's mother and Mary Magdalene went to the sepulcher. Behold, there was a great earthquake for the angel of the Lord descended from heaven and rolled back the stone.

The watchers were frightened. The angel was radiant and he said, "He is not here for He is risen. Come, see the place where the Lord lay. Now go quickly and tell the disciples that He has risen from the dead and He goes before you into Galilee; there you shall see Him."

Then Mary Magdalene runnith to Peter and John, and told them they took Jesus away and we know not where they laid Him. Then Peter ran to the tomb and stooping down, he saw the linen clothes lying by themselves. And the napkin that was about His head, not lying with the linen clothes, but wrapped together in a place by itself. (John. 20: 7).

Mary had followed and stood outside the sepulcher weeping and as she wept, she stooped down and looked into the sepulcher. She saw two angels who said, "Woman, why do you weep?" She answered, "Because they have taken away my Lord and I know not where they have laid Him."

AS soon as Mary Magdalene said this, she turned and saw Jesus and knew not it was He. "Woman why weepest thou?" She took a step forward and said, "Master."

Jesus said, "Touch Me not for I am not ascended to my Father, but go to my brethren and tell them that I ascend to my Father, and your Father, and your God."

(Did Jesus not want her to contaminate Him as He was to rise to heaven? Or did He not wish for her to become ill from radiation from the electromagnetic radiation. Radiation from his spirit being forced into His body that made an imprint negative on the shroud?)

Mary came to the disciples and told them that she had seen the Lord. Then the same day, they were assembled behind closed doors for fear of the Jews. Jesus came among them and said, "Peace be with you" He showed them His hands and sides. The disciples were glad.

Jesus said, "Peace be unto you: as My Father has sent Me, even so send I you. Receive ye the Holy Ghost. Go ye therefore and teach all nations, baptizing them. Teach them to observe all things whatsoever I have commanded you: and lo, I am with you always, even unto the end of the world."

The Shroud, God's Gift to Mankind.

The Sudarium was wrapped around His head which had fallen to the right, and pinned at the back. There were pin-point spots of blood there caused by thorns. The main stains on the cloth indicated a Oueraloedema caused by asphyxiation; jolting movements forcing blood out the nostrils.

The Sudarium, 84 by 53 cm (33" by 21"). It had no image, no facial stains of dried or drying blood. This proves it was not used to wipe His face, and it was removed, folded and put to the side. John. 20: 7. The blood on the Sudarium is the same as that on the Shroud; AB+. Also pollen found on it are the same found on the

Shroud. The length of the nose is the same on both cloths. Stains of blood on the beard, face, nape and blood on right side of the mouth are the same.

The Sudarium was in Palestine up until Jerusalem was attacked and conquered by Chosroes II, King of Persia in 614 A.D. It entered Spain at Cartagena. The Bishop Fulgentius welcomed the relic. He gave the box to Leandro, Bishop of Seville.

St. Isadore became Bishop of Seville, then became Bishop of Toledo until 718 A.D. It was taken north to protect it from the Muslims. It was kept in a cave in Monsacro near Oviedo. It was opened for King Alfonso. In the year 1113 A.D., the chest was covered with silver with the inscription that it contains Holy Blood. It has been kept in the Cathedral of Oviedo ever since.

The shroud, the burial cloth of Jesus is 14', 5" long by 5', 7" wide. The linen cloth was indigenous to Israel. Pollen found on the shroud is the thistle Gundelia which blooms in Israel between March and May, they were used for thorns for His head (the image of the plant can be seen near the image of the Man's shoulders on the Shroud). Also found were Zygophyllum Dumosum, and Cistus Creticus. These were also found on the Sudarium; These can only be found in lines linking Jerusalem, Hebron, Israel, Madaba, Kavax and Jorden.

The man was 5', 11" tall, muscular and weighed 175 lbs. (Determined by five doctors in 1959 who studied the image. They appeared on black and white T.V.) He had blue eyes and dark, reddish- brown hair and his complexion had a red cast (described by a centurion who was at His trial).

The image on the Shroud shows a badly beaten man. Stains of blood show He was crowned, pierced in the wrists and in the feet. It shows that He was severely beaten and covered with blood from head to toe. It was AB positive blood that was found on both cloths.

The coins on Jesus's eyes: The computer scientist, Velosino Nello examined the shroud and found the coin on the right eye depicts a lituis staff of the time of Pontius Pilate, 29 A.D. The disc on the left eye depicts the sacrificial cap during the time of Tiberias Caesar.

The Body of Christ, in the Shroud, would have to have been lifted at least six inches off the slab in order that the image could be transfixed on the underside of the shroud by a high-powered energy that took place, taking a picture of the Man.

(This was seen at the bombing of Hiroshima. A person standing near a wall when the bomb struck, left the image of a person on the wall).

The shroud in 36 A.D was taken from Jerusalem by Thaddeus to Edessa, Turkey. He was requested to heal Abqak of disease. He took the cloth with him and here it was hidden. In the 6th century, the walls of Edessa were repaired. The Shroud was discovered and a church was built for it and it was placed there.

944 A.D. Emperor Romanus sent an army to remove it to Constantinople. Looters eventually stole it. The next known public appearance is Liey, France in 1353-1357. Then hidden for 34 years. Then made its way to Austria and then to Chambery, England until 1578. In 1578, House of Savoy took it to Turin, Italy. In 1694, repairs made by Sebastian. In 1868, repairs by Clotilde of Savoy.

1898, May 28. Photographer, Secondo Pia, took a photograph of the Shroud. He processed the photo. It was faint and blurred with no contrast. In his dark room, lit by a dim red light, he processed the photo in his developing tray. He was utterly astonished to see appearing very slowly the clear, neat image of a dead person. The dead Jesus Christ, Savior of man, King of the Universe. The world was amazed.

1983 House of Savoy. 1997, the Shroud escaped another fire (Lucifer hell bent on Its destruction?).

1985, Monsignor Giulio Rucci said that the cloth of Oviedo and the Shroud of Turin had been on the same corpse. Studies were made, and it was found to be true and it is irrefutable.

Jesus said, "I go to prepare a place for you. If I go and prepare a place for you, I will return and receive you unto myself."

"SO THAT WHERE I AM, YOU MAY ALSO BE."

CHAPTER 15

THE BOOK OF REVELATION

And I saw a woman sit upon a scarlet beast, full of names of blasphemy, having seven heads (sitting on seven mountains of Rome) and ten horns (ten kings of the Old Roman empire named in chapter 14. The woman which thou sawest in the great city (Rome) **which reigneth over the kings of the earth.**

Rome is the fourth and last kingdom to rule the world. (Dan. 2: 31.). Dreadful and more terrible than the others. This kingdom has ten horns (kings), and a little horn (antichrist). So, from about 309 B.C., Rome and the Vatican has ruled the kings of the world until now.

Around the First Century, five million Jews lived outside Palestine About 80% of them lived within the Roman Empire, but they looked to Palestine as the center of their religious and cultural life.

70 A.D., 230 years before Rome began ruling the world, just as Jesus predicted, the Jewish second temple was destroyed by the Romans. They destroyed it in retaliation for an ongoing Jewish revolt. Jewish zealots were active for six decades because of the Romans financial exploitation of the Jews. Also Rome's contempt

for Judaism and favoritism that the Romans extended to gentiles living in Jerusalem.

The Jews would not defile God's Temple with a statue of pagan Rome's newest deity, Caligula. This infuriated the Romans and they dispersed and set upon the Jews a horrible orgy of war, killing about one million Jews.

135 A.D. A revolt: 580,000 Jewish soldiers were killed. Emperor Hadrian decreed that the Name Judea should be replaced by Syria-Palestine. In the ensuing years the greater part of the Jewish population went into exile as a captive, slaves and refugees. Galilee remained a center of Jewish institutions and learning until the 6th Century.

476 A.D. After the fall of the Middle ages, the papacy was influenced by the temporal rulers surrounding Italian province and Frankish papacy. The periods are known as the Ostrogothic Papacy, Byzantine Papacy and the Franklin Papacy.

566 Buddha was born into a wealthy family as a prince in present day Nepal. He is not god, but an enlightenment. It is one of the leading religions of the world known for its four noble truths: Identify suffering, Cause of suffering, Truth of the end of suffering and the Method for attaining the end of suffering.

570 A.D., Muhammad was born. In 622, The Birth of Islam started by the migration of Prophet Muhammad from Mecca to Medina and this marked the establishment of Islamic Religion in Arabia. Muhammad was flown to Jerusalem by an angel where he met Moses, Jesus and Abraham. At the height of its power, during the next one hundred years, Islamic rule extended from India to Southern France.

638 A.D., Arab conquest of Palestine which was Christian-Greek speaking and ruled from Constantinople as part of the Byzantine Empire, successor of Eastern Roman Empire. The sophisticated Arabic culture was developed; renowned for its science, philosophy, literature and architecture.

Marduk is no longer ruling the world but had influenced the papacy so much as for the Popes to wear the fish miter of his father, Enki. Also to have a statue in the Vatican to venerate Queen **Semaramus**, Marduk's daughter-in-law, wife of Astar/Osiris; mother of Horus/Horon. And the Popes end their prayers with the word Amen, to venerate Marduk, himself. It is important to remember that the underground Luciferians are still ruling the world through Rome. Rev. 18:17.

Over time, the Papacy consolidated its territorial claims to a portion of the peninsula known as Papal States. Thereafter the roles of the neighboring sovereigns were replaced by powerful Roman families during the Saeculum obscurum, the Cresentic Era and the Tusculan Papacy.

628-1099 Islamic Caliph Omar's completed conquest of Palestine with the capture of Jerusalem from Emperor Heraclius. On Enlil's Mission Control Center, Omar built the Dome of the Rock. Jerusalem was declared the third most holy site of Islam. Crusaders established Latin Kingdom of Jerusalem.

1099 A.D., Crusaders established Latin Kingdom of Jerusalem.

1187 A.D., Saladin, Kurdish, ruler of Egypt defeats the Crusaders.

From 1048-1257, the papacy had increasing conflict with the leaders of the Holy Roman Empire and the Byzantine Eastern Roman empire which culminated in the East-West schism.

1257-1377. The Pope resided in Viterbi, Orvieto, Perugia and then Avignon. He returned to Rome and was followed by Western Papacy.

1492, Population spread worldwide; an estimated 2 billion,300 million. Christopher Columbus discovered America. Jews were expelled from Spain.

1516 A.D. Sulejman, the magnificent of Turkey takes Jerusalem.

1517-1585. The Protestant Reformation. Martin Luther was an Augustine friar in Germany. He was a teacher in the University of Wittenberg. He developed a doctrine of Justification. He began to disapprove of the wrongs in the Church such as paying to have your relatives released from purgatory, penance, righteousness, and salvation.

Luther nailed his ninety-five Thesis of disapprovals on the door of the Wittenberg Church and sent them far and wide. The Pope was furious as this was a threat to his assets. They argued back and forth and the Pope declared he was a heretic and a bounty was put on his head.

Luther's thesis and pamphlets caused a turmoil. The Reformation spread. The Pope denied King Henry VIII an annulment of his marriage. Parliament declared King Henry supreme head of the Catholic Church in England. The Struggles continued for one-hundred years culminating in the Thirty-Year War.

The population of Europe was 65 million. About 300,000 people were killed each year due to the war. It ended with Peace of Westphalia and validated religious freedom for Protestants.

The Jesuit order was started in 1534 by Ignatius of Loyola, a Spanish soldier. Their plan was to convert the Muslims. In 1540, the Pope gave him permission to start the Jesuit Order. It grew and in 1556 there were one thousand members. In the 1600's, they set up ministries around the world. Thousands of priests were killed by those hostile to their mission of conversion.

The Jesuits played an important role during the Protestant Reformation. Their goal was to defeat Protestantism and regain world-wide Papal rule. They set up ministries all over the world.

The Jesuits give total adoration to the Pope; he alone do they obey. They are the Secret Army of the Papacy. They are sent all over the world to employ any method of pseudo-education, social programs, infiltration and all wickedness that could possibly be conceived and told to go into every school, church, organization, business, etc., pretend to be their friend, lie to gain their confidence to get every bit of information about them and their work and report it to 'Daddy', the Pope even if it means the death of those who trusted them. Betray even your mother, father, friends and anyone that is anti-Catholic.

In their writings they said, "We came like lambs and will rule like wolves." Read their Manifesto!! They then had 24,400 members.

Their Jesuit Manifesto is a shocking plan they will follow to attain the New World Order under the Jesuit Pope of Rome. In effect, it says:

I, (name of the Jesuit) in the presence of God and all His holy ones, Blessed Mother, St. John, by the womb of the Virgin and others. I swear that the Pope is Christ on earth.

I will defend this doctrine. I will wage a secret war against all heretics, Protestants, Masons, all those against the Catholic Church. I extirpate. I will spare neither age, sex, nor condition and I will hang, burn, waste, boil, flag, strangle and bury alive informers, heretics.

I will rip up the stomach and wombs of their women, crush their infant's heads against the walls in order to annulate their race. I will secretly use the poisoned cup, the strangulation cord, the sword or bullet, regardless of their authority, honor, rank, no matter what their condition.

I will send Catholic girls into Protestant families that they may give a weekly report. Also, I send our agents into all religions including the Jewish where they will be befriend them, get all the information, and then report to our Holy Father, the Pope. I defend this oath and write my name with this dagger dipped in my own blood.

!585-1689 Baroque Papacy led the Catholic Church through the Counter Reformation.

1773. The Jesuits were engaged in 740 schools and were totally dedicated to the Roman Catholic church. They lost their power and influence because of the problems they created. Pope Clement XIV issued a Dominus ac Redemptory Suppressing the Jesuits. He did so yielding from the pressure of the Bourbon courts, fearing loss of Papal States.

In 1814, The Society was restored by Pope Pius VII. They began to infiltrate the Catholic with pedophiles and homosexuals so they could blackmail the Catholic Church until they could gain full control. Little by little it worked. They are ruled by Lucifer.

1789. George Washington was elected president. The Vision of George Washington. Published in The National Tribune in December 1880.

The vision was reprinted in The Stars and Stripes Forever. December 21,1950. The aged Anthony Sherman told writer Wesley Bradshaw on July 1859 that he had something to tell him of an incident in Washington's life.

He went on to say that Washington after several set backs in the war, retreated to Valley Forge to pass the winter of 1777. He would cry over the conditions of his soldiers and went often to a thicket to pray for aid and comfort. One chilly, dreary day, he remained in his quarters all day. When he came out, his face was very pale and he seemed troubled. He had a conversation with the offer in attendance.

"I was sitting at my table preparing a dispatch and something in the apartment disturbed me. Looking up, I beheld a beautiful being. I asked him why he was there...no answer. A strange sensation spread over me, I couldn't speak, paralyzed was I and felt I was dying, I couldn't think or reason and couldn't move."

Presently, a voice said, "Son of the Republic, look and learn," as he extended his arm eastward. A white vapor rose, and dissipated a scene spread out on the table, all the countries of the world;-Europe, Asia, Africa and America. I saw rolling and tossing between Europe and America the billows of the Atlantic and between Asia and America lay the Pacific. "Son of the Republic, look and learn."

I saw a dark being like an angel floating in mid-air between Europe and America. He dipped water out of the ocean and sprinkled it upon America and Europe. With his left hand, he cast some over Europe. Immediately a cloud arose from these countries and joined in mid-ocean. Then it moved westward until it enveloped America. Sharp flashes of lightning gleamed through it at intervals. I heard the smothered groans and cries of the American people. The Revolutionary War that was then in progress.

"Son of the Republic, look and learn." I looked at America and saw villages and towns and cities springing up all over until the whole land is dotted with them. The mysterious voice said, "Son of the Republic, the end of the century cometh, look and learn."

The dark shadowy figure turned his face southward. From Africa, I saw an ill-omened specter approach our land. It flittered over every town and city. The inhabitants set themselves in a battle array against each other. I saw a bright angel on whose brow rested a crown of light, on which was traced the word "Union." He was bearing the American flag between the divided nation and said, "Remember, ye are brethren." The Civil War.

The inhabitants cast down their weapons, became friends once more and united around the National Standard.

Frightful- incredible WWIII.

Again, I heard the mysterious voice saying, "Son of the Republic, look and learn." At this, the dark shadowy angel placed a trumpet to his mouth and blew three distinct blasts; and taking water from the ocean, he sprinkled it upon Europe, Asia and Africa. Then my eyes beheld a fearful scene. From each of these continents arose thick black clouds that were soon joined into one. And through the mass there gleamed a dark red light put Russia by which I saw hordes of armed men. These men moving with the cloud, marched by land and sailed by sea to America, the country the men devastated, burned the the villages, towns and cities which had sprung up.

As my ears listened to the thundering of the cannon, clashing of the swords, and the shouts and cries of millions in mortal combat. The mysterious voice said, "Son of the Republic, look and learn." When this voice ceased, the dark shadowy angel placed his trumpet once more to his mouth and blew a long and fearful blast.

The shadowy angel for the last time dipped water from the ocean and sprinkled it upon America. Instantly the cloud rolled back, together with the armies It had brought, leaving the inhabitants of the land victorious.

Isaiah 18. Woe to the land overshadowing with wings,/eagle, America ... (V.1) which is beyond the rivers of Ethiopia: (in relation with Israel).That sendeth ambassadors by the sea). This alone eliminates all nations of Europe, Asia and Africa.

V. 2. That sendeth ambassadors by the sea, even in vessels of bulrushes upon the waters, saying, Go, ye swift messengers sent to a nation scattered and peeled, to a people terrible from the beginning hitherto; a nation meted out and trodden down, whose land the rivers have spoiled!

3. All ye inhabitants of the world and dwellers on the earth, see ye, when he lifted up an ensign on the mountain; and when he bloweth a trumpet, hear ye. For before the harvest when the bud is perfect, and the sour grape is ripening, he shall cut off the sprigs with pruning hooks and cut down the branches.

They shall be left together unto the fowls of the mountains, and to the beasts of the earth; and the fowls shall eat them and all the beasts of the earth shall winter upon them. In that time, shall the present be brought unto the lord of the hosts of people scattered and peeled, and from a people terrible from the beginning, a nation meted out and trodden under foot, whose land the rivers have spoiled.

America is the only nation on earth that fits that description. First of all, every country since the beginning of time has called their nation SHE, Mother Russia, Mother England, Mother Poland, etc. In Isaiah, this nation.

America is called HE, Uncle Sam. He that settith an ensign on the mountain THE FLAG ON THE MOON. He that is terrible (tenacious) from the beginning…The U.S. has never lost a declared war. One of the early flags bore the ensign, "Don't Tread on Me". America is the bully of the world and when he speaks, all listen.

A nation meted out and trodden down. No other nation on earth is so completely surveyed and "meted out". Every acre is accounted for in government archives, 9,435, 000 square miles.

Ezekiel 38, describes the One Day Nuclear War between the United States and Russia in which five-sixths of the Russian Army will be killed in the mountains of Israel. It will take 7 yrs. to burn the Russian weapons made of the tree lignostone. Is that why in

Washington's prophecy that as Russia begins attacking the U.S.; "Instantly the dark cloud rolled back with the armies it had brought, leaving America victorious." However, one third 3,145,000 square miles of the U.S. will be destroyed.

1789-1799. Age of Revolution witnessed the largest expropriate of wealth in the Church's history. The Roman question arising from the Italian unification resulted in the loss of the Papal States and the creation of Vatican City. Vatican means serpent.

1809, December 29, Albert Pike was born in Boston Massachusetts. He was a teacher for a short time, a poet and had a lucrative law practice. He retired and pursued his real interest which was the Masons.

1860, Lincoln was elected President of the United States.

1861-1865. Civil War A war between the North and the South over slavery. Slavery had become entwined in states' RIGHTS.

1871, Aug. 5th. A letter was written by Jesuit Albert Pike. It was sent to Giuseppe Manzini. In it, Pike said that a spirit guide (Lucifer's agent.) came to him in a vision that there must be three world wars, followed by unparalled economic disaster to establish the New World Order.

World War 1, Pike wrote, must happen so the Illuminati can overthrow Czar's power in Russia and making Russia atheist. The divergences caused by the agents of the Illuminati; between British and German Empires will be used to foment this war. Communism will be used to destroy other governments and to weaken religions.

World War II. Take advantage over the differences between Fascists and political Zionism. Nazism will be destroyed and political Zionism strong enough to institute a sovereign state of Israel in Palestine. A strong international Communism to balance Christendom, which would be held back until needed for the final social cataclysm.

World War III. Take advantage of the differences between Political Zionism and the leaders of the Islamic world. The war must cause the Islam (Modern Arab World) and political Zionism (the state of Israel) to destroy each other. (Word War 111 will be a **one-day** war).

Meantime the other nations, divided on this issue must fight to the point of complete physical, moral, spiritual and economic exhaustion. We will unleash the Nihilists and the Atheists, and we shall provoke a social cataclysm which will show its horror to all the nations, absolute atheism, slavery and bloody turmoil.

Then everywhere the citizens must defend themselves against the evolution, then Christianity will be without direction. Anxious for an ideal, will receive from the pure DOCTRINE of "LUCIFER" which will be brought out in public view. The reactionary movement will follow the destruction of Christianity and Atheism, both exterminated at the same time."

"We came in like lambs and will rule like wolves." So said the Jesuits.

1882 A.D., Five million Jews lived in Russia under Alexander III under anti-Jewish laws were in effect. Jewish boys of twelve years must spend 25 years in the Russian army. The first of the modern Zionism waves of immigration began with the establishment of agricultural settlements under Turkish rule. Jewish villages with a population of 85,000 were violently attacked.

1897. A.D., President Theodore Roosevelt calls the First Zionist Congress. He was shocked by the anti-Semitism in France. He concluded that that Jewish freedom and dignity could only come by with the restoration of a Jewish national homeland. He wrote the Der Judenstaat, a program for a Jewish State. He convened the first Zionist Congress at Basle in Switzerland which created the World 141 Zionist Organization.

1904 A.D., There was a second wave of immigration after another outbreak of pogroms in Russia. Thousands died.

1914-1918 A.D., WW1 began on July 28, 1914. The causes of the war were: Militarism, Alliances, Imperialism, Nationalism and the assignation of Ferdinand. 116,708 American soldiers died.

Militarism created an arms race out of competition and fear of neighboring Germany who tried to compete with Britain by building more and more ships.

Alliances created to check the balance of power between nations of power. In 1882 Germany-Austria-Hungary and Italy formed a Triple Alliance; In 1907, France, Britain and Russia created a Triple Entente. Imperialism caused much competition. Britain and France made Germany jealous as they tried to colonize parts of Africa.

Nationalism created the feeling that countries were better than others and promoted the anti Austria-Hungary settlements in Serbia.

Austria and Hungary declared war on Serbia. The small conflict spread rapidly. Germany, Russia, Great Britain and France were drawn into the war. They used bold attacks and rapid troop movements. In the West, Germany attacked Belgium and then France.

Russia attacked Germany and Austria-Hungary. In the south, Austria-Hungary attacked Serbia. This small conflict spread rapidly. Soon Germany, Russia, Great Britain and France were drawn into the war. There were bold attacks and rapid troop movements. In the West, Germany attacked Belgium and then France.

Russia attacked Germany and Austria-Hungary. In the south, Austria-Hungary attacked Serbia. After the Battle of the Marne, September 5, 1914, the western front became enthralled in Central France and remained that way for the rest of the war.

Late 1914, Ottoman Empire was defeated. After Germany tricked Russia into thinking that Turkey had attacked it.

1915. Allied actions against the Ottoman Empire in the Mediterranean. First Britain and France attacked the Dardanelles. Then Britain invaded Gullipoli Penibsula and the Turks in Mesopotamia.

1916-1917 There was trench warfare in the East and West with machine guns, heavy artillery and weapons. Millions of soldiers died on both sides but gained no advantage.

In early April, the United States, angered by attacks on the Atlantic declared war on Germany. Bolshevik revolution forced Russia to pull out of the war.

1918. New offense failed on both sides. The troops were exhausted, demoralized so the Germans began to fall back. A deadly outbreak of influenza broke out and took its toll, plus multiple mutinies from within lost control.

Fall of 1918, the Central Powers signed armistice agreements, so one by one, they conceded. Austria was broken into several smaller countries. Germany was punished under the Treaty of Versailles. Germany must disarm and is only permitted to have a small army and 6 ships. The Rhineland was to be demilitarized and land was taken away from Germany.

1903 Wilber Wright invented the airplane.

1908. Ford invented the Model T. He would make 15 million cars.

1920. Population of the world is 1 billion, 900 million. Population of the United States was 106.5 million. Fascism in Italy began with Mussolini in more urban dwellers than rural. Warren Harding was president.

1922. Fascism in Italy under the rule of Mussolini.

1925-1929. An era of good feelings existed.

Stalin in power in Russia.

1929. American Stock Market Crash which started a world-wide depression. Europe was affected by it more than United States. It was worse in Europe.

1931. Japan invades Manchuria.

1933. Hitler becomes chancellor of Germany. He withdraws from the disarmament conference and the League of Nations.

1934 German-Polish Non-Aggression Pact weakens France's policy of security. Russia joins the League of Nations.

1935. Germany rearms, Mussolini invades Abyssinia. 1936. Germany Sends troops into the Rhineland.

1936. Spanish Civil War. Germany sends troops into the Rhineland.

1938. Munich Agreement. Crisis over a large border regions. Germany annexes Austria.in Western Czechoslovakia.

World War 11 started September 1939, because 1. The Treaty of Versailles. Germany must accept the guilt and blame for starting the war.

Reparations of 6, 600 million dollars must be paid for damages caused by the war. 2. Failure of the League of Nations failed to settle problems. It had earlier successes but failed many times since. Germany could not pay. The majority felt that Germany was not being treated fairly.

Hitler armed his troops and began taking back lands that were taken from him during WW 1. He marched into Austria and remained under false votes. Germany invaded Poland followed by Britain, and France declaration of war on Germany. Russia stayed out of it because a week earlier they signed a pact with Germany. They used this pact to occupy in Poland, Baltic states and Romania over the next year.

1940, April 10, German victories in Western Germany that started on the 9th by occupying Denmark, Norway, Netherlands, Belgium and Luxembourg. France started a week later and established a new government, Vichy, that will do Germany's bidding and signed an armistice.

1941 Germany conquered Yugoslavia and Greece in a few weeks. She invades Russia and gains control of vast territories but failed to knock Russia out of the war. Germany is in a war it can't win Hitler begins a new invasion of Russia. Toorak in North Africa.

December 7, Japan attacks Pearl Harbor. President Roosevelt said, "We must find a way to get into war with Japan." He antagonized Japan by: restricting exports of scrap iron and steel, later, he restricted all exports of scrap iron and steel to destinations all over the Western hemisphere, then he froze Japanese assets in United States. Roosevelt then embargoed exports of oil in command flow to Japan: British and Dutch followed suit.

Early in the morning all officials of the area and officers of the United States Armed Forces were told to leave immediately. At 8: a.m., 183 planes flew over Pearl harbor and bombed. The United

States declares war on Japan and enters the war. 3,355 of our boys were killed.

1942. Germany suffers a set back at Singapore and Singapore falls to the Japan; 25,000 prisoners taken. American victory at the Battle of Mid-way. Mass murders of the Jews at Auschwitz begins.

1943. Stalingrad surrenders, Germany is majorly defeated. Invasion of Italy. Italy surrenders Germany takes over the battle. British and Indian forces fight Japanese in Burma.

1944. Monastery at Monte Carlo is bombed. Soviet offenses gather pace in East Europe. D-Day, allied invasion of France and Paris is liberated in August.

1945. Auschwitz is liberated by soviet troops. Russia reaches Berlin. Hitler commits suicide. Germanys surrenders on May 7. The atomic bomb is dropped on Hiroshima and Nagasaki, 291,557 American soldiers died in WW11.

1947, Feb. 19, Admiral Byrd meets Enki/Poseidon.

Admiral Byrd, G. Beckley and William Reed were on an exploration flight over the North Pole.

From 800 hours to 1130 hours, they experienced: a slight turbulence, then spotted vast ice of a yellowish color which turned to reddish-purple color Their magnetic and gyro compasses began wobbling. Over the next 15 minutes, they spotted mountains and had stronger turbulence.

They saw a small mountain range with green grass, and a small river running through the middle. The instruments were spinning. He left turned to examine the valley. The light there was different and he could not see the Sun. A mammoth was spotted, incredible. The temperature was 74 degrees F., more rolling hills.

At 1130 hours, the country side was more level than normal. Ahead, they were astonished to see a city, impossible. Their air craft was light and buoyant and now the controls refused to respond. They saw an air craft closing in on them, and they have the markings of a swastika on them. It was fantastic. "Where are we? We are caught in an invisible vice grip," said Byrd to his crew.

They were pulled into the city. At 1,135 hours, an English-speaking voice said, "Welcome, Admiral. We shall land you in 9 minutes. Relax, Admiral, you are in good hands." Byrd said that the engines were not running, the craft was turning itself. 1140 hours. "We are landing, the plane shudders and slowly touches down."

Byrd reported that several men approach on foot, they were tall with blond hair. The radio man and I boarded a platform which moves toward a glowing city made of crystal. We were taken to a large building and given a warm delicious beverage. The radio man was left behind, and my guide and I go onto an elevator; the walls emanated a rose-colored light.

We stepped off and there was the most beautiful surrounding to be seen. One host said, "Have no fear, Admiral, you are to have an audience with the Master."

I entered the room and saw the most beautiful sight I have ever seen, too beautiful to describe. A warm, rich voice said, "I bid you welcome to my domain, Admiral." A man seated at a long table had delicate features and the etching of years upon his face. He put his fingertips together and softly says, "We left you in because you are of noble character and well-known on the surface world." He smiled, "You are in the domain of the Arianni, the inner World of Earth. I have summoned you."

He continues, "Our interest begins just after your race exploded the first atomic bombs on Hiroshima and Nagasaki, Japan. We sent flying Flugelrads to the surface to investigate. We never interfered in your lives before in your race wars and barbarity, but we must now for you have tampered with a certain atomic that is not for man."

"Our emissaries have delivered messages to the powers of your world and they do not heed. Now you have been chosen to be a witness that our world does exist. Our culture and science is many thousands of years beyond your race. In 1945, we tried to contact your race, but were met with hostility. Our Flugelrads were fired upon."

Enki continued, "Your race has reached a point of no return for there are those among you who shall destroy your world rather than relinquish their power as they know it. Now I say to you, my son, there is a great storm gathering in your world, a black fury that will not spend itself for many years. There will be no answers in your armies, no safety in your science. All human things will be leveled. Your race war is only a preclude. We see it more clearly with each hour, Do you say that I am mistaken?" Asked Enki.

"No," answered Byrd. "It happened before in the Dark Age which lasted 500 years."

Enki answered, "Yes, my son, the dark ages that will come now will come over the earth like a pall. Some of your race may survive. Beyond that, I can't say. We see at a great distance, a NEW WORLD stirring from the ruins of your race seeking its lost and legendary treasures and they will be here, my son, safe in our keeping".

He continued saying that when that time comes, they will help renew his culture and race. By that time your people will learn the futility of war. He ended by sawing, "You, my son, are to return to the Surface World with this message."

The two beautiful hosts came to escort him out and the Admiral turned back to look at the Master. A gentle smile was etched on his delicate and ancient face. "Farewell, my son." Then he gestured with a lovely slender hand motion of peace, and our meeting was truly ended.

1947. Marshall Plan an aid in rebuilding western Europe, advances Cold War.

1949. Creation of NATO, North Atlantic Treaty Organization.

1950. Korean War. The North Korean People's Army backed by Russia and china crossed the 38th parallel that is a boundary line between the north and south and went into South Korea, backed by the United States. 36,574 American soldiers were killed.

1950. Five years after WW11 ended, the first Walmart was built by Sam Walton who was born March 29, 1918 in Kingfisher, Oklahoma. He joined the military Army Intelligence Corps where he supervised security at air craft plants and **prisoner of war concentration camps** at Fort Douglas in Salt Lake City, Utah. These camps held American Germans, Italians and Japanese who were thought to be a threat to America. Walton reached the rank of captain.

The New World Order has been planning for hundreds of years for a global take-over and depopulation. It can be seen now how they are achieving the New World Order by wars, riots, terrorism, hatred, distrust, etc. It is therefore logical to assume they have made plans for hundreds of years on how to herd 6.5 billion people to go to their deaths. What better place than food markets.

1951. United States tests hydrogen bomb. Russia launches Sputnik into space.

1954-1975. Vietnam War was the consequence of the Cold War. It revolved around the simple belief that communism was threatening to expand all over South-East Asia. 58,220 American soldiers were killed.

1954, Feb. 20. Luciferian aliens summons President Eisenhower for a meeting while he was vacationing in Palm Springs, California. They met at Edwards Air Force Base. Those present were; Franklin Allen of the Hearst newspaper, Edwin Norse of Brooklyn Institute, Gerald Light of Metaphysical Research fame, and Bishop Macintyre of Los Angeles.

Gerald Light described it in chilling detail. He had a distinct feeling that the world had come to an end with fantastic reality. He said that he had never seen human beings (his group) in that state of complete collapse and confusion as they realized that their own world had ended; with such finality. They decided it would cause too much chaos if the people were told of them.

A formal treaty was signed between the alien underground nation and the United States. The treaty stated that they would not interfere in our affairs and we not to interfere in theirs. They would give the United States advanced technology. They would abduct humans for medical examination and they be returned with no knowledge of their experience. Then the alien nation would furnish the Majestic Twelve with a list of all human contacts and abductees on a regular basis.

It was agreed that U.S. bases would be constructed underground for the use of the aliens and the U.S. government. A multi-million dollar fund would be kept by the Military Office of the White House. The fund was used to build 75 deep underground group facilities to build top secret alien bases. Eisenhower would have two more meetings with the aliens at Holliman's Air Force Base.

1961 East Germany raises the Berlin Wall. Cuban Missile Crisis.

1962, July, Sam Walton opened the first true Wal-Mart in Rogers, Arkansas.

1963, June 29, Lucifer was enthroned at the Vatican.

1963, Nov. 23, assassination of J.F. Kennedy. An army officer rushed to the camera man and said, "Five shots came from five different locations. I am an army intelligence officer and it is my duty to advance to see where enemy fire is coming from to protect my men before they go into a battle zone."

Kennedy was shot from the front as his brain matter flew to the back of the car. In 2010, a radio show was announcing the events of his death and they slowed the sound and five shots could be heard.

That evening, it was announced what time the next morning that Oswald would be taken from the jail. Anyone who heard this knew it was a set-up for his murder.

1960-1962, First Satellite launched. 1962 John Glenn was the first U.S. astronaut to orbit in the Friendship 7 Mercury capsule.

1963. The Supreme Court voted that the recitation of the Lord's prayer is unconstitutional. Alcatraz Prison is closed.

1965, Civil Rights Act.

1967, June 8. During the six-Day Israeli War, President Johnson gave orders for the Israelis to bomb the American ship, the USS Liberty, that he put there off the coast of Israel as a pretext for war. Johnson told the Israelis to sink the ship to the bottom of the Sea. At 2 P.M., the Israelites bombed the ship and it was a violent 67 minutes, killing 34 men and wounding 174. American boys died. Unexpectedly, the crippled ship made it safely to shore.

1968. Martin L. King and Robert Kennedy were assassinated.

1969. Gay Rights Movement.

1970 Americans landed on the Moon. Nixon invades Cambodia.

1978-79, The government of the U.S. set up a series of executive orders to have Fema Camps placed in various states. To begin depopulation in the future.

1980. Georgia Guidestone, ninety miles east of Atlanta was erected. It is a granite monument erected 750 feet above sea level. It has six slabs, one in the center and four arranged around it and a cap stone. It is a warning from the LUCIFERIAN ONE WORLD ORDER, the Luciferians, warning what they plan to do with the citizens of the world.

One year earlier, Robert C. Christian on behalf of a small group of loyal anonymous Americans, who for twenty years planned the Guidestone, went to the Elberton Granite Co. Company to erect the monument. it is a message to the world warning beforehand, as the Luciferian-Illuminati/Shadow government do in a mocking, "I told you so."

It is a message consisting of 10 Commandments; guidelines or principals engraved in eight languages: English, Spanish, Swahili, Sanskrit, Hebrew, Arabic, Chinese and Russian: 1. Maintain humanity under 500,000,000 in perpetual balance with nature. 2. Guide reproduction wisely-improving fitness and diversity. 3. Unite humanity with a living new language. 4. Rule passion-faith-tradition and all things with tempered reason. 5. Protect all peoples and nations with fair law and just courts, 6. Let all nations rule internally resolving external disputes in a world court. 7. Avoid petty laws and useless officials. 8. Balance personal rights with social duties. 9. Prize truth-beauty- and love-seek harmony with the infinite. 10. Be not a cancer on the earth. Leave room for nature--Leave room for nature.

This shouts out **Depopulation** and **Pike's Luciferian One World Order.**

The Anunnaki still need slaves to work underground digging for gold for Nibiru and working in their cities and buildings. There are 900,000 children go missing every year; 100,000 world-wide, 800,000 from the United States; 80,000 of these are suspected of a parent stealing one's own child, or kidnapping, serial killers, sex slaves. I believe 720,00 of them are working for their master, Enki, of whom the Pope wears his Miter, the fish hat.

CHAPTER 16

THE CURTAIN WAS RENT

We have determined that Lucifer owns Planet Earth. We also know that he and Jesus were adversaries in the Upper Universe. We can therefore assume that Lucifer, through his New World Order and the Georgia Guidestone, is intent on making Earth like those planets of the orderly Universe that he once oversaw.

It can be assumed that Lucifer as Christs adversary, hates Him and will do anything to despoil His words, undermine His crucifixion and disprove the Shroud and the coming rapture/ evacuation.

An example of under mining Christ when He said, "Call no man father except my Father which is in Heaven." Matt. 23: 9. The Vatican told its peons to call their biological father dad and call the priests father. So, we who have experienced the hard knocks of life: wars, tribulations in the work force, lay-offs, bill-paying, food and clothing for and raising our children to call a 26-year-old child, or any priest, Father. This is a deliberate defiance and a slap in the face of Jesus.

We can also be certain that with Lucifer's trained Luciferian Jesuits who take an oath to do the following things to those who will not conform to the New World: rip out their intestines, rip the child from the womb and bash its head against the wall, torture, boil and bury alive all those who will not conform or bow down to the Pope; even kill their own parents, and to go all over the world creating hatred, turmoil and riots can't succeed to create a serene New World Order.

They can never succeed; they can't change because of the evil psychopathic nature of the Jesuits and their god, Lucifer… We can proceed now to show how they intend to create their New World Order.

1990's. In Madison Georgia, in Morgan County, millions of black body bags and 500,000 of plastic coffins were delivered to the Fema Camps. Around the country is stored thousands in Fema Camps.

1993. After sending their astronomers from the Vatican to Mt. Graham in Phoenix, Arizona in 1981, the Jesuits made plans to build an observatory on Mount Graham's peak in Phoenix, Arizona, 11,000 feet above sea level. Vatican means serpent and they called their telescope Lucifer. It costs them 1 million dollars a year to operate it. They say they are there to collect data.

2001, 9/11. Bombing of the Twin towers by those power, who create the problem for the masses, give the solution and are worshiped by them.

2005, March U.S. Congress passed a law that the government can control weather. Mar. 5., Government passes a law that it is illegal to feed the homeless.

2013, Jan. 90 year-old Arnold Abbott in Fort Lauderdale, was arrested twice for feeding the hungry. Jean Cleever was fined $2,000 for feeding the hungry. Government ordered 1.6 billion rounds of ammunition; enough to fill 16 Olympic swimming pools. It intends to purchase 21.6 million over the next 4-5 years.

2013, Mar. 13. **Jesuit** Pope Francis was elected the 112th Pope. He is of Bishop Malachi's Prophecy as to be the last pope. This Catholic prophecy says that he will betray the faith and he will oversee the destruction of Rome. When he was elected, he said to those who elected him, "May God have mercy on you for what you have done" He knew the prophecy that he is the false prophet, and what he must do.

Pope Francis is ruled by the Jesuit black pope, Arturo Sosa, who is ruled by Lucifer. Pope Francis is the false prophet of Rev. 16:13. And I saw three unclean spirits like frogs come out of the mouth of the dragon, and out of the mouths of the beasts, and out of the mouth of the false prophet. He will usher in the new religion, the Whore on the Scarlet Beast of Rev. 17: 3. And upon her forehead was a name written, MYSTERY, BABYLON THE GREAT, THE MOTHER OF HARLOTS AND THE ABDOMINATIONS OF THE EARTH.

Pope Francis will be followed thereafter by the antichrist who will not be revealed until after the destruction of Rome by Russia, and after 'that which restraineth' be taken, out of the way (true Christians with Saint Michael will be raptured/ translated; Rev. 2: 7. For the mystery of iniquity/antichrist already at work.

2014, Apr. 33 American cities passed restrictions on feeding the hungry. Wal-Mart now has 4,177 stores throughout the United States 2016. Fort Lauderdale Military facility; U.S. soldiers expose U.S.A. Fema Camps saying there are 30,000 guillotines that were purchased by our government; 15,000 sent to Georgia and 15,000 shipped over the country to Fema camps.

2017. Wal-Mart has closed 183 stores, claiming each one was closed for plumbing problems. Hurricane Harvey struck and victims were taken to prison barges off the coast of Texas. This facility will be used in 2018 when migrant children will be taken from their parents.

By now, there are 1,200 Fema camps in the United states, 400 Fema Camps and 800 Fema prison Camps. Alaska has the largest which can house up to 2 million people. It now houses 500,000 people.

2017, 180,0000 prison barges costing 7 billion dollars. One came to the shores of Texas after Hurricane Harvey and it was filled to capacity; housing 300 people. The barges are being sent all over the world.

2018. Wal-Mart erected a store in Brownsville, Texas at the border. This facility is now being used to house 1,417 migrant boys, torn from their parents at the border.

It is very large. There are 4 beds to each room, a gymnasium, games to play. They must stay within the walls for 22 hours a day. There are 130,000 skilled workers, reserves, veterans and active duty soldiers. They will be sent over the U.S. Some are there to teach reeducation to the boys.

2018, The prophecy of the young Evangelist in 1954 is now an appropriate time to reveal it.The young Evangelist visiting New York City, went atop the Empire State Building to view the magnificent city. Waiting in line to look through the telescope, he felt a sudden surge of the Holy Spirit come over him. The voice of God said that His eyes run to and fro over the earth and sees the foolishness of men so from thenceforth thou shalt shall have wars. He dropped in his dime and he was caught away, overpowered by the Holy Spirit.

He did not see Manhattan, but a vision of a struggle and the fall of the Statue of Liberty. A vision of WW111 came and then the fall of the statue. He did not see Manhattan, but the Atlantic and Pacific Oceans. I saw the Statue of Liberty standing far out in the Gulf of Mexico. She was between him and the United States.

Suddenly he saw a giant hand reach out toward the Statue, her torch was torn from her hand and replaced with a cup from which came a giant sharp, glistening, dangerous sword that threatened the whole world. The great cup was placed in her hand and he heard these words, 'Thus saith the Lord of Hosts....Drink ye and be drunken, spew and fall, and rise no more because of the sword which I will send."

The Statue replied, "I will not drink."

Then with a voice of thunder the Lord's voice said, "Thus saith the Lord, "Ye shall certainly drink."

Then suddenly, the giant hand forced the cup to her lips, and she was powerless to defend herself. The hand forced her to drink every drop of the cup. She drank the bitter dregs. The Lord said, "Ye shall not be unpunished: for I will call for the sword upon 'all' inhabitants of the earth."

The cup was withdrawn from her lips and the sword was missing. This meant that the contents of the cup were consumed and the sword typified war, death, sudden destruction which is no doubt on its way.

The statue becomes unsteady from too much wine, she began to stagger and lose her balance. She splashed into the Gulf, trying to regain her balance. She staggered again and again and fell to her knees. She desperately tried to regain her balance and rise to her feet, but as she struggled in the Gulf, he heard the words of God say, "Ye shall drink and be drunken, and spew and fall and rise no more because of the sword I shall send upon you." She was struggling until she rose and continued swaggering.

Then coming from Alaska was a huge black cloud in the shape of a man's head. The cloud began to take the shape of a skull with a gaping mouth. Shoulders and long black arms appeared. The skeleton bent toward the United States, stretching forth its hands to the west and east toward New York and one toward Seattle. Its entire attention was focused upon the United States, its one interest was to destroy the multitudes.

He watched in great horror as the black cloud set its face upon New York City. From its mouth came white wisps of white powder which looked like smoke. The smoke covered the eastern part of the United States.

The skeleton turned to the West Coast until the entire West Coast was covered with vapors. Then upon the Central States it forced white vapors. Then it began to cover the head of staggering Statue. She took one breath; gasping for breath she began to cough to rid her lungs of the horrible vapors; the painful coughing told that they had seared her lungs. (horrible nerve gas).

God spoke again, "Behold the Lord maketh the earth empty and turnith it upside down and scattered the people. And it shall be with all people, the land will be spoiled. The earth mourneth, the haughty people languish; they have transgressed the laws, changed the ordinances, broke the everlasting covenant. Therefor the curse devoured the earth, and they that dwell therein are desolate, the inhabitants of the earth are burned, and few men left."

The Evangelist watched as the Statue was moaning and groaning; in mortal agony. The pain was terrific; again, and again, she tried to clear her lungs. She staggered, clutching her lungs and her breasts. She fell to her knees. She gave one final cough, made one last desperate effort to rise and the fell on her face, never to rise.

Suddenly the silence was shattered by the screaming of sirens that screamed, Run fir your lives!" The shrill was terrible coming from everywhere, all corners of America. People were screaming and running and falling. Millions of people, running, falling, coughing; moaning, groanings of the doomed and dying.

The Lord Spoke, "Behold, evil shall go forth from nation to nation and a great whirlwind will be raised up from the coasts of the earth. The slain shall be at that **day** from one end of the earth to the other end of the earth: they shall not be lamented.; neither gathered nor buried, they shall be dung upon the ground."

Then from the Atlantic and the Pacific and out of the Gulf rocket-like objects like fish leaping out of water. High into the air they leaped, each heading in a different direction, but everyone toward the United States. The sirens screamed louder. Up from the ground, I saw similar rockets beginning to ascend.

To the evangelist, he thought they were interceptor rockets arising from different parts all over the United States. The rockets reached their maximum height and fell back down. Then suddenly, the rockets that leaped out of the oceans like fish exploded all at once. The noise was ear-splitting. He saw a huge ball of fire which resembled the Hiroshima H-bomb.

The evangelist thought on these words, "Blow ye the trumpets in Zion and sound the alarm in my holy mountain: let all the inhabitants of the land tremble for the **day** of the Lord cometh, for it is high at hand: A **day** of darkness and gloominess, a **day** of clouds and thick darkness."

Then, the young Evangelist said, "And then to my ears came another sound- a sound of distant singing. It was the sweetest music I ever heard; joyful shouting and sounds of happy laughter. I knew immediately it was the rejoicing of the saints of God. I looked and there high in the Heaven above the smoke and poisons gasses above the noise of the battle, I saw a huge mountain. It was God's own people **who were found worthy to escape these things**, were rejoicing, safe from harm which had come upon the earth."

This sounds like George Washington's vision of a horrific one-day war. The WW111, a one day war.

Rev. 1: 2. He that has an ear, let him hear what the Spirit saith to the **churches**. This is said seven times from Ch. 2: V. 7 to Ch. 3, V. 22. And in Ch. 13, V.9 it states, "If any man has an ear, let him hear." This certainly lets you know that the Church is GONE.

Revelation, Ch.8 and 9. On the island of Patmos, Jesus opened the seal to tell John what would happen. There were seven angels with seven trumpets. An angel had a golden censer with burning incense and cast it down to earth, an earthquake occurred and the seven angels prepared to sound.

The first angel sounded the trumpet and there followed hail and fire mingled with blood; they were 'cast' to the earth and the third part of the trees were **burned** up and all the green grass.

1914, 6/28. WW1, bombs were 'thrown' from planes. A **scorched** earth policy was used by Germans and Russians.

The second trump sounded and as it were a great mountain burned and cast into the sea; and a third part of the sea became blood. And a third part of the creatures in the sea died and the third part of the ships were destroyed.

1939,9/1-1945, 9/29. WW11. First atom bomb dropped on Hiroshima. And a great mountain burning with fire was cast into the sea, and a third part of the sea became blood and a third part of the creatures in the sea died, and the third part of the ships were destroyed.

The third angel sounded and there fell a great star from the heavens burning as a lamp and fell upon the third part of the rivers and upon the fountains of the water and the name of the star was Wormwood; a third part of the waters became wormwood, and many died of the waters because they were bitter.

1986, June 26.**Chernoble**, Russian name for **wormwood**. Russia had the worst nuclear disaster in history, 4,000 died and many more from the after affects. One third of the waters were affected by radiation. Torch Report. One third of the waters became wormwood and many died from drinking it.

The fourth angel sounded, and the third part of the Sun was smitten, and the third part of the Moon and the third part of the stars, so the third part of them were darkened and the day shone not for the third part of it and the night likewise.

1991, June 15. Mount Pinatubo erupted causing reduction of the Sun, Moon and stars. NASA reported a global dimming of 3, One third reduction of light during the day and night.

"Woe, Woe, Woe to the inhabitants of the Earth," said an angel in a loud voice. The first four trumpets were woes upon the people in localized areas. Now, this concerns the whole world.

And the fifth angel sounded and a star fell to earth and to him was given the key to the bottomless pit which he opened and there arose smoke of a great furnace and the Sun and the air was darkened because of the smoke from the pit. From the smoke, locusts/helicopteres came upon the earth and to them was given power as a scorpion. It was commanded that they should not hurt the grass, nor trees, but only those men without the seal on their foreheads.

1991, January 16. Saddam Hussain started 610 oil well fires, causing enormous amounts of smoke and out of the smoke came locusts/army helicopters with stingers in their tails (missiles).

January 17, war was declared. The men in helicopters were not to kill them but torture them. So, they will seek death and not find it. Their shape was that of locusts. Their faces were that of men, they had hair like a woman and teeth of a lion and hair like a woman. They had breast plates of iron and the sound of their wings were the sound of many chariots and tails like the sting of the scorpions. They had a king over them, the angel of the bottomless pit.

This is a perfect description of the Army Apache helicopter. Their shapes were like locusts (helicopters).The faces were that of men as one can see the pilot's faces through the windshield. Teeth as lions; painted teeth on the front of copter. Hair like a woman; Apaches have long, thick-flattened hair. Breastplates of iron and the sound of their wings like many chariots (blades of the helicopter). They have tails that sting, missiles and machine guns.

The sixth angel was told to loose the four angels at the River Euphrates. The four angels were loosed and told to slay the third part of men. The number of the men were 200,000,000. John saw the horses they 'sat' on. They had breastplates of fiery red, hyacinth blue and sulfur yellow. They had heads of lions. Out of their mouths came fire, smoke and brimstone and coming from their tails were like serpents that had heads and with them, they hurt.

Isis, their chariots are: tanks, jeeps and trucks, some are painted fiery red, others are hyacinth blue and others sulfur yellow. The men 'sit' on them. From the front of the vehicles are Machine guns, from the back, missiles.

The angels loosed: Turkey 74,000,000. Syria 22, 400,000. Iran 76, 420,000 and Iraq 32,580,000. Total = 205,400,000.

To slay one third of men with weapons upon the chariots with fire/incendiary bombs, ; smoke/ chemical weapons and brimstone/ chemical weapons which shoot put from the front and backs of the vehicles/chariots.

(Luke. 21: 36.). Watch thee therefore and pray that ye shall be **accounted worthy** to escape these things that shall come to pass, and stand before the Son of Man.

Trumpet Seven is about to blow. This Trumpet is announcing Christ coming for His own. "I will come again and receive you unto myself that where I am, you may also be."

"COME"

O, Lucifer, son of the Morning Star / Jesus, you have fallen, fallen, and have but a short time left.

APPENDICES

*Jonah did not go into the belly of a whale.

In 1891, a sailor, James Bartley, while aboard the ship, Star of the East was accidentally swallowed by a harpooned whale. Some fifteen hours later, as the fishermen cut open the whale, James was still alive, but unconscious. After a month, he regained consciousness, and recalled the whale had swallowed him. He lost all the hair on his body, his skin bleached whiter than normal and his eyes had been badly damaged.

351 years earlier, Enki made the first submersible boat on Earth. The god of the Old Testament prepared a fish to swallow Jonah.

*What happened to Malaysia, Flight 370?

On March 8, 2014, Malaysia Flight 370 took off from Kuala Lumpur Airport in Malaysia. It was headed for Beijing. It was seen on radar shortly after take-off, being followed by two planes as it made a complete left U-turn and headed for Diego Garcia, an American owned island. A passenger, Philip Wood, was taken off the plane and placed in a shed from where he called a friend and took a picture from a small opening in the door.

Obama ordered Putin not to go into Ukraine. The following day, Putin did so. And on April 15, 2014, Ukraine declared Crimea a territory occupied by Russia.

On July,24, 2014, Malaysia Flight MH17/MAS17 supposedly left Amsterdam heading for Malaysia and was shot down near the Ukraine border. Immediately the United States blamed Russia.

But, the unexpected happen; hikers came upon the scene. To their shock they saw passengers still buckled in their seat belts and all the bodies were **putrefied**.

*There is an error in the longevity recording of Pre-Diluvial patriarchs.

According to the Bible, pre-diluvial patriarchs lived about 1,000 years. This accounts for the 1,656 years from Adam to the deluge.

Age of Adam when he begot Seth.................... 130 years.
Age of Seth when he begot Enoch.................... 105 years.
Age of Enoch when he begot Kenan.................. 90 years.
Age of Kenan when he begot Mahalalel............... 70 years.
Age of Mahalalel when he begot Jared................ 65 years.

Age of Jared when he begot Enoch.................. 162 years.
Age of Enoch when he begot Methuselah .... 65 years.
Age of Methuselah when he begot Lamech........... 187 years.
Age of Lamech when he begot Noah .... 82 years.
Age of Noah when the Deluge occurred .... 600 years.
Total time from Adam to the Deluge................ 1,656 years.

This is incorrect. This does not match the Sumerian, nor Enki's account of his own history. In the Sumerian Hexadecimal base of 60 Mathematical system, the cuneiform sign for "1" could mean 60 depending on the position of the sign. Just as "1" could mean one or could mean sixty, depending on the digits position in the decimal system. The distinction depending on the position of the sign. The distinction is easy by the use "0" to indicate position writing 1, 10, 100 etc.

Having this knowledge, and Enki's own account of his autobiography and history, the numbers: 1,656 (birth of Adam, 1,526 (birth of Seth) and 1,421 (birth of Enosh/Enoch) are converted:

Adam/Adapa born 110,000 years ago, Seth born 104,560 years ago and Enosh born 98,160 years ago, etc. Adapa born 110.000 years ago in chapter 7 in this book.

This solution leads to astounding results. It places Adam, Seth, and Enosh/Enoch right in the time-frame when Neanderthals and Cro-Magnon walked the Earth, both who passed through the lands of the Bible as they spread toward Asia and Europe.

Neanderthals (Those who ventured away from the camps of the original creation of Adamu and Tiamat, born about 300,000 years ago). And Enoch, who was born 98,160 years ago. His name means 'human', the first biblical term for what we call Cro-Magnon; the first homo- sapiens-sapiens.

This fits in perfectly with Enki's recorded autobiography and history as told to his scribe, Endubsar.

*3,453 B.C. Tower of Babel (a launching tower to shoot a rocket to Mars). Marduk/Nimrod said, "Let us make a shem for ourselves. He meant rocket. The Bible says, he said, "Let us make a name for ourselves." Rocket and name have the same word, shem.

*#1

Face on Mars. 412,000 years ago,
Alalu's face was carved on Mars.
Here, he could forever see Earth
Where he ruled Eridu for 8 shars and
See Nibiru where he ruled as king
For 9 shars as it passes every 3,600 yrs.

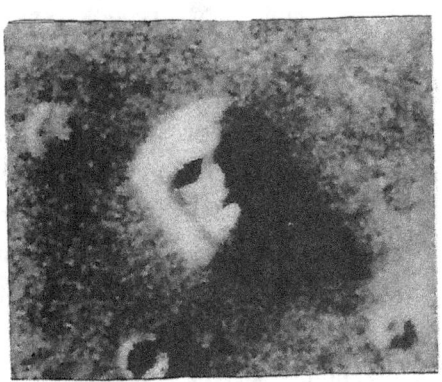

*#2

"THE EVERLASTING GROUND PLAN,
THAT WHICH FOR ALL TIME
THE CONSTRUCTION HAS DETERMINED.
IT IS THE ONE WHICH BEARS
THE DRAWINGS FROM THE OLDEN TIMES
AND THE WRITING OF THE UPPER HEAVEN
THE CITIES ARE:

1. ERIDU
2. LARSA
3. NIBIRU-KI
4. BAD-TIBERA
5. LARAK
6. SIPPAR
7. SHURUBAK
8. LAGASH

PRE-DELUGE FLIGHT PLAN

*#5 THE NEW FLIGHT PATTERN

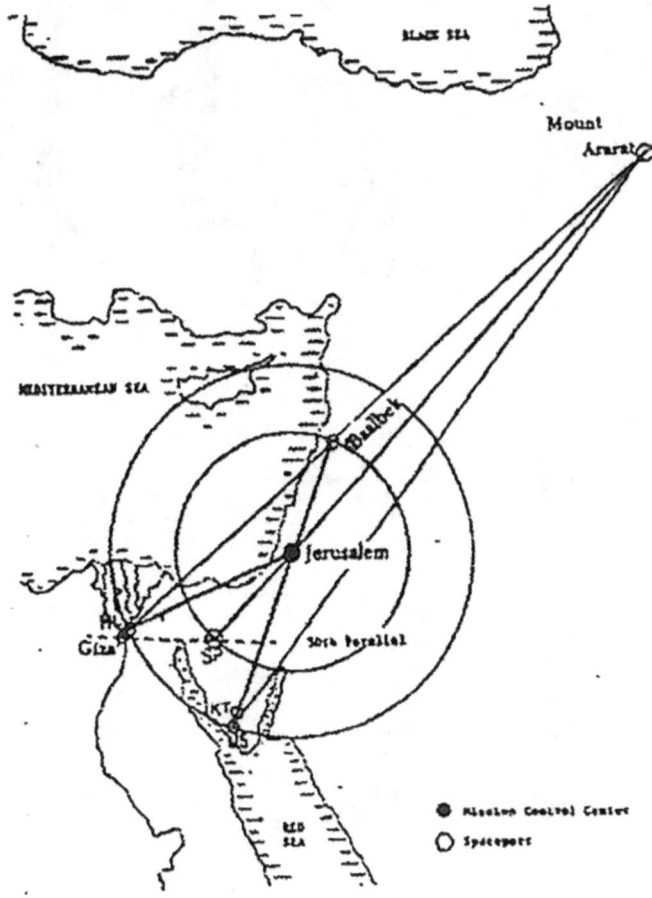

*#3 "LET US MAKE MAN IN OUR IMAGE AND LIKENSS." AND SO IT WAS DONE!

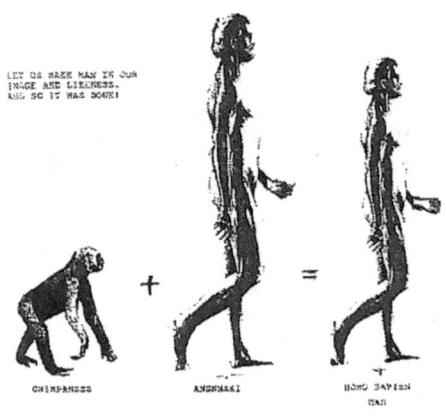

*#4

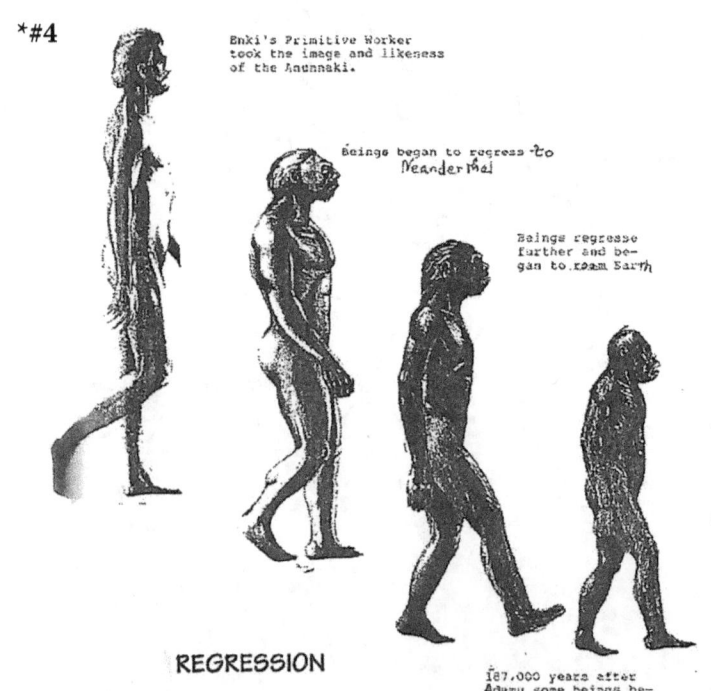

Enki's Primitive Worker took the image and likeness of the Anunnaki.

Beings began to regress to Neanderthal

Beings regresse further and began to roam Earth

REGRESSION

187,000 years after Adamu some beings began living in caves.

#6

#7

Pyramid War, 9,400 years ago. This was a war of ferocity between the two brothers; the Enkiites and the Enlilites over the death of Dumuzi, Enki's son. Inanna, to avenge her lover, flew in her craft and a fleet of sky ships to destroy the pyramids. Ninurta, Enlil's son, with his laser destroyed the crystals on the way up to the pyramid's top. There, he lasered loose the compartment's lid that housed the gug stone (the detector of enemies approaching and air traffic controller for in-coming craft). Tourists wrongfully call this compartment a sarcophagus.

www.ingramcontent.com/pod-product-compliance
Lightning Source LLC
LaVergne TN
LVHW021700060526
838200LV00050B/2432